PRAISE FOR
NEVER HAVE I EVER

"Katie's prose illustrates her life events by letting the voice in her head reveal all. Everything that ever crossed your mind while you were with your friends and crushes will echo back to you as you read about moments like a messy kiss with Eric or the feeling of helplessness when finding out that a friend of the opposite sex likes you and you just are not ready for that kind of information."
—HelloGiggles

"Her stories are relatable and pretty damn funny—she brings you along on all the moments of over-analysis, self-doubt, and personal triumph that make dating both a little bit soul crushing and totally worth it."
—Refinery29

"Brims with sharp observation . . . Her memoir, which takes as its subject liking and being liked, has all of the easygoing, intimate cheerfulness that verb implies."
—*Slate*

"*Never Have I Ever* is a strikingly profound and brilliant memoir that presents on-point observations about growing up, friendship and the confusing world of dating. Katie writes with such ease and skill that it's hard not to become completely wrapped up in her many relatable adventures. Her wit and intelligence effortlessly place her amongst today's great writers, and readers will be left thinking, "Finally, someone gets it." If you're a fan of Mindy Kaling, the New Adult genre or are simply looking for your next great read, *Never Have I Ever* is the book for you."
—*RT Book Reviews*

"You won't be able to put down her hilarious debut."

—*Teen Vogue*

"The most compelling dating memoir of the last few years...The book resists pretty much all of the stock narratives about single-hood that romantic comedies, women's magazines and the like have led us to expect. it's the story of a young woman navigating a space lots of people find themselves in but fewer talk about—one where dating is something to think about, but certainly not the only thing, and certainly not something worth overhauling one's life or self for."

—Salon

"Every twentysomething woman will relate to at least one of the disastrous attempts at courtship in this memoir. And then she'll want to buy copies for all of her girlfriends so they can discuss it over a few glasses (bottles?) of wine at book club."

—*Library Journal*

"A Judy Blume-meets-Carrie Bradshaw memoir about how, despite boys and growing up, friendship between women endures."

—*Publishers Weekly*

"Reading *Never Have I Ever* is a bit like reliving your most awkward moments—but in the best way, because this time, the cringeworthy moments are happening to someone else. Anyone who's ever swooned over a boy whose name she didn't even know or overanalyzed a text message from a crush will see herself in Katie Heaney. You'll relate to her frustrations and admire her confidence, and probably wish she was your best friend."

—Rachel Bertsche, *New York Times* bestselling author of *MWF SEEKING BFF*

"I challenge any reader to not feel like one of Katie Heaney's closest girlfriends as she examines, in the most charming, honest, original and amusing way imaginable, how she's managed to never have a date. But don't let the breezy language or topic fool you—this is also a brilliant examination of what it means to be a friend, a girl, and a human being. The first guy to take Heaney out will be very lucky; in the meantime, we her readers are the lucky ones."

—Anna David, *New York Times* bestselling author of
Party Girl and *Falling For Me*

"No one has ever captured the angst and frustration of crushes as perfectly and humorously as Katie Heaney. Anyone who has ever fallen in love with a cute stranger on a train, on the street, in class, or at work, will instantly identify with it, and laugh and cringe along with her dating misadventures. But what is most admirable and impressive about this book is how unflinchingly Katie is able to examine herself. As hilariously cutting as she is when describing the male objects of her desire, she's also self-deprecating and introspective. And the book manages to point towards another (oft overlooked) great love in a woman's life: that of her friends."

—Chiara Atik, Author of *Modern Dating: A Field Guide*

"Katie's writing is hilarious, and warm, and thoughtful, and reading this book is like having a little version of her to hang out with. What's that, Miniature Paper Katie? You don't like the bath??"   —Edith Zimmerman, founder of TheHairpin.com

DEAR EMMA

WITHDRAWN

katie heaney

GRAND CENTRAL
PUBLISHING

NEW YORK   BOSTON

Copyright © 2016 by Katie Heaney

Grand Central Publishing
Hachette Book Group
1290 Avenue of the Americas
New York, NY 10104

www.HachetteBookGroup.com

Printed in the United States of America

RRD-C

First Edition: March 2016
10 9 8 7 6 5 4 3 2 1

Grand Central Publishing is a division of Hachette Book Group, Inc.
The Grand Central Publishing name and logo is a trademark of Hachette Book Group, Inc.

The Hachette Speakers Bureau provides a wide range of authors for speaking events. To find out more, go to www.hachettespeakersbureau.com or call (866) 376-6591.

The publisher is not responsible for websites (or their content) that are not owned by the publisher.

Library of Congress Cataloging-in-Publication Data has been applied for.

ISBN: 978-1-4555-3460-9

For R.

DEAR
EMMA

Dear Emma,

I am a freshman, and everything is going great: I'm pledging my first-choice sorority, I love my major and my classes, and my roommate, while extremely emo, goes home every weekend to visit her boyfriend and parents, leaving me the room—not that I have much time to spend there. I'm having an amazing time, and would have absolutely nothing to write to you about if it weren't for my best friend, "Kelly." She and I have been best friends since we were 12. We applied here together and were super excited when we both got in. I actually wanted to be roommates, but Kelly thought it would be good for us to have space and make ourselves meet new people. But now that I'm actually doing it, she's not happy. I know there are reasons—her roommate is practically a nun and only leaves the room for class and church, and Kelly didn't get into the sorority she wanted, which is the house I'm now in. Instead of pledging the house that did bid her, like I thought she should, she decided not to pledge at all. But now she doesn't do much, and asks me to hang out all the time, and gets mad when I have other stuff going on (especially Greek stuff), which I usually do. She'll always be my best friend, but I want to do my own thing. All her moping is kind of driving me nuts. Help!

Sincerely,
Get a Life

Dear GAL,

The first thing you need to do is talk to her about this, which, from the sound of things, you haven't yet done. Why? What's the worst that could happen—she'll get upset with you? She already is! Stop blowing her off thinking she'll just stop asking you to hang out. For one thing, I don't think you really want her to stop completely. For another, it's not an efficient plan. All you're doing now is pushing off talking to her one day at a time. Text her or email her and find at least a two-hour block you both have free, and meet somewhere quiet. Don't tell me you don't have two hours free because you do. If you don't think you do, it's because you don't want to find it. I know full well what freshman schedules are like. Most of you are barely in class after one PM.

When you do talk to her, I suggest not starting, or finishing with, or ever mentioning again, any phrase remotely resembling "Get a life."

What you do tell her is the truth. You know you haven't been super available lately, and you're sorry that's been hard on her. You're very busy. You need to put in extra legwork now so your new sisters like you and don't kick your butt to the Greek Row curb before May. You want to make new friends and you want to do well in school. Then listen to what she has to say. Most of the time, it's easier to find a resolution for this kind of thing than you think. It might not be a permanent one, but I promise it will help for at least a while. You can ask her for patience until things calm down for you—unless, of course, you don't really want her to wait it out at all.

I want you to think about something for me: What does it mean to say that she (or whoever) will "always be your best friend"? I hate it when people say that. It's very presumptuous. "Best friend" isn't a fixed status. It's not like you guys reached that point and now you never have to work at it ever again. Kelly is having a hard time. She needs you. She hasn't had your luck with roommates or the somewhat arbitrary approval of fifty girls who wear the same T-shirt. She will feel better eventually, but not right now. I can't make you be a good friend, especially if it's to someone you don't really want to be very good friends with, but I want you to remember that you will be where Kelly is one day. Not in exactly the same way, necessarily, but close enough. I know that asking you to understand that is a tall order, because most of us can't imagine anything that hasn't already happened to us. But one day, you will feel lonely and left out and ignored, and you will be like, "Huh, I get it now."

And at that point you might really want to rely on the person who's known you for what will soon be half your life. And in order to ensure she's still there, you might have to give up just a little of your precious time now. Not tons! You may still have to say no to her sometimes, or even most of the time. At least this semester. That's fair, and I think it's fair of you to ask her to do her best to understand that.

I'm definitely not saying the only reason you should be there for her now is for your own future benefit. You should do it because she's your best friend and you love her. But because most of us need the promise of some amount of personal benefit to make us do much of anything, sure, do it for your sake, too.

And finally: Never underestimate the value in having friends from nonintersecting social circles. Who else will so willingly and vehemently agree that your friends are crazy and annoying when they're being crazy and annoying, if not your other friends who don't know them at all?

Most humbly yours,
Emma

1

I guess what I am wondering is: is he dead?"

I clutched my phone in my left hand and squinted at its screen, as if, like a Magic 8 Ball, it might produce a response to my question. Instead, my roommate Logan did. "It doesn't seem that likely to me that he is not texting you back because he is dead," she said.

"There's a first time for everything," I said. "I could be the first girl who can say, 'The guy I was seeing stopped texting me back, and I didn't know why, but then I found out he fell off of a mountain before he could hit send. He text-walked off a mountain.' There could be a tragic movie about me, like *A Walk to Remember*."

"This is not like *A Walk to Remember*."

"It has some similar elements," I said.

"Not really."

"Well. Whatever. The last time I checked, last night, he hadn't done anything on Facebook in forty-nine hours. So I think his continued survival is very much uncertain."

"I just saw him on Friday," said my other roommate, Mel, who walked out of her bedroom, where she had been, I thought, watching something on her laptop—YouTube videos of international boy bands I'd never heard of, probably—with head-phones on.

"You always join conversations in the middle," said Logan. "The moment you start listening is the moment you should come out here. Instead of lurking."

"I was catching up from my bed. I was like, 'Oh my god, maybe he IS dead and Harriet knows something I don't,'" said Mel, who took two chocolate chip cookies from a package on top of the refrigerator, poured herself a glass of milk, and sat down next to Logan, across from me. She lowered one of the cookies into her glass and held it there.

"Where did you see him? And what time?" I asked her. I flipped my phone over on its face, as if to punish it. For a moment I thought about getting up to put it on the floor in the corner of the kitchen, to give it a proper time-out, but the dull pulsing behind my forehead confirmed that standing up right now, or making any unnecessary movement, was a bad idea.

"Ummm, I'm not really sure," said Mel.

"What?" said Logan.

"WHAT??" I said.

"You guys know I don't recall narrative details well!!" said Mel, repeating a phrase we'd often told her ourselves.

"Yeah, but, this was two days ago," I said. "Right? Are you sure it was Friday? Or could it have been upward of . . . sixty-one hours ago?"

"No, it was definitely Friday, I think. Because, I remember"—and here she pointed first at me, and then at Logan—"I was in the hallway on the upper level of NSC, so I must have been on my way to TA hours for Organic Chem," she said. NSC was the Natural Sciences Center, where she and Logan practically lived. Mel crossed her arms and smiled proudly.

"Congratulations," said Logan, putting her hand on Mel's right shoulder. "You have a modest capacity for placing events from your own life in chronological order."

"What did he look like?" I asked Mel, already imagining it—he'd have been limping, first of all. He'd have been wearing a torn shirt and jeans, and had one arm in a sling, and gauze wrapped around one eye. Or both eyes. It would actually explain a lot if he'd become blind in both eyes. I felt a little better.

"Ummm, I think he was wearing, like...some shirt?" said Mel.

"*Mel*," said Logan.

"What! It was like, two seconds! I didn't even notice that it was him until he had already passed me. All I registered was that it was him," said Mel.

"But did he seem, like...sad, or anything?" I asked her. "Or... disoriented at all?"

"I don't know, it was two seconds."

"Just try to remember anything."

"I guess he could have been sort of frowning," she said. "Yeah. His lips must have looked extra tiny, because as I passed him I was like, 'Did that guy even have a mouth?'"

"What do you mean by '*extra*'?" I asked.

"He has the smallest lips I've ever seen on anyone in my whole life," said Mel. "Including babies."

"Maybe that's why he can't communicate," said Logan.

"OK," I said. "This is all beside the point, which is that UNLESS something terrible happened last night, which is something I personally believe is a very real possibility, Keith is alive and, presumably with free will, choosing not to respond to my texts."

"I just don't see how that could be it," said Mel.

"Why?" said Logan. "It happens all the time."

I groaned.

"Look, he's weak," said Logan. "Like all guys. He's just lucky we're not living in the Stone Age. He'd never be able to provide for you."

"I can't believe *you* of all people would suggest Harriet couldn't take care of herself in the Stone Age," said Mel.

"Yeah!" I said. "I'm self-reliant."

"You definitely couldn't prepare your own food," Logan said.

"That's fair," I said, crossing my arms on the table in front of me and burying my head in the crook of my elbow.

"All I'm saying is that if you're going to willingly participate in our society's regressive mating rituals, the partner you select should at least bring some survival skills to the table," she continued. "Keith has no useful skills. He's a philosophy major."

"I didn't *select* him," I said into my elbow. "I just want to make out with him again."

"Read us your last message again," said Mel.

I sat up and very slowly turned my phone over onto its back. I unlocked the screen carefully, like either it or I could explode at the slightest wrong touch, and pressed "Keith."

"One twenty-two AM—technically earlier today," I said. I sighed. "I wrote: 'heyyyy'—I remember thinking, 'four Ys is a good, not-crazy amount of Ys'—'heyyyy, am I going to get to see you this wknd?' W-k-n-d, to be casual," I said.

"Right," said Mel. "Totally the right vibe."

"I'm worried it was a little too direct," I said, reading it over again to myself. Maybe I shouldn't have framed it as a question. Maybe I should have only used three Ys. In daylight, four Ys looked weird. The more I looked at the word, the more it started to look like a bug. Like a disgusting centipede. I put my head back down in my arms.

"Don't worry about that. Seriously," said Mel. "At some point you had to say you wanted to hang out again, because otherwise he might've thought, like, 'maybe she doesn't like me anymore!' You guys were, like, going out! You're allowed to say you like him!"

"It doesn't seem like that's true," I said.

"He didn't say anything?" said Logan.

"No!" I said. I sat back up, checking to see if anything had come in—silently, somehow—in the last ten seconds. "No," I said again.

"I'm telling you," said Logan. "Weak."

"I don't know what to do," I said. "I guess that's . . . it?"

"Well," said Mel. "What would Emma say?"

I thought about it for a second. Emma was no-nonsense. She had zero patience for anyone's bullshit and would find Keith's tepidity repugnant. Emma told the people who wrote to her asking for advice to have a backbone for once in their sorry lives, and I knew she'd say the same thing to me.

I knew this because Emma was me. To everyone else at school, she was a pseudonymous sage with a weekly column in the student newspaper. Aside from the paper's editor-in-chief, a senior named Alexia Collins, Mel and Logan were the only ones who knew the column was mine. I'd started it as a sophomore, and written it for a semester and a half before breaking down and telling them. It was briefly very exciting that they knew and I could talk to them about it, until they started using her against me.

"She'd probably say 'Tell him to go fuck himself,'" I said. I could see myself writing the response to this letter, and I knew that I/Emma would not give Keith the benefit of the doubt. I would tell me that I was wasting my time.

"Exactly," said Logan. "So don't stress out over him. He's unworthy."

"I think you should text him again. Write 'See you in HELL!'" said Mel.

"That implies that Harriet will also be there," said Logan.

"I already am," I said. "I think I need to go back to sleep for a little bit." I got up from the table to refill my glass of water and swallowed a second Advil. "Are you guys going to the library later? I work two to six."

"Yeah, I'll probably head over after I shower," said Mel.

"Me, too. Except for the shower part," said Logan.

After closing my bedroom door, I picked up my laptop off my desk, placed my water on my nightstand, propped up my pillows, and slid into bed. I did not plan to go back to sleep, exactly. I planned to resume my now-multi-day, ongoing investigation into Keith's whereabouts, physical and emotional.

The last I'd heard from him was ten days earlier. A Thursday. Two days after we'd studied for a quiz together in the library. I'd texted him to ask if he was going to make it out to the bars, and, forty-seven minutes later, he'd texted me "Nah, I think I'm in for the night. Have fun." Except there was no period. "Have fun" was an unclosed statement, wide open with potentially infinite space after the n. "Have fun" without an exclamation point, the more I looked at it, seemed an almost ominous command. Or maybe it was just sad. "Have fun…like you used to be able to, once." "Have fun…on your own, specifically not with me." Was "have fun" without the period a kind of good-bye? Did he think that counted?

I'd texted back "Ah, okay, goodnight (and thanks)!" Exclamation point. And then I'd waited. I didn't see him out on either weekend night. He didn't come to the class we had together on Monday, either. So that evening, I'd texted him to ask how his thesis was coming, and he didn't ever respond. On Wednesday, he showed up late to class and sat down several rows from me, near the door. "It was just because he was late," my friends told me, and I tried to believe them. Then, last night, at 1:22 AM, after consuming approximately 1.5 shots of tequila, 2 whiskey sours, and 2.25 beers, I'd texted him a centipede.

I didn't have to think of what I did today, or tomorrow, as "waiting" for him to respond. I knew he wouldn't. I still sort of believed he might, but I knew he wouldn't.

I looked at the exchange again, scrolling back to two weeks earlier, back to the last time it had seemed good. I tried, again, to find anything telling, anything that seemed like a warning, but I still couldn't. A couple weeks back there was a good day of texting each other needless emoticons and giggling sounds, and then he stopped gushing: periods over exclamation points, the smiley face disappeared altogether. Mel and Logan had told me I was imagining things, and reading too much into texts, and that his shift in tone didn't mean that he hated me now. And maybe it did not. But now I felt I had been right to think it didn't mean anything good.

Before opening my laptop, I started my search with a cursory examination of the sources available on my phone. Keith wasn't much for Instagram. His last post was eleven weeks ago, before we even knew each other. He'd taken it at home over winter break. The picture was of an open book in his lap and his dog's head resting on his outstretched leg, and I remembered that when I saw it for the first time (whenever it was I first looked him up), I considered it proof positive of his intellectuality and sensitivity. I was like, *Wow, I cannot believe I found someone who also likes dogs and books.*

Next I checked Twitter, which he did not have. A few of his friends did, though, and if he *had* suddenly died, I thought they might be tweeting about it ("RIP Keith"). Instead I found only a handful of days-old tweets about cross-country practice and *New York Times* articles. A tweet from Keith's friend Jake reading "Yoooooo this is too real" seemed mildly promising, but the timestamp and surrounding context kind of made it seem like it probably referred to something that had happened on *Game of Thrones.*

Next I checked AstrologyZone to see if it had any relevant-seeming predictions about my day and/or love life. "Work now, play later" began today's entry. "This is a hard pill to swallow for an adventurous fire sign, but it's important—especially for your financial well-being." I sighed.

Having consulted all relevant phone sources, I lifted my laptop screen and opened a new tab for the main locus of my search: Facebook. For serious searches, I never dared look at it on my phone. The risk of accidentally "liking" someone's post seemed far too high. Not that the web version was without its various stresses, though—as always, I was struck with overwhelming panic that I'd accidentally type Keith's name into my status bar instead of the search box. (Sometimes the fantasy would carry on for several minutes, through several possible outcomes. Maybe I wouldn't notice my mistake, and his name would sit up there for hours, and I wouldn't know until he commented with a single question mark. Or maybe I'd delete it right away, but he'd still get a notification.) I took a deep breath, triple-checked that my cursor was in the search box, and, as if typing his name extra slowly would provide added protection against embarrassment, pecked the letters of his name out one by one using only my forefingers. K-E-(quadruple-check the box I typed in)-I—and at that point his full name (Keith Rapp) appeared auto-completed in the box, in what I felt was an aggressive and accusatory move on Facebook's part.

Keith's profile picture was not of him, or any human being, for that matter. It was, as it had been for a year and a half, according to the timestamp, a modernist painting. Though I didn't care much for the piece itself, I'd found this choice and this consistency charmingly self-effacing. It was odd and discomfiting to have a crush on someone and, partway into it, watch him change his profile picture. It forced a reevaluation ("What does he think this picture of him hiking in the woods says about him that the other picture, of him lying in the sun with a T-shirt draped over his face, did not?"), and a recognition that his presentation was something he actively participated in. To come upon an already made Facebook profile was one thing, but to realize its owner, like you, sat there wondering which picture to use, and which facts about himself to include, was nearly heartbreaking in its exposed vulnerability. *Do I think about Facebook too much?* I wondered.

I was somewhat relieved to find nothing new in Keith's recent activity, or on his wall—the latest post was still a link to a campus environmental event that had taken place the previous Friday. He'd linked a reminder the night beforehand: at 8:13 PM. I looked at the clock on my laptop's navigation bar—10:09 AM, Sunday, March 15. As far as I could see, Keith had now gone a little over sixty-two hours without doing anything on Facebook. It wasn't so long, or so far off his typical usage rate (not that I kept a log or anything), but it was starting to feel conspicuous.

But maybe that was only because I'd never before paid quite this much attention.

I could pretend that the inactivity pointed toward something temporarily all-consuming in his life, like an exam, or a serious (but not fatal, or too sad) family issue, or some deep, emotional self-examination from which he'd emerge a better man. Or something. But the explanation that seemed most likely was that he hadn't used Facebook in a while because it didn't matter that much to him. Just like the reason he hadn't been texting me back was probably that I didn't, either.

We met in January in HIST 365: Special Topics: The Spanish Civil War—Mondays and Wednesdays, 1:10 PM. It was a very specific class, but it was a popular choice among humanities students looking to satisfy their modern history prerequisite because it was moderately easy and because the professor, who was from Spain, made charming, cheesy jokes. I liked to sit near the back of the lecture hall and write them down on the last page of my notebook.

On the fourth day of class, Keith moved past me to sit in my row, and when I stood up to let him by, he smiled at me in polite thanks before taking a seat that left one empty chair between us. That's when I noticed that he a) was even hotter than he'd looked from across the room, where I'd noticed him the first day, and b) smelled the way all guys should smell, though I hadn't known I thought so until just then. (The only way to describe it was that he smelled like a Christmas tree, including the lights.)

I didn't write a single word in my notebook that day. Instead, I stared straight ahead at the whiteboard, trying so hard to appear fully absorbed that I went too far and slipped over the edge into something that must have looked more like hysteria. A few minutes before the end of the lecture, I looked in Keith's direction with my peripherals, first trying not to move my head at all and then, when that proved dizzying, turning it only very slightly to my right. He looked up from his notebook, where, I noticed, he'd been drawing in the margins, and then he looked right at me. He smiled again, and I kind of half smiled and half grimaced, I think, and quickly looked down at my completely blank page. I picked up my pen and held it point down on the paper, like a prop, until we were dismissed.

The next two classes proceeded about the same, with him one seat away.

After the seventh class, a Wednesday, I had a work-study shift at the library from 3:00 to 6:30. I worked at the circulation desk and did very little but check out students' books, show them how to work the photocopier, and answer the odd phone call about our hours from people who apparently didn't know how to check them online. I considered it an ideal campus job because it provided me with several blocks of time a week during which I could reasonably argue that I had almost nothing to do but look at the Internet and people-watch.

The collection of four-person tables near the circulation desk, an area that was inherently noisy and ripe for distraction, had long been unofficially designated for unambitious, performative studying. On the weekends hungover students brought snacks there, sat with their unopened books in front of them, and gossiped about the night before, while I eavesdropped. Weekday afternoons were usually less interesting—the overheard gossip more academic, less boozy and sexy—but still, sometimes, something exciting would happen. Once I overheard a trio of statistics TAs plan a mutiny against an absent fourth one. "It's like he thinks he's George E. P. Box," one of them had said, and they'd all laughed for like two full minutes. For months afterward, anytime anyone acted like a know-it-all in one of my classes, I thought to myself, *It's like he thinks he's George E. P. Box.*

On that February Wednesday, though, it had been 12 degrees outside, and the library was totally dead. I exhausted all my various Internet time-killers within the first hour and became so bored that I was practically forced to do some actual work. Instead, though, I started drafting the following week's Dear Emma, answering a letter from a freshman who hated her roommate because the roommate's boyfriend slept over at least four times a week. In the top bunk.

I had only managed to type "Dear SSH"—Sleepless in Seaver Hall—before I noticed Keith approaching the circulation desk from the right. (My peripherals had, apparently, learned to recognize his distinct blur.) Reflexively, like a deer who has just noticed she's been spotted by a human being, I stopped moving. I stopped typing. I sat up straight. My fingers hovered over the keyboard for a second before I realized that looked weird, and then I resumed frantic mime-typing: "Dear SSH, a;lsdfkja;leifaow;eiffasdl;kfjasl;kdfjas;lkdfja;lskdfj;."

"Hey," he said, having traversed the thirty or so feet between the front entrance and the desk in what seemed to me an inhuman speed. "Oh, hey!" he said, again, in apparent recognition.

"Oh, hi...hey!" I said. I figured I should probably pretend not to know his name, because I'd only learned it by looking up our class's registered student list and then searching for all the guys in it on Facebook, one by one, until I found him.

"Spanish Civil War, right?" he asked, which I liked as a question out of context.

"Right!" I said. "I'm Harriet."

"Keith," he said, extending his hand over the stretch of desk between us. I shook it. He had a really great grip. For the first time I felt free to look at him directly: He was tall and skinny with broad shoulders, and was wearing a too-small plaid button-down shirt and jeans. He had deep-set dark eyes and long eyelashes and a pronounced jaw. His hair was very dark brown, and so was the partial beard growing in on and around what I must state again, for emphasis, was truly a stellar jawline. We smiled at each other for another beat.

"I was hoping to check out one of the special texts back there," he said, pointing to the racks behind me, where professors put aside their harder-to-find or too-expensive books for students to photocopy or check out for a few hours at a time. He told me the professor's name, and the name of the text's author, and I said, "Sure, one sec." I stood up, turned around, and immediately forgot everything he'd told me. I stopped in my tracks, then turned back to him.

"Um, sorry," I said. "What . . . were the names again?"

Keith laughed and picked up a pen and a small slip of paper from the little plastic containers that sat behind my computer screen. He wrote down the two names and, next to them, a smiley face.

(I kept the slip of paper. The professor's name was Kendall, and the author's name was Reuchlin. The smiley face had vertical dashes for eyes and the mouth was sharp, almost like a v.)

He pushed the paper facedown across the desk to me like someone making a deal with a Mafia boss in a movie, and I laughed as I picked it up. I headed back to the stacks, a little slower than I would have otherwise, trying to make the encounter last. I saw the book he wanted right away but pretended to look for a few moments longer, making a concerted facial expression that, to me, said "Hmmmmmmm, where could that book be?" I picked it up and walked back over to the desk, where I was disappointed to see that Keith was scrolling through something on his phone. But then he looked up, and smiled, and said, "Awesome, thanks, Harriet."

It was thrilling to hear him pronounce my name. It doesn't matter how simple your name is; it's always a surprise to hear it spoken aloud for the first time by someone new, how the specific arrangement of syllables sounds coming out of their mouth. Hair-ee-it, he pronounced it—just like everyone did, but different. He said it like it was the first time he'd said "Harriet" in his life. Like it was a word he'd never thought about, or needed to know before, but that he would from now on.

I'd handed Keith the sign-out form on the book, which told him he needed to return it within two hours. I'd hoped he'd sit at a table near me so I could cautiously observe him for that entire period, but he headed up the stairs to some unknown floor and corner. I was disappointed, but I also had to admire his work ethic.

In an hour and forty-two minutes he came back, said "Hello again," and handed me the book, which I traded for the form. Then he stood there for a second—maybe even half of one—and to fill the interminable space I said, "Well, see you on Monday! In class!"

"Yeah!" he said. "It's been kinda slow but it seems like things are about to take off."

"Yes, I think Nationalist tensions are running high," I said.

He laughed. "I don't think I trust that Franco guy."

"Me, either," I said, legitimately beaming.

"OK," he said. "See you Monday."

"Yep!" I said, which was not cool. I could have said "See ya" or "Monday!" or something flirtatious, like "I can't wait." Any of those things would have been better than the curt, dorky half word that came out of my mouth. But then he did a kind of awkward half wave/salute-type gesture, and I figured we were basically even. He smiled, and I smiled, and he picked up his book bag and walked out of the library. I spent the rest of my shift looking at my restricted, nonfriend view of his Facebook page and wondered what he was trying to say with that painting.

The next Monday Keith sat next to me in class without the open seat in between. Instead of writing Professor Ferrer's jokes in the back of my notebook, I took actual notes on the lecture. But after he made a particularly cheesy pun involving the Fascist Falange, I noticed Keith writing it in a word bubble next to a cartoon drawing of Ferrer's face. And then something very exciting happened: Keith elbowed me. It was a soft jab, his flanneled elbow just barely meeting my sweatered upper arm, but it felt like a jolt that ran through my entire body. He nudged his notebook an inch or two closer to my desk, indicating that I should look at it, which I did, more overtly now. I smiled. I should have looked up at him but I was afraid of how close our faces would have been.

At the end of class, Professor Ferrer announced that we'd have a quiz on Wednesday.

"Maybe we should study," Keith said when we stood up at the end of class.

"That would be good," I said.

"Cool," he said, and then he turned around and bounded down the stairs so quickly I could not have caught up if I tried. I stood there for a moment, confused as to whether or not we had made an actual plan, since we hadn't given each other any way to get in touch.

When I got home in a panic and told Mel and Logan what had

happened, they urged me to at *least* add him as a friend on Facebook. After ten minutes of deliberation, I slid my laptop across the coffee table to Mel, who pressed the button for me.

He accepted my friend request eight minutes later.

That a month had passed since seemed both too much and too little. I checked my laptop's clock again: It now read 11:07. My laptop, which still sat open on Keith's Facebook profile, had slid halfway off my thighs and rested at a distraught-looking angle on my comforter. I slid it back into an upright position on my legs and looked at his timeline and recent activity one last time. Still, nothing.

63+ hours now.

I clicked on the "Post" button and watched my cursor flash in the little box. It's not like I was really about to write something on his wall, obviously. It would be embarrassing, and pathetic at this point, and people barely used Facebook walls to say hi anyway. (Except for aunts and uncles and weird people you hadn't seen since high school.) But there was still something territorial about posting on someone's wall, like claiming a small plot of their land, like you had to earn it somehow. Because everyone would see it, you needed a good reason. You needed to be close, or at least to have been close once. Part of me wanted to try to make that true.

Instead I closed out of the browser window, shut my laptop screen, and pushed it off to the side. I took another Advil, set my phone alarm for 1:00, and lay back down to sleep. But first, for exactly the ten minutes I gave myself and no more, I read through my texts to Keith just one more time in case I found something that might explain everything.

2

I woke up to the sounds of my phone alarm harp and eased myself out of bed, relieved to note that my headache had subsided to a more tolerable muted pressure. I walked through our shared bathroom, which led into the kitchen, and peered out, but nobody was there. The dirty lunch dishes in the sink told me that Mel and Logan had already left. I stood looking in the bathroom mirror for a few minutes trying to decide between a shower (the underdog) and dry shampoo (the favorite). I opened the cabinet, took out the bottle of powder, and dumped some of it over my head, making my dark brown hair slightly gray in this process. I combed it through my hair, pulled the whole thing into a high bun, and fixed the mascara smudged under my eyes.

I got to the library five minutes before my shift and dropped my bag on the floor below my usual seat at the circulation desk. On Sundays I worked with a sophomore named Lara, who wanted to be an actual librarian after graduation. She had a lot of pretty, drapey cardigans and was quietly menacing, so I thought this seemed like a wise choice. But today, her seat was empty. I walked over to check the work study schedule that was pinned up next to the staff librarian's office door, but it was the same printout that had hung there all semester. As far as I knew, Lara should've been there since one.

I sat down again, feeling increasingly frustrated by how infrequently everyone kept me updated on where they were all the time.

I took my notebooks and folders out of my bag. My plan was to first work my way through the two readings I had for Victorian Era Prose and Poetry and then to write the 1000-word reading recap I had due the next day in Spanish Civ. I had arranged my books in front of me and uncapped my favorite blue highlighter when a girl I didn't know pushed open the swinging circulation gate and sat three feet down from me at the long desk.

"Hey?" I said.

"Hi," she said, smiling more at the book bag in her lap than at me. I paused, waiting for her to explain herself.

"Are you filling in for Lara...or ...?" I said finally. "I'm Harriet, by the way."

"Yeah—well, we swapped shifts for the semester, actually. I guess she had a conflict with a new study group or something," said the girl.

"Sorry, what was your name?" I asked.

"Oh! Right. Remy," she said.

Remy? I thought. But of course her name would be Remy. She was short and fair-skinned and thin, with an angular, jagged bob dyed jet black. She was wearing a loose, dark purple sweatshirt over floral-patterned leggings and ankle boots. She had on about ten bracelets and she looked amazing.

"I really like your leggings," I said. She smiled, said nothing. I went on. "I always want to wear things with flowers on them but I don't think I have the right vibe, if that makes sense?"

"I think the vibe comes after you put them on," said Remy, which was easy for her to say.

"No, really," I said. "I've tried. I just end up looking like I'm going to church."

"I'm sure that's not true," said Remy.

"Well," I said, and then I shrugged, because I didn't want or know how to argue with someone I'd just met about whether or not I could pull off florals. I needed to change the topic. "What do you study?"

"Art," she said. Of course. "Well, and English writing minor, though I always feel dumb saying that because it's like three classes."

"Cool," I said, pausing again. "I'm an English lit major," I said, when it became clear she wasn't going to ask me the same question. "Because it's *extremely* practical, career-wise."

"Oh, cool," she said. "Are you . . . a sophomore?"

"Junior," I said. Like I looked young enough to be a *sophomore*. "And you are . . ."

"Senior," she said, and I thought, *well*, if she and I get trapped in this building by a sudden nuclear war, and we sit here for years and years, and this conversation never starts to feel normal, at least she will probably die a little bit before I do.

Remy pulled her bag onto her lap. I half expected her to produce a canvas and oil paints, but instead she took out a notebook and folder not unlike mine. I sat there dumbly for a moment with my hands folded in my lap, looking between her and my computer, because I didn't want to seem like I was in a rush to get to studying. Lara and I had not been best friends or anything, but we had established a nice, routine camaraderie with each other. We'd start our shifts complaining about things like books being returned with creased pages and how cold it was in there. She always had a small plastic container filled with Earl Grey tea bags in her backpack, and sometimes she'd disappear into the staff kitchen and come back with mugs for each of us, the little tags hanging out over the sides. I don't really like tea, but I always drank it anyway.

Remy, on the other hand, opened her notebook and started scribbling with a pen, her face hovering just above the paper and her body definitively faced away from me.

I could not really see Remy making us tea in the foreseeable future.

I opened my email and typed a quick note to Lara: "You dropped your Sunday shift!! :(" I looked over at Remy and saw that she'd already filled nearly a page in wide, loopy writing. She put down her pen and stretched out her writing hand, and then sat up to use her computer. I quickly looked back at my own. I decided to reverse the order of my homework plan and opened up a document for my recap. I'd already read the assigned text during my Friday shift and was now able to get to 340 words through memory recall and overly long sentences. At 2:28, I decided I deserved a quick break.

I logged into Facebook, where, unsurprisingly, I had no personal news. I looked at Remy to make sure she couldn't see my monitor screen, and typed "Remy" into the search bar. "Remy Roy" popped up right away. I couldn't see very much of her profile, but her main picture, of course, was beautifully lit and interestingly cropped.

I returned to my own page and sat there staring a moment before reflexively checking Keith's page. I scrolled down quickly, hardly looking, and had already clicked back to my profile when I realized that I'd registered something new. The link to the environmental event had been just a little lower on the page, and above it, something else.

I felt my pulse quicken, which was so stupid. It was probably nothing, at least not anything helpful or telling, and in a moment I'd click back and I would feel silly for letting Facebook rule my circulatory system. I took a deep breath and a sip of water from my water bottle. I clicked over to my Spanish Civil War recap and pretended to reread what I'd written. And then, casually, I clicked back over to my browser, and typed K-E-I into the search bar for what felt like the four hundred millionth time that day.

I scrolled down as slowly as humanly possible.

The first thing I saw was the post, a link to a YouTube video for what looked like some kind of stop-motion animated short. In itself, this seemed innocuous enough. Links were impersonal and unoriginal; this was not a movie made FOR Keith but simply something someone else saw, either liked or hated, and sent over to him. There was no personalized message that accompanied the video. It sat there unadorned, with no likes or comments beneath it. It was posted twenty-seven minutes ago.

I checked the name and gasped involuntarily.

Remy looked up at me and I panicked.

"Sorry," I said, forcing a weird little laugh. "I was just watching this video of ..." I hesitated, unable to think of literally anything plausible. *What about snakes??* said my brain. *SOMETHING ELSE*, I thought. *Snakes. Snakes. Snaaaakes*. "...snakes," I said. Whatever.

"O...kay," said Remy, smirking back down at her notebook.

I watched her a moment to make sure she wouldn't come over to check out this very interesting alleged snake video, but she had resumed her scribbling and seemed likely to continue doing so. I realized I'd been holding my breath and I exhaled, and then I looked back at my screen.

It seemed impossible, but the person who was apparently

responsible for having posted this video on Keith's wall twenty-eight minutes earlier was Remy Roy.

Did she post this while she was WALKING to the LIBRARY? I wondered. *Are they on a POSTING-on-each-other's-FACEBOOK-while-WALKING basis??*

My face felt hot and flushed, and my heart thudded dully against my chest, then dropped, as far as I could tell, completely out of my body. I knew it was just a link. It didn't say "I think it is so great we had sex last night!" or "Pretty cool that we are now in love!" above it. But I worried, and my body worried *for* me, overruling whatever pathetic attempts at rationality and caution I might have otherwise made, throwing me into full-throttled panic, that it might as well have.

I clicked on the name "Remy Roy" in the post, just in case there were secretly two of them out there, two Remys with very similar profile pictures, but of course it took me back to the page I'd visited only minutes earlier. I wanted badly to add her as a friend if only to find out anything more about her, any small detail that might have helped me determine how she knew Keith and what he might think about her, what role she played (or what role he wanted her to play) in his life. I clicked on her profile picture and realized I could see a few more—there she was studying abroad in what looked like Greece; there she was making a funny face with red lipstick on, holding up a peace sign while standing in front of what looked like some kind of light show; there she was a year or two earlier, standing behind a beer pong table with two teams of two guys on either end, holding a plastic cup and smiling with her mouth closed, looking down. The common theme among these photos was that she looked fucking great in all of them. Rarely had I been moved to use the adverb "exquisitely," but Remy was *exquisitely* beautiful.

I looked over at her and noticed she now appeared to be text-ing. *With Keith?* I wondered. I tried to surreptitiously evaluate her expression. Did she look happy? Infatuated? Stressed, but in an antsy-crushy sort of way? Her face was unreadable until she laughed and I felt my face get hot all over again. For just a mo-ment, I wondered if there was some way I could rush her chair and knock her out of it so that she and her phone would fall to the floor, and I could pick it up, and apologize, and read it very quickly while handing it back.

No, I decided. That would probably come off poorly.

Remy put down her phone and I realized I hadn't stopped star-ing. How had she not noticed? It was weird. One could argue that it was actually weirder to be stared at that long without noticing than it was to be the one staring.

I clicked back to Keith's profile and, after making sure the computer's sound was muted, took a careful screenshot of Remy's post, which I then attached to an email and immediately deleted from the library computer's desktop. I addressed the email to Mel and Logan. In the subject line, I wrote: "WTF IS THIS HORSESHIT." In the body, I wrote: "Help me I am sitting next to this girl RIGHT NOW in the library and I just saw that she wrote on Keith's wall within the past hour?????? Do either of you know her?? If you guys are here you need to come to the desk and like...look at her, I don't know, HELP." I pressed send and sat back too hard into my chair. This, finally, made Remy look up. She glanced over at me. I looked over and whispered "Bored" by way of explanation. She smiled thinly and looked back down at her notebook.

What the FUCK was she writing about that was so all-consuming is what I wanted to know.

A few minutes later I saw Mel and Logan coming down the

central stairwell and relaxed. They walked toward me slowly, gaping at and evaluating Remy.

"Hey!" I said, almost hissing. The subtext was *get over here now*.

"Heyyyy, Harriet, how are you doing today?" said Mel, who was incapable of acting natural in situations that called for it, and would start to speak too formally, and use people's names too often.

"Good," I said, "just slow, you know."

We sat there nodding at each other for a moment.

"Were you guys studying on three?" I asked. I was pretty sure the answer was yes; Mel, a pre-dental major, and Logan, who was pre-med, frequently had overlapping classes, and would hole up together somewhere on the third floor and come visit me when they needed a break. Mel looked back over at Remy.

"Yes," she said. "We do not know *anyone*"—she paused significantly—"else here."

"Um, OK," I said. "Cool. Do you guys think you'll leave before my shift ends?"

"Probably not," said Logan. "Exam tomorrow. So we'll meet you here at six?"

"Sure," I said. "See you." I looked at Remy out of the corner of my eye, confirmed that she wasn't looking at any of us, mouthed *email me*, and tilted my head in her direction.

"What?" said Mel.

"OK, later!!" said Logan, gently shoving Mel back in the direction of the stairs.

A few minutes later I received a short email reply from Logan: "As you may or may not have gathered from Mel's extremely subtle hint, neither of us knows her. Neither of us thinks that link really means anything. (Except that it seems insufferably twee, but, maybe that's up his alley.) She is hot though."

Why couldn't she have just left off that last sentence? I thought. I clicked "Reply" and wrote back, "I knowwwwww, ughhhhhhhh-hhhhhh."

I clicked over from my email to Keith's Facebook, scrolled down, and sharply inhaled. Sometime within the last few minutes, he had liked Remy's link post. There was his name below it, the approving little thumb to its left. So, yes, it *was* up his alley.

I watched it for a moment to see if a comment from him would immediately follow, and when it didn't, I felt mildly consoled. A like could be genuine, but it could also merely be a way to acknowledge that you saw something you didn't care much about. It could be a way of ending the interaction—of saying "Thanks, that will be all." Maybe Remy had a crush on him, and, however implausible it seemed that any guy could resist her charms, Keith didn't have one in return. Or maybe they had been friends once, maybe their freshman year, and now had the kind of relationship sustained only by sporadic, near-thoughtless link-sharing.

I scrolled down farther, to his recent activity, and saw that I could safely rule out the latter: Keith and Remy had only become Facebook friends a few hours ago.

I really hate this website, I thought, and closed out of the whole window. Left with no other alternative, I returned to my Spanish Civ assignment. And they say the Internet isn't good for productivity.

At six on the dot, Mel and Logan returned to the front desk, coats and backpacks on.

"Hey," I said. I looked over at Remy, who was now wearing headphones and mildly bouncing along to whatever she was listening to. She did not look as stupid doing this as any normal human being would have.

I walked toward the gate with my things and was just through it when I heard Remy say, "Oh, are you done?"

"Yeah," I said, a bit too cheerily. "Two to six!"

"Oh, okay," she said, moving to put her headphones back on.

"See you next Sunday," I said, and she nodded.

Mel and Logan and I made it into the vestibule before any of us said anything.

"She seems easy to talk to," said Logan.

"GOD," I said. "It's like pulling teeth. Eh??" I elbowed Mel.

"Good one," she said. "I haven't heard that before."

"Thank you," I said, pushing open the doors that took us outside. We walked in silence for a few seconds, adjusting to the cold. "He liked her post. So I guess he is alive."

Mel and Logan didn't say anything but exchanged looks.

"What?" I said. "What was that?"

"Well," said Logan. "We may have had prior confirmation of that fact. More, I mean."

"We saw him upstairs," explained Mel.

"WHAT?" I said. "Why didn't you tell me??"

"It's not like you would have done anything about it," said Logan.

"How do you know that?" I asked. "I could have done a drive-by with the reshelving cart or something."

"Would you have said anything to him?" asked Mel.

"I don't know!! I don't *know* what I would have done, because you didn't tell me," I said, feeling hurt for reasons I couldn't specifically name.

"Who cares where he is? He sucks. You shouldn't even care whether he lives or dies," said Logan.

"Thank you, Logan, that's very reasonable," I snapped. "I'll just stop caring. Good idea."

"I still bet he'll say something in class tomorrow," said Mel. "I mean, you'll see each other in class for the rest of the semester."

"I bet you he won't," said Logan. "I mean, maybe," she added when I glared at her.

"OK, look," I said, coming to a stop and waiting for them to stand still, too. "I don't want you guys not to tell me things about Keith, or anyone, to protect my feelings. OK? Because they're already hurt." I paused to look at my feet. "I'm not stupid. I know he isn't going to text me back. Ever. But I don't know why, and I'm sad, and I'm angry about it, and I'm going to want to know where he is, what he's doing, until I stop caring. I will tell you when I stop caring. OK?" I felt my eyes brimming with tears and I blinked them away. "I don't want you guys conspiring to keep things from me."

"We weren't *conspiring*," said Logan.

"I'm sorry," said Mel.

Logan sighed. "I'm sorry, too," she said. I could tell that, in spite of herself, she meant it.

We started walking again, crossing half a block in silence.

"Just, tell me about something else, something science-y," I said.

"Ummm," said Mel, "oh my god, OK. Wait. I know. There is some *prettyyyy* juicy drama happening with the Tri-Beta leadership," said Mel. Tri-Beta was the biology department's honor society. A fraternity for nerds, according to my roommates.

"Peter Dorffman is positively tyrannical," said Logan. "He wants us to have a singles mixer."

"Ew, why?"

Katie Heaney

"I think he thinks if he plans it with Nora, they'll fall in love or something," said Mel.

"You can't have a couple as Tri-Beta co-presidents," said Logan. "It's a conflict of interest. And you can't make us court each other. The entire system is going to crumble."

It took five more freezing minutes for us to speed-walk our way home, but I was grateful for them. Those were five minutes during when I couldn't check my phone, or my laptop, or think about Keith and what might have happened. I knew that as soon as I got home it would be all I was able to do.

3

One of the things I liked most about Keith was his quickness. Not just physically, always speed-walking a foot or two ahead—the way he'd run out of class after asking me to study, because he'd accomplished one task and didn't want to waste time getting to the next. It was also that he never made me wait very long. He'd asked me to hang out on the first day it occurred to me to think it might be possible for the two of us to hang out. Once we'd started texting, he wrote back immediately. At least at first. Every other boy I knew said so little, and 80 percent of what they did say was "I don't know" and "*Ummmm*." Keith never said he didn't know.

On the night he accepted my Facebook request, promptly, I shrieked, pacing around the kitchen and asking Mel and Logan what I should do.

"Nothing," said Logan. "It was his idea to study. He should give you actual details."

"I don't know," said Mel. "Sometimes boys need a lot of encouragement."

"As a people, they need to get over that," said Logan.

"So, what, should she never speak to any of them, to teach the entire sex a lesson?" said Mel.

They were still arguing about how I should proceed when I heard the sound of a message arriving in my inbox. I stopped and gasped, leaning over my laptop to look.

"What?" they asked.

"He just wrote to me!!!" I said.

"Read it!" said Mel. "Open it!!!"

"Are you insane??" I said. "There's read receipts. He can't know I read it immediately after getting it. I will seem like a murderer."

"That's not a trait of murderers," said Logan. "If anything, you would take longer to read it, because you would be out murdering people for the night."

"Oh my god," I said. "You're right."

"Harriet," said Logan.

"I DON'T KNOW," I said, almost yelling. "Someone needs to give me a solution that doesn't raise the question of murder!!!"

"Literally none of the solutions raise the question of murder!" said Logan.

I sat down at the table and Mel got up from it. She removed three shot glasses from the cabinet, took our half-empty bottle of tequila out of the freezer, and set the items in front of Logan and me.

"Do we have any chasers?" I asked.

"Umm, orange juice?" she said. Logan and I hesitantly agreed by grimacing. Mel didn't use chasers herself—not because she didn't think she could benefit from them, but because having to swallow different drinks in quick succession stressed her out.

"Thank you," I said, and waited a moment while she poured shots for the three of us. I poured the orange juice. I swallowed half a shot, coughed, followed it with some juice, and repeated.

"OK," Logan said. "Now: how many minutes has it been since he sent the message?"

"Six," I said, checking the clock.

"OK," she said. "He accepted your friend request pretty quickly, right?"

"You were here!" I said.

"I know that," she said. "I'm, like, presenting the case."

"OK," I said. "Correct."

"Don't you think it's true—?"

"Objection!" yelled Mel. "Leading the witness."

Logan and I both turned to look at her gravely.

"Overruled," she said. "I overrule myself. Proceed." She uncapped the tequila bottle and poured each of us another half shot, and we all paused to drink.

"When Keith accepted you after eight minutes," Logan started again, "you didn't think *he* was crazy, did you?"

"No," I said. "I was excited."

"And why is that?" asked Logan.

"Because it made me feel like he couldn't wait," I said, simultaneously starting to grin and trying to make myself stop.

"So might he not then feel the same way if you were to read and respond to his message in a comparably short amount of time?" she asked.

I hesitated. "Entrapment," I said.

"It's not," said Mel. "You just know she's right."

I sighed and pulled my computer closer to me. I clicked on the message and it opened in a pop-up on my screen. It was over—now I'd really have to respond, because he'd know for sure that I saw it. I read aloud:

"Harriet," I said, "[exclamation point]. I'm planning to study for Spanish Civ tomorrow night around 8ish. I prefer the reading room on the 3rd floor because the lighting flatters my features. Come by if you're around, I'm a great quizzer. [Hyphen] Keith."

"Wowww," said Mel. Even Logan looked mildly charmed.

"Really?" I asked. "'Come by if you're around' seems kind of ambivalent to me. Like 'Don't come for *me*, but if you somehow just *happen* to find yourself at the library tomorrow night, I will also be there, unrelatedly.'"

"Yeah, I'm always telling people I hate to stop by my specific location in the library so I can sexily quiz them on history facts," said Mel.

"I have been waiting my whole life to quiz a hot guy in the library and now that it's here I'm like, not ready," I said. I touched my neck with my middle and ring fingers to feel my pulse, which somehow felt normal. "People shouldn't study with hot people. I don't think it's a good idea, academically."

"It'll be a good way for you to assess his intelligence," suggested Logan.

"What should I write back?" I asked.

"I don't know. You're the writer! We're bad at this," said Mel.

"You're not *that* bad," I said. "She is." I gestured at Logan.

"I wasn't even going to try," she said.

"I just want a template to work off of," I said. "If you suggest something I hate, it's helpful to me, because then I know what I don't want to say."

"Nice," said Mel. "OK. Um. Just say, like, 'Cool, see you then maybe.'"

"That's it?" I said.

Mel glared at me.

"OK, I'm going to say: 'Interesting. I always think people on the third floor look slightly jaundiced. I will try to stop by (I'm a great quizzee). [Space down, no hyphen] Harriet,'" I said, typing the words as I read them.

"That's good," said Mel. "See, I helped."

"Not writing his name at the beginning is a good call," said Logan approvingly.

"Thank you," I said, and pressed send.

I closed Facebook to prevent myself from staring at the message window until his read notification appeared. But when I opened it again eleven minutes later, it already had. He didn't write back, but I supposed he hadn't needed to.

I started panicking the next afternoon around four. Though he'd mentioned a time and a place, and, if I was being reasonable, I knew that meant he actually did want me to stop by, or at least wouldn't be shocked and dismayed if I did, the distance between talking about it and the time it would allegedly happen seemed enormous, and it seemed very plausible that he could have changed his mind or plans.

"What do I do if I go to the library and he's not there? Just leave??" I texted Logan.

"Yes. That is literally the worst-case scenario," she texted back. She seemed to not understand how devastating that would actually be. And what would be even worse is if I went to the library, and saw Keith sitting at the table, and, as I walked closer, realized there was another girl sitting with him at the table, and then they both egged me. I decided not to text all of this to Logan. What I had wanted her to tell me was that there was no way on earth he wouldn't be at the library waiting for me, no way it wouldn't work out as perfectly as I'd started to allow myself to hope for. I wanted her to tell me to calm down, to stop being an idiot, that it was obvious he was interested in me and surely thought I was very cute and funny. But that kind of thing wasn't really Logan's style; everything to do with boys had always bored her completely.

So I'd put my phone away and walked home from class, and, for three hours, found ways to (attempt to) distract myself while I waited. I watched the Food Network. I made toast. I touched up my hair for twenty minutes. I listened to Rihanna and made sexy music video faces in the bathroom mirror. I felt embarrassed and changed my outfit. And then again.

At 7:33, I was ready to go to the library and stood with my backpack on in the kitchen in front of our house's side door. I looked over at the microwave clock and sighed impatiently. I entered into a small internal argument with myself in which one part of me reasoned that I'd walked to the library many times, and knew it would take fifteen minutes at most, and the other part of me asked myself whether today might not be the first time I encountered several time-consuming obstacles along the way that merited leaving now. (Like an impassable traffic jam, or a turtle that needed to be carried to safety.) In the end I made myself sit down, on top of my hands, in the living room. Because I thought it would seem too eager to get there at eight on the dot, I didn't let myself leave until 7:52.

(I am trying to memorize the details. When I go back over it in my head, I make myself remember *everything*, start to finish, because I know it wasn't long, and if I don't walk through it again and again, I am going to forget. If I leave it up to my subconscious, I will only remember a few of the more obvious moments. I'll forget about how I felt before any of that happened, when I was waiting alone with my hands under my legs. And in some ways that was the best part.)

The study date was neither as bad as the worst version nor as seamlessly spectacular as the best version I'd spent that afternoon imagining. It was somewhere in between, uncomfortable and good in ways I couldn't have foreseen to daydream about. I walked up the stairs to the third floor, turned a corner, walked between the JA–KE humanities stacks, and found him there on the other side, exactly where he'd said he'd be, alone. He was wearing a gray T-shirt and jeans, and his normally wavyish hair looked flat on his head, like maybe he hadn't done anything to it that day but wake up, shower, and head off to class.

Keith looked up to see me standing still, watching him, ten feet away from his table. He smiled at me and waved, and though it was very difficult, I lurched back into movement.

"Hi," I whispered. "How's it going?"

"Oh, you know," he said. "Just making some note cards." He gestured to a pile in front of him on the table. The term "note cards" was really more of a euphemism—he was using torn-up pieces of notebook paper, all different sizes and shapes, covered in the boyish-est of bad, boyish handwriting. I found this mess of his to be both aggravating and profoundly adorable.

"That seems like a generous term," I said.

"*Harsh*," he whispered, grinning, and I felt myself flush. It was going to be really annoying if that was going to happen every time he smiled at me.

I had taken out my own study guide, a single sheet of printer paper with color-coded blocks of text I'd drawn boundaries around using a ruler, and Keith had snatched it up, half marveling at and half mocking its precision.

"The colors *mean* something, don't they?" he asked. "Is it a CODE?"

"No!" I laughed, taking the paper from him, wishing there was a way for me to touch his hand but unable to come up with anything reasonable. "I just thought it looked nice. Using different-colored pens makes studying feel less boring."

This was a lie. Each of the colors represented a different category of knowledge. Purple was for people, green was for places, blue was for dates, and so on.

"OK, OK," he said, and I'd wondered if he knew I was lying. I felt transparent. I was afraid to think anything complimentary about him because I felt sure that by sitting that close to me he could read my thoughts. I tried to keep my eyes on the table, on the study materials, where his left hand, I noticed, was pressed flat against his textbook to hold it open. *God, he has sexy hands*, I thought. *No, wait, I mean—dammit.*

We talked a little about our professor and a little about the sophomore in our class who, whenever he'd raise his hand to ask questions, which seemed to happen at least three times every class, would pronounce the Spanish names and places with a comically pronounced accent—José Sanjurjo becoming hgho-ZSAY sahn-HGGHOOR-hghgho. He'd even say the Spanish words a little louder, which we didn't think he knew he was doing. We were sure that Professor Ferrer hated him.

That led to talking about who was the most annoying student in each of our classes, each of us trying to one-up the other with increasingly exaggerated stories of our nightmarish classmates. Keith had claimed that there was a girl in his 8:00 AM East Asian Philosophy lecture who sat behind him and clipped her nails during every class. "She puts the nails into a plastic sandwich bag," he said, his eyebrows raised, as if to convince me of the severity of the situation. "She is *collecting them*."

"She is not," I said, laughing until my eyes started tearing up.

After that we decided we were starving and needed a "break," and, leaving our books set out to claim our table, we walked downstairs to the basement, where there was a vending machine and an instant coffeemaker. He made coffee and bought a Twix, and I bought a bag of pretzels even though what I wanted was Pop-Tarts.

"Won't that keep you up all night?" I asked him.

He'd leaned in closer to me, conspiratorially, and I worried I might legitimately faint.

"It's decaf," he said.

"What is the point of THAT?" I'd asked, horrified, because I didn't think anyone under the age of fifty even drank decaf coffee, and he'd laughed. There was a kind of laughing boys did at girls more because they were being cute than they were being funny—not that whatever it was wasn't funny, but that its cuteness mattered more—and I had thought this might be one of those times. I was never one to think very much about any particular boy's interest in me, because I generally assumed that few of them had any. But there were clues even I could not ignore, and I was starting to think it kind of, sort of seemed like Keith might like me.

Back upstairs, we realized that it had somehow gotten to be 9:12 without us having done much with our study materials except pick them up and put them back down.

"OK, be serious now," Keith told me. "I mean it."

"Me, be serious?" I asked. "I believe you were the one to suggest a break."

"That doesn't sound like me," he said, and we'd smiled and picked up our pens. And then put them back down.

The amount of time we'd spent studying in any meaningful capacity could probably have fit easily within a half-hour slot of network television, not including commercials. It was just a quiz anyway, we reasoned at 10:42. It was, like, a negligible part of our grade. And it was so early in the semester. Probably it was even good to do a little bit poorly on this quiz, because then we'd only be able to go up from there. We agreed that setting too high a precedent for oneself early on in a class could actually be dangerous for one's achievement potential.

We left the library slowly, I thought because neither of us knew exactly how to proceed from there. Was he going to walk me home? It was a little late, kind of, but I lived close enough, and I walked home by myself, often at later hours, all the time. Of course, he didn't know that.

"Where do you live?" he asked.

"Kind of off John Street and Locust?" I said.

"Oh, okay," he said. "I'm by, like, Pennsylvania and Orchard."

"Oh, nice," I said, cursing internally. There was no way for us to pretend either of our houses was a convenient stop along the route to the other's. We stood there for a second, mentally confirming this fact, considering the Springfield grid. At least, I was. A gust of wind blew the snow, shoveled into piles alongside the sidewalk, around in the air, and I shivered.

"You're cold," said Keith, and for a brief, crazed moment I wondered if he'd offer me his jacket. But it was 20 degrees out. And I was already wearing one. "You should go."

I thought that was strange, because we were both leaving, and him saying it like that made me feel disappointed about doing what I'd already planned to do. I was going. I had made that clear by leaving the library. Did he think I'd been hoping to be invited to his house or something? I looked down at my boots, at the snow stains streaked across the tops. *I NEED to clean these when I get home*, I thought. *I am not kidding around this time.*

"This was fun," Keith said, and I felt so much better so quickly.

"Yeah!" I said, trying to come up with the courage to say something else (ANYTHING, HARRIET) about seeing him again in some context outside our class. Say *Let's do it again.* Say *I think we have a great future as study partners.* Say *Next time, preferably, we will make out.* Instead I just smiled and said "Yeah" again. "It was."

"Next time we'll be very productive," he said, and he looked at my eyes so directly I wondered how I'd never noticed how infrequently I'd felt that looked at. It felt like that thing where you press your face up close to a screened window and alternate between focusing on it and on the outside world past it. It felt like having that done to me, me as the screen.

"Definitely," I said. "This was essentially a practice round, and everyone knows those don't even count. Except for...uhh... grade-wise."

"Right, just that." He laughed. We were still just *standing* there. It had to be almost the next day by that point, I thought.

"I guess we'll see how it goes!!" I said. "So. See you tomorrow!!" I sort of half waved in Keith's general direction.

"OK, bye!" he said, and turned around.

I walked home quickly, half running both to keep warm and because I'd wanted to tell Mel and Logan everything as soon as possible. I got home to find Logan's door shut and her presumably asleep on the other side, but I found Mel reading a textbook in her pajamas in the living room, and I recounted the study date for upward of twenty minutes while she ate most of a box of plain Cheerios. Mel had dated the same boy, Jacob, all throughout her junior and senior years of high school. Halfway into the summer after graduation, she'd calmly broken up with him because she could tell they wanted "different lives." As a result, I trusted her assessment of any relationship's potential implicitly, often viewing her more like a savvy, divorced woman of forty-seven than a peer. I'd asked her that night if she thought things with Keith seemed "good," by which I meant worth getting hopeful about, and she'd said no, and I'd freaked out, even though part of me knew she was teasing me. "Of course," she'd said. Of course it was good. He'd referred to "next time."

So we'd crafted a Facebook message, figuring it was late enough at night to seem mildly sexy just by virtue of the hour it was sent, but early enough that he might still be awake, and respond. Mel had told me to write something short and practical— like "That was fun, I'm glad we're study buddies now"—but I ignored her, mostly, and wrote something I thought was cute and funny: "OK I lied: the colors do mean something. Maybe (MAYBE) I can tell you what that is next time."

"That's better than mine," said Mel.

"I hope so," I said. I pressed send and felt exhilarated, and immediately after that I felt like I wanted to die. Mel sat back in her chair and took her book into her lap. It was an unspoken agreement that we'd sit vigil out there together until he wrote back, or until it became late enough that we'd tell ourselves he must have already gone to bed, and would respond in the morning. I was prepared to give it an hour, but I heard the little beep of a new message just a few minutes later. Both of us sat up abruptly.

"What does it say?" said Mel.

"You can see me, right? I haven't touched my laptop yet!!" I said, leaning forward to pick it up off the coffee table.

"I'm just anxious!!" she said.

"SO AM I," I said, yelling as loud as I could, given that I was partly whispering and trying not to wake up Logan.

"*OK*," she hissed. "*God.* Read it!!"

I clicked on the message button (there was simply no way, at this time of night, at this level of anticipation, to wait a cool-seeming amount of time to read it in order to delay his knowing that I had) and watched the window pop open.

Below my message was Keith's, which read: ":)". I scrolled down to look for the rest of it. It seemed like there was probably more of it somewhere, maybe really far down the page. But I scrolled down as far as it was possible to go, and found nothing but that tiny little face.

"It's just...a smiley," I said. "A smiley face."

"That's it?"

"That's it," I said. "Believe me, I have looked everywhere."

"Well, I guess that's...friendly?"

"Mmm," I agreed. "Verrrryyyyyy FRIENDLY."

"We are saying the same word."

I huffed.

"I don't know," she went on. "If I were him, and I had just gotten home from a library study date with this cute girl, and she sent me a Facebook message after, and I'd already basically told her I wanted to study with her again, and she sent me a nice message that again referred to studying together, I would definitely maybe just respond with a smiley face." I gave her a look. "It's nice! It's literally a picture of a face of happiness."

"Maybe," I said. I had been joking, sort of, but I also felt disappointed and embarrassed—for having tried to prolong the night's charm beyond its natural endpoint, for not having been better able to manage my expectations. "OK, good night," I'd told her, closing my laptop and carrying my things to my bedroom. I put on pajamas and, picking up my laptop again, I snuck through the bathroom and stood outside Logan's bedroom door, trying to assess whether she was actually asleep or just watching Netflix in bed. I listened for a moment before hearing a little thud, like she was setting her water glass back on the nightstand, and I tapped lightly on her door and heard a muffled "Come in."

Logan was awake, her laptop on her stomach, lying flat on her back with her head propped up slightly by a balled-up sweat-shirt.

"Where are your pillows?" I asked.

"I haven't been using them lately," she said. "I think they coddle my neck."

"OK," I said. "Is it OK if I read you an interaction really quickly?"

"Sure," she sighed, pushing her laptop off to the side and sliding her body toward the wall so that I could sit next to her.

I gave Logan a brief recap of the night's events—with a minor derailing taking place over Keith's choice of decaf coffee, which she felt was possibly "indicative of deeper moral failings"—and read to her my Facebook message and his (if you could call it a message). I read it to her dramatically: "And all HE wrote back...his entire reply...was a singular...small...emoticon."

"Which one?" she asked.

"Oh," I said. "A smiley face."

"Oh," she said. "I mean, the way you said that I was expecting like, the frown with the angry eyebrows. A smiley is good.... Right?"

"Really?"

"I mean," she said. "It's...smiling."

"I know, but, what about? In what way?"

Logan rolled her eyes. "You need to go to bed."

"Ugh, fine," I said. I closed my laptop and stood up, hovering near her bed, hoping for one last piece of encouragement. "So it's not bad?"

"It's not bad," said Logan, sliding her own computer back onto her stomach.

Logan wasn't very touchy, but still I felt compelled to lean over and hug her with the arm that wasn't holding my laptop. The hug was a mess, my hand ending up essentially in her armpit and my face in her neck, neither of our torsos even touching. She reached a long, skinny arm out from the trap I'd placed her in and patted me twice on the back. "OK," she said.

We said good night and I went back to my room—sneaking through the bathroom again, though I didn't know exactly why; sometimes I didn't want one of my friends to think her advice hadn't been enough, and that's why I'd needed to ask the other's.

The next day I walked to the history building and into class, took the one-sheet quiz off the pile sitting on the podium in the front of the room, and sat down in my usual spot. Keith came in moments later, took his own quiz, and sat down next to me. Before starting, he elbowed me. I looked up and he gave me a two-finger salute—possibly the most sexless of all hand gestures. I smile-grimaced and quickly looked back at my quiz.

The quiz took the class twenty minutes to take, and we graded them together immediately after. I got an 81. Keith got a 90. "Ohhhh," he whispered. "Damn. You must feel really bad."

"Did you study more in secret??" I whispered back. My outrage was largely feigned, but my competitiveness kicked in reflexively.

"Nope," he said. "But it's OK. I'm sure you have an excuse."

"Yes!!" I said. "My study partner was intentionally distracting!"

"Oh yeah?" he'd said, as I blushed, and then I hadn't had a chance to respond, or dial back the flirtatiousness of what I'd just said, because Professor Ferrer started up his lecture. I'd sat there fidgeting, pretending to listen, writing phrases and historical figures down haphazardly, dooming myself to more 81s. At the end of class I'd stood up abruptly, nervously. But then Keith stood up, too, and, as if it were nothing at all, he'd asked if I wanted to go to a party he was going to that Friday. I did. I'd paced around my living room—only slightly less nervously than I had two days earlier—until he texted me to say he was on his way and asked if I wanted to meet him there. When I'd walked up to the house he was sitting on the steps out front, waiting. We drank beer from a keg and stood unnecessarily close to each other and drank some more, and then we left the party together and made out against the brick exterior of the hardware store on Baker Street. Then he walked me to what I was starting to think of as our corner and no farther. He asked me what I was doing the next Monday, and when I said, "Like, apart from school?" he asked if I thought I might want to drive with him to Chicago to see a show his friend's band was playing that night.

"What about Spanish Civ?" I asked, and regretted it immediately.

"We're gonna play hooky," he said. "Come on. I could use the company for the drive. Especially on the way back, when it's dark."

"Well, if it's a safety issue," I said.

"Yes!" he said, grinning. "We can leave early, make a day of it."

"OK," I said. "That sounds fun."

Then we stood there a minute smiling at each other, apparently feeling it was too soon to kiss each other good-bye, even though we'd technically already kissed. The twenty minutes we'd spent walking and talking had reopened too much nervous distance between us for it to happen again that night.

"Cool," he said. He started to walk away, backward and slowly. "I'll text you Sunday night to plan."

"OK," I said. "I'll be . . . around." By my phone. Holding on to it for dear life.

"Good night, Harriet." He smiled and put his hands into his pocket.

"Good night, Keith," I said. Then I waved for some reason, but it was fine.

When I got home, Logan and Mel were waiting up in the kitchen and when I told them about the making out, Mel grabbed my arms and shook me. When I told them about the Chicago trip, she screamed.

"Isn't that kind of a lot for a second date?" said Logan. "That's like, a three-hour drive."

"You're *definitely* going to have sex," said Mel.

"Really?" I asked. She seemed likelier to know than me.

"Um, yes," she said. "People don't just go on, like, romantic weekday jaunts to the city and then not have sex after."

"How many people in this exact situation do you know?" asked Logan.

"I'm just saying," she said. "I hope you still have your condom."

I did, of course; it had rested untouched and unseen in the zippered pocket of my purse, alongside my emergency tampons, since it was given to me two and a half years earlier at the campus health center. I'd gone in after twice having quick, perfunctory sex with Scott Dunleavy—first, to get my first time over with, and second, to pretend I'd been more excited about the first time than I had. I was pretty sure he hadn't had sex before either, but he'd told me after the second time we slept together that he wanted to see someone with more experience, heavily implying that what he meant was a match to his own. So I'd wanted to be sure. The nurse had handed me a printed-out and folded-up copy of my clean bill of health, a single condom attached to it by paperclip. It would expire two months after I graduated, a date that I viewed as something of a personal deadline—who would die without having sex first: the condom, or me?

"I have it," I said. Of course, now that the possibility that I might need to use it in the near future was vaguely tangible, I wasn't sure I wanted it in my purse that day, riding along to Chicago, beating like some Telltale Condom. Now that we'd acknowledged it was there, it felt like I was *committing* to sex. And even though I'd done it already, and it had been a long, sometimes-arduous time since, and I was sure I'd want to do it soon*ish*, I wasn't sure I'd be ready in a mere three days. So when I said good night and went to my room, I took the condom out of my purse and folded it into a sock in my dresser. I got into bed, telling myself that surely he had his own supply anyway.

Three hours later I had yet to fall asleep. I got up, opened the dresser drawer, slid the condom out of the sock, and put it back into my purse. Just in case.

4

He had told me he liked me so many times. Or at least it was a lot considering the time frame—how many instances over two weeks? It had to have been ten or more. He'd said it unprompted, making it clear much sooner than I ever would have: He texted me "hi I like you" the day after we first made out at the party. I thought this was devastatingly cute, almost too much to tolerate. I'd been watching TV hungover in the fetal position on the couch with Mel, my feet in her lap. I was giddy from the kissing, disbelieving and excited and nervous, my phone parked near my side, even though I hadn't actually expected to hear from him until Sunday.

But then my phone had buzzed, and Mel and I turned our heads sharply to look wide-eyed at each other, which made us burst out laughing.

"It's probably, like, my dad," I'd said, stretching my arm out to grab it.

Mel said nothing, wanting neither, I assumed, to wrongly get my hopes up or to agree it couldn't be Keith. And then it had been. I'd read the message to myself, my face flushing up so severely it felt like I'd start sweating. I'd shown my phone screen to Mel and she'd screamed.

Nobody had ever said it that directly before. There had been a couple times I'd figured it out, or heard from a third party—though being told, in my freshman year of high school, that Neil Bishop, whom I hadn't spoken to since fourth grade, liked me, and each of us then continuing to never speak to the other hardly felt like it counted—but nobody had ever said *I like you* to my face. Or, I guess, to my phone. But Keith made it seem so easy to say. It quickly became something he did provocatively, knowing and liking how flustered it made me. We'd play-argue about something by text, and he'd make some joke, and I'd write "Keith," pretending to chide him. And then he'd write back, always the same way but somehow never any less disarming: "hi I like you."

When Keith picked me up that Monday morning at 9:22 (we'd planned on 9:15), I'd already read the phrase three separate times. As a result, I found it difficult to look at him, even through the protective barrier of his car's windshield. But when I got into the car he said, "Good morning! I hope you've already peed," and I'd been horrified enough to turn and stare—half-jokingly appalled by both his use of the word and the preemptive accusation it implied.

"Um, yes," I said.

"Good," he said. "Then one of those is for you." With his thumb he pointed at the two water bottles sitting in the cup holders between our seats.

I'd worried the day before about what we'd talk about during the approximately 190-minute drive from Springfield to Chicago, but I hadn't needed to. We argued about pizza (I was pro–deep dish and he, blasphemously, was anti-) and somehow, that turned into a discussion about free will. (Neither of us was sure exactly how much we had, but it was clear Keith had thought about it much more.) He told me about his sister, who was in law school at U of C.

"Actually, maybe we can stop by and see her!" he said.

"Sure!" I said.

"Eh," he said, "it's probably too far out of our way."

"Mmm," I said, knowing U of C wasn't really all that far from where we were going, but not wanting to seem either too eager or too opposed to the idea of meeting one of his family members.

"Do you have siblings?" he said. He kept his eyes fixed on the highway when he asked me things, which helped.

"No," I said. "Just me." I paused, feeling I ought to contribute more to the conversation but dreading it all the same. "My mom had me kind of late, I think that's why."

"How old is she?"

"Well," I said, "she died when I was sixteen. But she was thirty-six when I was born."

"Oh wow," he said. "I'm so sorry." Then he turned to look at me, catching me looking at him to see if he would. It was just a second, but I was sure it would have been longer if he hadn't been driving.

"It's OK," I said. "I mean. You know what I mean."

"Can you talk about it?" he asked. I had thought that was nice, to acknowledge I might not want to.

"Yeah," I said, "I mean, there's not a whole lot to say. It was five years ago. She got breast cancer and found it late. And it sucked." It wasn't true that there wasn't a lot to say, but I had found that it was easiest for everyone involved if I offered the other person as many escape routes as possible.

"That's awful," he said. "My grandma just died from that a couple years back."

I said I was sorry, and we talked about whether we thought

anything major would be cured in our lifetimes, and that turned to talking about politics, and that was that. We'd moved on.

When we first saw the city skyline I got heart palpitations, having apparently forgotten that there was somewhere we were going, that we weren't going to just drive on infinitely, and that we were going to have to get out of the car. I could deal with the car. I'd gotten used to the setup of the car. It was safe. We were wearing seat belts.

When we parked in a ramp downtown—after Keith refused to let me pay for the day pass, or for gas, or anything—I got out of my seat only reluctantly. It was just after 1:00. The show was at 6:00. At the bottom of the ramp on the sidewalk, we stood and looked all around ourselves, blinking confusedly in the bright sunlight, like we'd been returned to the middle of nowhere post–alien abduction.

"So what should we do?" I said.

"I've got an idea," he said, "but it might be dumb."

I'd wanted to reach out and grab his wrist, wanting to reassure him even though I was certain I had to be twice as nervous as he was, though he was more nervous than I'd expected. But I grabbed my own instead.

"I'm sure it's not," I said. "I mean, I'm not sure, but."

He smiled. "Do you want to know now or just head there?"

"Don't tell me," I said.

So we walked a bit and got on the El and walked some more, and then we were outside a building with a sign that said Harold Washington Library Center. I started laughing as soon as I saw it.

"Oh my god," he said, "we can just leave." He pretended to storm off and leave me there and that time I ran to catch up, and I did grab his arm. I let it go after he turned, looking at my hand and then back at the library.

"No," I said, "come on. I've never actually been inside."

"And you call yourself a librarian," he said.

We walked in and headed for the directory, my boots' wooden heels echoing across the marble floor. Halfway across I slowed down, trying to walk instead on my toes.

"*Nine* floors?" I said, looking at the map.

"Yep," he said, and he stood up straighter, proud.

"Oh, did you help build it?" I said, and he grinned.

"OK," he said, "I think we should split up"—here I tried not to let my face fall—"and find three books each: one that looks interesting to us personally and two we think would be interesting to the other. And then we'll see who did a better job." I nodded, my adrenaline beginning to rush at the hint of competition. "Meet in the Winter Garden in . . . how long, do you think?"

"Half an hour?" I said. I'd felt torn between not wanting to spend too much time without being able to look at him and wanting enough time to win.

Keith looked at his wristwatch. "It's one thirty-two," he said. "Let's say, Winter Garden at two."

"OK."

"Ready?"

"I'm a librarian," I said. "I've trained for this all my life."

He laughed, and I blushed, and then he bolted in the other direction, toward the stairs. Because I didn't want to run up directly after him, I opted for the elevator. I waited two full minutes for it to reach the ground floor: a waste of precious time.

I stopped off first at the children's book floor, scanning the display racks like a madwoman while families tried to keep their kids mollified all around me. I saw *Why Is the Sky Blue?* and laughed, a single "HA" I tried quickly to cover up as a cough. I maneuvered through a gaggle of three- and four-year-olds still wearing their puffy marshmallow coats and picked it up off the shelf. I checked the time—1:38—and decided to switch to the stairs.

I climbed to the seventh floor, which, per the directory, held literature, short stories, fiction, and plays. I knew what my own selection would be, so I rushed there, plucking the familiar book off the shelves without allowing myself to stop moving. In the middle of the floor I stopped still, checking my phone (it was 1:43) and allowing myself thirty seconds to consider my next move. I wasn't sure I had time to go to another floor, but picking out a novel for him felt intimidating, and strangely intimate. Then again, if I pulled it off, it would be very impressive. I turned in slow circles, looking up at the placards dividing the floor into sections. Realizing how frantic I must look, I laughed to myself again.

I checked the time again (1:45) and decided I'd risk switching floors. I was always worried about being late and I was always early anyway. So I ran down a flight of stairs to the Social Science and History floor, scanning the signs until I found the one I wanted. I speed-walked through the racks, running my fingertips along the plastic-wrapped spines until I found something I thought might work: *History of Milwaukee: Wisconsin, From Prehistoric Times to the Present Date*. I'd only just learned Keith was from Milwaukee on the drive up. Considering just how few people at our school were from places outside Illinois, even this fact lent him a degree of intrigue.

The book was not perfect, I thought, but it was personalized, and it was now 1:53, so it would have to be good enough. I half ran the three remaining flights up to the Winter Garden. I pushed open the doors and stopped still in my tracks, gaping at the nearly cobalt sky visible through the greenhouse-like glass ceiling. Shadows from the mint-green beams crisscrossed the room so that the trees standing in marble-encased planters around the room seemed to shine.

My attention was only drawn downward again by the sound of a hissed whisper: "*Harriet!*"

Keith was at my side then, having apparently beat me there.

"Hi," I whispered. "This is so pretty!"

"I know!" he said. "It's the best." Then he pointed at a table across the room, where I saw his coat draped over a chair. When we got closer I saw his own trio of books, but when I tried to peek at their covers he caught me looking and swept them off the table, pulling them into his lap as he sat down.

"OK," I said, "relax." But I kept my books in my own lap, too, between both hands, suddenly terrified to show him what I'd picked out.

"You show me first," he said.

"Absolutely not," I said.

"Come on," he said. "The whole game was my idea."

I sighed. "Fine," I said. "I'm going to start with the one I found for me, though." He nodded, and I picked it up and held it in front of me like I was giving a presentation. The sun beat down on my face, forcing me to squint. Keith, meanwhile, was in the shade. "This is a book of poems by Christina Rosetti, which might be considered mild cheating, because it's assigned for my Victorian Prose and Poetry class later this semester," I said.

Keith laughed. "So you're doing homework right now?"

"I just saw it as a two-birds, one-stone–type scenario," I said.

"OK," he said. "Now mine."

I slid both books quickly across the table. "Here."

"What do we have here?" he said, slowly, in a little voice like a cartoon surveyor.

"I got you *Why Is the Sky Blue?* because it struck me as very existential. Since you're a philosopher," I said, blushing when he laughed. "And then I got a book of Milwaukee history, for more obvious and boring reasons. But I skimmed it and there are some cool pictures."

"This is great," he said, pulling them closer to him, paging through the Milwaukee book and letting it fall closed when he reached the end. "Now I'm nervous," he said.

"I'm sure yours are great," I said. "If a little less great than mine."

He grinned and tossed all three books onto the table and covered his face in his hands, groaning a little.

"OK, let's see," I said. I spread out the titles in front of me and reach each aloud. *"An Anthology of Spanish Poetry, Little Women"*— on this one I grinned and looked up, and he peered back at me with one eye between his fingers—"and, uh, *The Political Psychology of Democratic Citizenship.* I'm going to guess that last one is yours."

"Unless you hate one of the other ones, in which case, mine is that one," he said.

"I don't hate them!" I said. "Technically I don't know any Spanish, but—"

"I just picked it because it was like a nice blend of your major plus our class," he said, pulling his hands away from his face to lock his fingers together in the businessman hand-speak symbol for words like *synergy.*

I laughed. "It is," I said. "You're right. And I adore *Little Women.*"

"Me, too," he said, and I raised my eyebrows. "My sister used to read it to me," he explained. "I pretended not to like it but I totally did."

"Aw."

Then we looked at each other for a couple moments, and back at the piles of books in front of us, and back up. I cleared my throat and looked around the room—nearly every other table was full, most of the people at them reading in earnest. I made eye contact with a girl who looked at me and then very pointedly back at her dense-looking textbook, and I thought how nice it felt to be the one the serious people were mad at.

"Well," he said, "we can either stay here for a bit and read, and then go do something else until the show, or we can go do something else right now."

"OK," I said, "what do you want to do?"

"Are you hungry at all?"

"Yes," I said, aware of its severity as soon as he said the word.

"Me, too," he said. "Let's go find something to eat."

We stood up and I took a picture of the ceiling with my phone—because it was beautiful, mainly, but also because I wanted to create a tangible record of having been somewhere so cool and far away, on a school day no less, with someone I liked.

We dropped our books in a return slot on the way out, and once we were back on the sidewalk Keith asked me if I thought I could survive another twenty minutes without food, because Millennium Park was close, if I hadn't been there before. I hadn't, and I was starving, but I'd seen pictures of half of everyone I knew reflected in the park's famous shiny bean sculpture, and so as a resident of Illinois I figured I ought to see it, too. We stood in front of it together, looking at ourselves stretched out in its surface. I didn't want to be the one to take out my phone.

"It's actually kind of lame," he said.

"I mean," I said, "I think it delivers on its promise of being a big silver bean."

"Ha," he half laughed. He took a hand out of his coat pocket, scratched the back of his head, and burrowed it back inside. Each time he took it out I reflexively looked over to see what he would do. "That is true. It just seems nuts that *so* many people come see it."

"Well," I said, feeling defensive, "you're the one who said we should come."

"Also true," he said. "Now you've seen it and you never have to come back."

"Oh, I'm actually going to come back every day," I said. I looked over at him, and when he saw that I was watching him he grinned. Out came his hand from his pocket again. But he just shook it around, trying to read his watch. "Ready to eat something?" he asked.

"Very."

At the restaurant, nearly empty in the midafternoon stretch between mealtimes, we sat across from each other in a two-person leather booth and talked about everything. The pizza place was famous—his favorite, my second favorite, and the one that was inarguably closest to the concert venue. We got thin crust, half sausage (him) and half cheese (mine), and whenever the server brought a steaming deep-dish to one of the booths behind Keith's head or on the other side of the frosted glass divider that ran between the rows, I noticed, but I didn't mind. We each ordered a glass of red wine, and then a second glass, and leaned in closer. Keith told me how much he hated Springfield, how small it was, and how flat. It was true, I said—you could practically see all the way across Iowa, but who would ever want to do that?

Keith also had strong opinions about the TV shows his friends watched, and sometimes the friends themselves, and the unhealthy, ultra-processed food they served in our cafeteria—that's why he'd moved off campus sophomore year, just as soon as the school had let him. He'd had to fill out a petition. He hated trendy pop-environmentalism and e-books and his own name. Most of the time, his name excepted, I more or less agreed with him, but whenever I disagreed and argued, he was delighted. His eyes would widen, and he'd say *"Harriet,* how could you," pretending first to be appalled and then softening, always willing to concede that I had a very good point. To me it seemed he was incredibly discerning, and one of the very few things he liked, perhaps the only thing good enough to merit his unreserved approval, was me. It was enchanting. We only noticed it was time to go because the sun went down.

Keith's friend's band was opening for a band everyone else in the audience was there to see. While we waited for the show to start in the back of the smallish ballroom-style theater, we complained about having to wait.

"If they're actually going to start at seven, why not just say it starts at seven?" he said.

"Because being late is very cool," I said.

"We can leave right after they play," he said. "Unless you... want to stay for the rest." It was clear he didn't want me to want to stay for the rest. Fortunately, I didn't. I shook my head and he smiled.

His friend's band—were they really called Noodles, or was I remembering that wrong?—was fine. They played either one very long song or about five that sounded exactly the same. The singer, Keith's friend Colin from high school, sang in a plaintive mumble, expressing a lot of complicated feelings about his ex-girlfriend. When they were finally done, Keith leaned over and whispered, "I am so sorry for making you endure that," and I laughed. In the lobby he told me he just had to pop backstage for a second to say hi to his friend—"so he knows I was here"—so I said I was going to find the bathroom before we headed out.

"OK," he said. "It'll be only a minute." I found the women's restroom downstairs and stood in front of the mirror fixing my hair and attempting to re-create facial expressions I'd made earlier to see how they really looked. When I got back up to the lobby, Keith was already there waiting to go. I asked him if he needed to use the bathroom before we left, teasing him, but he just said no, he was ready. An hour into the drive back home, he pulled into a rest stop. "OK," he said, seeing me smirk, "you were right."

By the time we got back to Springfield, it was almost midnight.

"Do you want to come hang out for a little bit?" he'd asked, as soon as we could see the campus streetlamps through the windows of his car.

I had class at 9:45 the next morning, but I wasn't tired. I was too excited to be tired. We'd spent so much time together already that to end it then—to ask to be dropped off at my house instead—felt in some way like a concession. What was fourteen hours together if I insisted on getting home by my normal bedtime?

So I said sure, and when we unlocked his front door, we found three guys playing a video game, sprawled across the floor and two couches, an empty pizza box sitting open on the coffee table among them. They looked up but didn't say anything, and Keith didn't address them. He led us through the room to the back of the house, offering me a glass of tap water and shutting his bedroom door behind us once we were inside. I surveyed the room: walls bare apart from an unframed art print taped up, beige comforter splayed haphazardly on top of a double bed, a small black desk I recognized as the same IKEA model that Logan had in her room, and an old-looking leather chair in the corner by a small wooden bookshelf.

"This is really nice," I said, perching on the chair and patting the caramel-colored cushion with one hand.

"Thanks, it was my grandpa's," he said. To both my dismay and my delight, he sat not at the desk chair across the room but at the foot of his bed, leaving no more than two inches between our knees.

"Were all those guys your roommates?" I asked.

"Yep," he said, "all three."

"Are you... not friends with them?"

"Oh, no, I am," he said. I tried to imagine walking into my house, past Logan and Mel, and into my room without saying a word. It was impossible.

Keith looked over at his bookshelf, apparently scanning the rows of books and movies, and started to drum his fingers on his knee. And because I didn't want to wait and see how long that could go on for, and because we'd been "accidentally" grazing limbs all day already, and because I didn't feel so nervous around him after all that time, I scooted a little closer to the edge of the chair, reached out, and tapped him on the knee he wasn't using. "Hey," I said, and when he looked up, I kissed him.

We scooted from the bottom of his bed to the top and fooled around on top of its lumpy surface, on our sides and facing each other. He was too tall for the bed, curling up like a tilde, and whenever we stopped kissing to talk for a minute or two I found myself addressing his chin.

"I'm so glad you came over," he said.

"Me, too."

"So where's our next road trip gonna be?" he asked, a little while later. "I feel like we set a precedent."

"I don't know," I said. "Where else is cool in Illinois?"

"Who said it has to be in Illinois?"

I'd started to worry, a little, about what all would happen between us that night, afraid I'd have to declare out loud that I didn't think I was ready to have sex quite yet. But I never took off my pants and he didn't try to take them off for me, so it didn't come up. Mostly we just kissed and talked. He asked me if I'd ever been to the strawberry festival in Long Grove, and when I said I hadn't, I hadn't even heard of it, he said we should go. It happened every May.

"There are *lots* of fun things we can go to in the spring," he said. It seemed soon to me to be saying things like that—making plans for months from then, specific and cute ones that would have made me roll my eyes if I'd heard other people making them. (A strawberry festival, for god's sake!) It had always been my understanding that you weren't supposed to freak a guy out by mentioning anything happening more than three days in the future, and the truth was it hadn't even occurred to me yet to think about it myself. I was just trying to keep it cool through the next five minutes. But Keith sounded so confident when he said it, so natural, that I couldn't help but agree and believe it a little myself.

"I can't wait," I said, and that was when I decided I'd have sex with him the next time I slept over, which I hoped would be very soon.

But Keith wasn't around the following weekend—he mentioned in class that Wednesday that he was going back up to Chicago, alone this time, to visit another friend. The next Tuesday, when we studied in the library, I couldn't focus, too busy hoping he was going to ask me to come over afterward. But he didn't. When we both lost steam around eleven, he walked me to our corner and said, "Talk to you soon?" I nodded, and he hugged me, and that was the end of that.

5

When Mel and Logan and I got home from the library, we separated into our bedrooms to put our things away and put on pajamas. I set my laptop on my desk and my books on the shelf next to it. I folded my jeans into my dresser, and when I'd put on a T-shirt and gym shorts I noticed that the word-a-day calendar I kept on top of it still read February 23.

I fell into this trap with daily calendars every year. For a few weeks I'd incorporate the daily tearing-off into my morning routine, but then, toward the end of the month, I'd start to feel increasingly hostile about the added responsibility. *This is literally a paper-wasting device*, I'd think. *Its actual design is to throw away a piece of paper!!!* One morning my schedule would be different in some way, and I'd forget the calendar, and the next thing I knew, it'd be weeks or months later and I'd wonder what I'd been doing with all that time. But this time, I knew. February 23 was the Monday I went to Chicago with Keith, and the thing that was different the morning after was that I wasn't home. I'd walked straight from his house to my 9:45 class, not to think of my calendar again until this very moment. I stuck my thumb under a chunk of its pages and flipped them to March 15, and then, thinking better of it—

the day was almost over—I skipped to March 16. Three weeks later, to the day.

I took the chunk of pages still in my left hand and carried them to the recycling bin we kept under the kitchen sink. Mel and Logan were already seated at the table making sandwiches from a loaf of bread, mustard, turkey, and cheese, and, for Logan, an avocado smashed up with spices. I stood there for a moment watching her assemble the layers and squeeze a lemon over the whole thing before placing the second slice of bread on top. I thought about asking her to make me one too, but she'd just pity-made me dinner the night before.

"Did you actually look at all of those?" asked Logan.

"No," I said, slumping my shoulders guiltily. Sometimes I told myself I would collect the words in a binder, laminated, and study them in my free time. Except I didn't want to have to think about the days I held in my hand ever again. I stood up straighter. "I think I've been through enough as it is without having to teach myself like twenty new words right now!"

"Are you going to eat with us?" asked Mel, though they were already eating.

"I think I'm just going to have some cereal in my room," I said. "I still have to write tomorrow's column."

"What's it about?" asked Logan.

"WELL," I said, "it's from this sorority girl who was hooking up with this frat guy who strongly led her to believe he was going to ask her to his spring dance, but apparently he's taking his ex-girlfriend instead."

"Jeez," said Mel.

"It's these dances, I'm telling you," said Logan. "They make people crazy."

*   *   *

In my room I held my cereal bowl in one hand and picked up my computer with the other. I set it down on my bed and put the cereal on my nightstand. *I shouldn't eat in bed*, I thought as I sat down on top of it and carefully picked up the bowl. I opened my dedicated *Dear Emma* email inbox and reread the girl's email while I ate.

Dear Emma,

I've been sort of seeing this guy for a few months now, including like every day over Christmas break. Last month, after we'd gone to a movie and gone back to his place and had sex, he told me he'd decided who he was going to ask to his fraternity's spring dance. I tried to play it coy, so I was like, "Oh yeah, who?" and he was like, "I can't say," and it was super cute because he obviously meant me. He started acting a little weird last month, but we were still hanging out and sleeping together at least once a week, and I thought maybe he was just stressed about the new pledge class because they're honestly kind of subpar. But THEN, last week, he has me over to his house, and we have sex, and he tells me he's sorry but he has to take his ex-girlfriend (who is in another house I won't name but it's the slutty one) to the dance because of some bullshit promise he made her when they were together. (They broke up in early December.) I asked if they were getting back together, and he said no, it's just for the dance, but formals have a way of reuniting people. What should I do? Sincerely, F- My Life.

I felt, as I always felt when reading a letter, a little thrill at knowing something nobody else who read the letter in the paper a week later would know, unless they were told by the person who wrote it: the author's name. In the paper, the whole trans-action was anonymous—they signed off with an acronym, and me, a pseudonym. But here in my inbox, it was anonymous in one direction only: me to them. They emailed a mysterious en-tity called Emma at a Gmail address I'd created, but they did it using their campus email accounts. In the beginning, I'd won-dered if anyone would ever send me a question from a burner account made just for the occasion. But nobody ever did. They either trusted Emma, or I guess they wanted advice so badly they didn't mind divulging their identities to get it.

I felt jealous of Jess because she could write to Emma and I couldn't. I knew I could never say that out loud, not even to Lo-gan or Mel, because Emma was me and I wouldn't be able to explain what I meant without sounding like an ouroboros made of self-absorption. But it wasn't about the actual advice, really, so much as it was the chance to get a clear-cut answer from some-one whose job it was to give clear-cut answers. I couldn't write to Emma for an explanation of what happened with Keith because I had to be her, and I had no idea what happened.

I typed Jess's name into Facebook—I liked to put a face to the name, do a little research, if it was available to me—and clicked on the top result. We had a few mutual friends, so I was able to see a lot of her profile. She appeared to be a sophomore, one with fair, freckled skin and pretty red hair. In her profile picture she was hugging another girl around the waist, their T-shirts two va-rieties of the same sorority-stripe brand: V-necks that bore their house's letters on the chests in one bright color, two stripes of another rung around each sleeve. Their shirts revealed them to be members of Alpha Gamma Delta. *Wife material*, I thought. That's what everyone said, wasn't it? Neither Logan nor Mel nor I had ever considered rushing—in fact, we'd started spending more time together because of it, seemingly waking up one day that first spring to find most of the other girls on our floor "lost," as Logan had said, "to the war with Greece." But over a third of the students at Springfield were Greek, so an accumulation of strange details about their culture was inevitable even to outsiders. Everyone said AGDs were the ones who got boyfriends right away freshman year, who were broken up with on and off during sophomore and junior years, and who were nonetheless engaged at graduation. I had no idea if this was even partly true, but it seemed true: even non-Greek students, whenever they knew a sophomore or junior-year AGD who got dumped, cited it as statistical fact.

I scrolled a bit down Jess's wall, looking for clues as to the guy in question. He was Greek, I knew, and, according to their mating patterns, probably Sigma Chi or Phi Gamma Delta. But Jess's wall appeared exclusively dominated by other girls, and her tagged photos were, too. Scattered among the shots of her at events and dances with her AGD sisters were just a few taken at mixers, little crowds of guys in the background, and one of two standing on either side of her, their arms around her waist. It was impossible to tell if either one was him.

I opened a new document and wrote "JESS—HOOKUP TAKING EX TO DANCE" in the title bar. I kept all my letters stored away like this, labeled by name and subject, in a folder I labeled Calc 2 Spreadsheets, because in the event I ever accidentally left my account open on a campus computer, I didn't want anyone to be tempted to open it.

"Dear FML," I typed.

The thing was, it was just so fucking typical. Here was this girl, Jess, and she was pretty, and seemed funny or at least artfully mean, and from what I could tell she had a lot of friends who really liked her. Sometime earlier this winter she'd probably been minding her own business, dancing with those same friends at the, like, AGD Christmas Spectacular or something, and all of a sudden this dumb-ass guy had wandered into her life and completely ruined everything. He'd probably walked into whatever dumb bar wearing whatever dumb frat T-shirt and said whatever dumb thing, and because he'd been cute, and tall, and he'd touched the small of her back, Jess liked him anyway. Or maybe she'd liked him *because* of all those things. Maybe he was exactly her type, and she'd had a crush on him for months, but hadn't been able to do anything about it, because he'd had a girlfriend. And then maybe he'd broken up with that girlfriend and started flirting with Jess, and she couldn't believe how lucky she was to have her impossible crush turn possible. He'd probably said a whole bunch of really simple, sweet things the first few times they hung out, like "I always had a little crush on you, too," or "I'm so glad this happened," or even just "I like you *so* much."

And then, sometime after Christmas break, he probably started taking longer, and then longer still, to respond to Jess's text messages. Probably, sometimes, he wrote back nothing but the letter "K." And Jess had told herself not to worry, but she had, and she'd asked her friends what they thought was going on, and they'd said *nothing*, don't *worry*. He is just busy with X Generic Disappearing Boy Activity, like school, or sports. And then he'd probably invited her over some night, and she *had* felt better, and they'd slept together, and then right after that, probably while she was still in his shitty little twin bed, he'd told her that he was taking someone else to his stupid dance that was probably taking place in a stupid barn, where everyone would wear stupid plaid shirts and cowboy hats.

I was snapped out of my trance by the sound of Mel and Logan coming into the bathroom, laughing and moving their various bottles and tubes off and back on the metal shelves we'd bought together and screwed crookedly into the wall. I wanted to go in there with them and get ready for bed together. We'd made friends this way, freshman year—always ending up in our dorm floor's communal bathroom around midnight or one, eventually drawing out the process of taking out contacts and washing faces and brushing teeth for nearly half an hour, giggling. It seemed like every night that year someone said the funniest thing any of us had ever heard, and you just had to stay up long enough to be there for it. Nobody wanted to be the first to go to sleep, in case we missed it.

But looking back at the open document on my screen, I saw that Emma's response had not yet written itself. I sighed loudly, almost hoping Mel and Logan would hear me and open the door to my room. They did not. I put my fingers on my laptop keys, waiting for the right next word to come to me. I clicked back over to Jess's email, which I scanned quickly. I got mad all over again. I typed:

Dear FML,

Here is a list of letters whose corresponding curse words I'd use to describe this young man if only this newspaper would allow it: F. D. A. C. M. S. As these names are not available to me (though I hope you'll know I think he deserves EVERY one, as well as any hurtful future slang terms we haven't yet invented), I will call him "Benedict Arnold."

Benedict, like so many young men his age, is an infant without object permanence. He can only deal with one thing at a time, and that's whatever is right in front of his dumb little face.

The minute he's separate from that object, it's virtually gone from his mind. It is replaced by the new thing that's there right now. It's not that he didn't like that other thing! It's just that his brain is too simple to manage two things. (The "things" can be people, though they aren't always. They could be a person and a job, or a person and school, or a person and drinking and football. God help those that try to manage *three* things!)

If this guy's motives appear unclear to you, it's probably because he doesn't have any. He himself doesn't even know what they are. Don't waste any more of your time wondering what he's going to do next. He doesn't know. He is a Class A Pathetic Flailer, and he'll go wherever his half-developed, uncontemplated impulses take him next. Literally at that very second. And that's not because you aren't enough for him, but because he will always, for the foreseeable future, do whatever is easiest. He's like a human game of Pin the Tail on the Donkey.

Because he is a small, tiny baby, the mild assertiveness required in breaking a "promise" he made to an ex, even though she is his ex, is impossible for him. He will always, always take the path of least resistance. If you wanted to really throw down over this, present an ultimatum, make him rue the day he thought he'd take someone else to that dance—you probably could. Quite possibly, it would work. But it's worth thinking about what having it "work" means to you. Is it just getting to go to the dance, or is it getting to go to the dance with someone who really wants to take you and who will make it fun? Because, to me, this does not sound like the kind of guy who makes a dance fun. He probably wouldn't sit with you on the bus ride over. This is the kind of guy who, after you've boarded the bus together, in front of everyone, will be like "Hey, I'm gonna sit with TJ and Blaze if that's okay?" and then act like you're the one who's uptight if you display anything less than backward-bending chill in front of his buddies. Picture him the way you saw him last and then add red-rimmed droopy eyes, slurred speech, and beer breath. At the stroke of midnight, that is who he'll turn into. Only on the way home will he be content to sit next to you, because he will need a shoulder to rest his dead-weight head upon.

My advice is to let him go to that dumb dance. If he tries to talk to you about it again (though my guess is he won't), say, "Who, me? Why would I care about this?" I don't know whether or not this will lead to a reunion between him and his ex (though I think you're right to suspect it's possible), but I'd suggest not waiting around to find out. This baby is not worth being fought over. To invite you over, have sex with you, and then tell you he's taking someone else to a dance he'd strongly suggested he was inviting you to is incredibly cruel. It's unacceptable.

Another option you might consider is to get one of his so-called brothers to take you to that dance and show up looking hot as…well, you know. F. And then don't talk to him at ALL. You have a real opportunity here to make this dude miserable, and I suggest you take it. But either way, remember this: You are a fun, cool babe who will no longer be saddle-bagged by an inferior baby-man. And *that* is something worth dancing about.

I paused, stopping to read over my response, fixing a few typos and making sure I'd answered everything as best I could. I signed off, as I always did, "Most humbly yours, Emma."

I opened Facebook in a new tab, looking briefly at my own page before checking Keith's. Remy's post was still there, which I supposed was likely proof that I had not fever-dreamed the entire thing while in a hangover coma at the library. Keith still had not commented on it, which wasn't especially comforting. It didn't make anything worse, really, but at this point I almost hoped for it—something firm, some undeniable proof that I didn't mean anything anymore and she did—just so I could stop waiting. I wanted him to tell me that he hated me, if that's what it took. No—I wanted him to tell me he was sorry, he fucked up, it was always me. But if he wasn't going to say anything like that, I wanted him to tell me it was done, it never even started. Anything had to be better than the silence.

I slowly pressed the top of my laptop closed and leaned over to rest my head on its overheated surface. It occurred to me that I was probably loading my head full of radiation. *Take me*, I thought, but the back of the screen got too warm on my skin and I sat up. I listened for a moment. The bathroom was quiet.

I picked up my empty bowl and walked out to the kitchen. Mel's door (ahead of me) and Logan's (to the right) were both closed, though light seeped out from underneath both. It was only about ten thirty, which meant Logan was probably watching a show and Mel was reading one of her textbooks in bed. I stood there for a moment deciding whose door to knock on, if either. I didn't even know what I wanted. Or, well, I did: I wanted to recap the entire series of events between Keith and me, up until the previous night's text, and I wanted one of them to tell me exactly what was going to happen tomorrow in class, when I'd see him for the first time in five days. If I talked to him, if he sat next to me, it would be for the first time in a week and a half.

I stood there in the dark kitchen, holding my empty bowl, standing up on my toes and then back down onto my heels. I felt pulled toward their rooms, both at once, but still I didn't move from my spot. I wanted to be in their beds next to them and hear them tell me versions of what they'd already been saying these past several days. But each time they did it they sounded a little less encouraging, and seemed a little less invested, and each time I asked anyway, I felt a little more pathetic. I was afraid they'd run out of patience before I stopped needing them.

I walked over to the sink, washed the bowl, and put it back in the cabinet. I hesitated once more outside the bathroom door, and as I looked at their doors, Mel's light went out. I walked into the bathroom, washed my face, brushed my teeth, and went to bed. The last thing I remembered doing before falling asleep was clutching my phone, wishing that by squeezing it tightly enough, a message—or email, or something, from anyone—would appear.

6

"He didn't even look at me," I said.

The three of us were sitting around the kitchen table, eating frozen pizza together like we'd done every Monday night since moving in. We'd decided it was the best reward for living through yet another Monday, as well as the best way to get through the rest of the week. It was also the only night that was ever relatively safe from our respective work-study jobs and extracurriculars, and it was a big exam day for Mel and Logan's classes, so they'd usually come home relieved, or at least defeated. We considered it our scheduled time to debrief—by Monday night we'd have gone nineteen or twenty hours at most without speaking to each other, but there always seemed to be so much we had to say.

I, for one, was practically foaming at the mouth.

"Did he sit by you?" asked Logan.

"No!!!!!" I said, shrieking somewhat.

"I guess that makes sense," she said.

"Does it??? To not sit by me, all of a sudden, when we've been sitting together for basically two months?" I said. "He was on TIME. There were plenty of seats. It wouldn't have been disruptive to come sit in the back by me. But he sat in the first one he saw by the door. It was just so *stupid*!"

"He's probably embarrassed," said Logan.

"He should be," said Mel.

"OK, but, what, he's just going to slink away from me for the rest of his LIFE?"

"Well, for the two more months you're in it," said Logan. "Sure."

"That's literally insane!" I said. "That is the behavior of a crazy person. You can't just pretend someone doesn't exist."

"I didn't say it wasn't crazy," said Logan. "I just think that's what he'll do."

"I really thought he'd wave or something," said Mel.

We each took another slice of pizza, taking a minute to eat and think.

"Do you want us to help you plot some kind of revenge?" asked Logan.

"Yes," I said, "but I don't want him to think I care or even notice that he's not speaking to me. What I really want is for him to evaporate into the atmosphere, and nobody notices, and he has to hover there, in little particles, realizing that nobody cares."

"Maybe you could like, booby-trap his room," said Mel.

"To do what?"

"I don't know," she said. "I haven't gotten that far."

"Do you think you'll see him out tomorrow?" asked Logan.

"What's tomorrow?" I asked. My heart rate took another precipitous leap upward. Surely, at this rate, I would have ten heart attacks before the month was out.

"St. Paddy's Day! How could you forget one of the great traditions in our great state's binge-drinking culture?"

"It just came up so fast," I said, closing my eyes and pressing them with my fingertips. "God. Of course he'll be out."

"OK, but there's, like, eight main bars to choose from," said

Logan. "Statistically, the chances that he'll end up in ours are fairly low."

"You literally just jinxed it, by saying that," I said. "Now he will one hundred percent for sure be in the same one as us."

"You did," said Mel. "You ruined it."

"IF I believed in determinism—which I don't—Keith would go to whatever bar he was predestined to go to regardless of me saying anything about it," said Logan.

"Maybe I won't go out," I said. I was exhausted by even the thought of it. Surely all I'd be able to do would be to watch the door. I could see it in my head—me standing in Mavericks, our favorite bar, and seeing him walking in. I'd drop my glass and sprint away, out the back door, so quickly I wouldn't hear it hit the ground. This was a big fantasy of mine: running away dramatically from unpleasant situations. In my head, it always looked fantastically tragic, my hair a wind-whipped frame for the serene sadness of my face. Sometimes I'd run through a moonlit forest into a clearing. Sometimes I'd run out onto a dock—also moonlit—and then jump off it. It always ended there. I didn't know what I'd do after I stopped running.

"You know you're going to come with us," Logan said, and I knew she was right.

On Tuesday I woke up feeling excited and nauseated. The first time I'd thought about seeing him out that night, I had felt abject dread. I wanted escape routes in place; better yet, I wanted to be unavoidably detained somewhere far away. Nobody could say I didn't go because I was too afraid if I was trapped at the time—not by anything or anyone life-threatening, but maybe under a pile of lightweight branches arranged in such a way that it took me exactly one night to work my way out.

Overnight, my position had shifted. I was still nervous, and restless, but I wondered if seeing him might resolve something for me. He could ignore my text messages and there wasn't very much I could do. He could pretend neither of us knew I was being ignored. He could avoid me in class too, but doing so in a packed, small bar would be tougher, and more obvious. There was something satisfying in knowing that if I saw him there, he would see me, too. Maybe he would have to look at me.

So I got through my classes, paying more attention than I had for what felt like the whole semester thus far, determined not to let my boy-related anxiety derail my productivity any longer. I was a competent woman. I was self-assured, and strong, and today was the day I'd get the answers (of whatever kind, I told myself; I'd be OK with answers of whatever kind) I'd been waiting for. And then tomorrow, no matter what, I would be fine.

Like always, we started getting ready much too early. By seven, I was trying things on: a dark blue chambray shirtdress, a forest green sweater and jeans, and then another sweater. I took it all off and stood in my bra and underwear in front of my closet door, willing something new to appear. I tried on a greenish gray, drapey boatneck shirt I'd gotten on sale six months earlier and then never worn. This happened to me sometimes: I'd buy things that didn't look like things I'd normally wear, because I wanted to break out of the types of things I normally wore, and then I'd never wear those things. I looked at myself in the mirror on the back of my bedroom door. "Tonight is just not the right night," I said to myself, again, and took it off once more.

I settled on jeans and a green-with-white-polka-dots button-down and walked into the bathroom, where Mel and Logan were completing their respective hair and makeup routines: for Logan, this meant straightening the very ends of her long, dirty blond hair, pulling it all into a low ponytail, and dabbing Vaseline onto her lips. For Mel, this meant brushing her thick eyebrows smooth with a little comb and putting eyeliner on her lower lids only. Soon she'd go lie down in bed and press her pillow over her head for five or ten minutes, a process which she claimed "flattened" her hair, but also, I thought, served as the only time she ever really let herself do nothing.

"Is this OK?" I asked them, gesturing to my outfit.

"It's a little prim for St. Patrick's Day," said Logan, who, though she never strayed much from T-shirts and jeans herself, was an unusually good and particular judge of style.

"I picked this one because whenever I wear the plaid ones you say I look like a boy," I said. "And it's green."

"Are different kinds of button-downs the only options?" she asked.

"Practically!!" I said. "You should know this!"

"What about that one shirt—"

"No," I said.

"OK," she said. "Then wear what you have on! You look fine!"

"Fine," I said. "Is not. Good enough."

"I meant great!" said Logan, unconvincingly.

"Logan!!" I said. She sighed, waving me back toward the direction of my room and following me into it.

I flung myself onto my bed and watched the ceiling while she sifted through my various tops and dresses.

"OK," she said, after a few minutes. "You have two options." She held up each of her hands: in the left was my secret-weapon dress, which, while deceptively plain (navy, cotton, long sleeves) was extremely tight in an unusually flattering way; in the right was my black oversized blazer and a green tank top whose neckline scooped low on my chest. "I know the dress is navy, but you can wear like, green eyeliner or something. And I think these are both on-theme anyway, if slightly different tonally," she explained.

"The dress is more like 'You're going to regret ignoring texts sent by THIS body,' and the blazer is like 'Who are you? Go get me a martini,'" I said.

"Exactly," said Logan, obviously curious about which message I'd choose. Maybe it was my imagination, but I thought I saw her extend her right hand slightly forward.

"The dress," I said. Logan did a very good job appearing impassive about most things; most of the time, nobody but Mel or me could tell if she was feeling anything other than contentment. And sometimes even we didn't know. She didn't say anything when she handed me the dress, but I knew she thought I'd chosen wrong.

Logan left the room and I changed into the dress, which was clingier than I remembered, but not in a bad way. I turned in half circles in front of the mirror, examining myself. I'd never worn the dress in front of Keith, though I'd had plans to; I'd assumed, at some point, that eventually he'd ask me out on a "real" date, a normal one, just to get dinner somewhere in town, and I thought I'd wear it then.

I walked back into the bathroom. Mel and Logan oohed and aahed appropriately. Mel walked out into the kitchen and came back with shots for each of us.

"To justice being served," said Logan, and we clinked our glasses.

Even from outside, through the tinted windows, I could see the bar was especially packed. I held my breath as I walked through the door, surveying the crush of people standing around the bracket-shaped bar counter, two or three deep in places. Mavericks was one of the biggest bars downtown, which was why we liked it better than Butler's, which was long and narrow, with barely six feet between a handful of booths on the left and the bar on the right, and two dingy pool tables in back. There was no such thing as a night at Butler's that didn't involve standing shoulder to shoulder on all sides. Mavericks was comparatively spacious, with an elevated row of booths around the perimeter (a good area from which to spy on the ground-level bar and table area), and, importantly, a women's bathroom with three stalls, which meant you could sit and pee within reasonable time frames. Except, it seemed, on St. Patrick's Day.

"I already want to go home," said Mel, looking around with furrowed eyebrows.

"What?? You MADE me come here!" I said, halting our trio in the entryway of the bar.

"I knowwww," she said. "I always think I want to go out, and then I do go out, and it's just like ..." said Mel, waving her hand vaguely. "All these people."

"Well, we're staying," I said. "At least for an hour. This is your fault."

"Let's get drinks," said Logan, grabbing each of us by a wrist.

We waded through a sea of people, most of them wearing piles of green and silver and gold beads around their necks. Halfway to the bar, I was hit in the face by a bright green one, being shook around in the air in what appeared to be a trade.

"Uh," I said.

"OH MY GOD ARE YOU OK?!?!" screamed the girl holding it, as if, rather than having tapped my cheek with a string of plastic beads, she'd hit me over the head with a brick. I immediately felt bad for my annoyed half reaction. There was nobody—nobody—nicer on the entire planet than a happy drunk girl.

"I'm fine!" I said. "Really." I reached my hands out as if to say *there, there*.

"I LOOOOOVE your dress," said her friend, the necklace's new owner.

"You look like Kim Kardashian," said the first girl, nodding in approval. It was a ludicrous statement. What she meant was that my hair was dark brown, and I was sort of short, and wearing a tight dress. But still, so nice.

"THANK you!" I said. "Can we squeeze past you guys to get a drink?"

"Yes!!" the girls said, parting like the Red Sea to create a path forward for us. "Go!" they said, waving us forward, like they were seeing us off on a long and dangerous journey.

As we brushed past them, Mel and I instinctively hung back to let Logan, who was tallest among us by several inches and therefore the appointed drink-getter, get to the bar first. It was her visibility, but it was also something about her default waiting face—serious and serene, interested but not eager. If she wasn't so openly hostile when approached by strange men wanting to buy her drinks, she'd have been besieged by them. Within moments the bartender, a tanned and pretty girl in her early twenties wearing a green tank top and her beachy blond hair in a high ponytail, was serving up three shots of tequila and a pitcher of beer. We weaved back through the ever-expanding crowd and found a recently evacuated booth in the back corner near the bathrooms.

Mel and Logan slid into the side of the booth that faced the back, quietly giving me the side facing the front doors. Once seated, I did another survey, looking not only for Keith but for anyone I knew to be associated with him. I didn't see anyone, but it was still early.

"Oh, there's Peter," said Mel.

"Oh god. Where? Is Nora with him?" asked Logan, swiveling around to look.

"I don't see her," said Mel. "I kinda feel like she's too cool to go out on St. Patrick's Day."

"Again, you're sending a lot of mixed messages about going out on St. Patrick's Day," I said.

"You know what I mean. Most girls, if they don't go out on weekends, or holidays, you don't think, like, oh, well, that's because they're doing something amazing that we just wouldn't know about. With Nora, you do. But nobody would think that about us," said Mel.

"Hey!" I said.

"I think, if we're being honest with ourselves, that's fair," said Logan.

"Is Peter still trying to make that singles mixer thing happen?" I asked. Secretly I hoped so. It was fun to hear about, and it wasn't often that I was able to make much sense of Mel and Logan's gossip. I didn't know their crowd or their science cliques or their professors. As freshmen we'd had a whole little world of friends, made by dormitory proximity, all of us taking the same 100-level classes and studying for them together. But over time we'd splintered off into tighter, smaller squadrons. Mel and Logan and I had been a team since the start, but I didn't have any classes with them anymore, and very few of the same friends, and sometimes it seemed all we had in common was each other.

"I think he's backed off the mixer aspect and is now just trying to convince us to do a spring dance of some kind," said Mel.

"It's absurd," said Logan. "There are like, barely thirty of us. It will be lethally awkward."

"Apparently Peter wants it to *be beach-themed*," said Mel, leaning as far forward as the booth's table would allow. "He wants us to wear, like, *leis*."

"Oh, good," said Logan. "Just what this event needed: cultural appropriation."

"Why does it even need a theme?" I asked. "Why can't you guys just have a semiformal end-of-the-year banquet like all the other honor societies?"

"THAT'S A VERY GOOD QUESTION," Logan yelled, not that it registered as especially loud. The bar nearly vibrated with Top 40 pop. You couldn't hear any voice or word in particular beyond the edges of our booth. She picked up the pitcher and divided the remaining beer equally among our plastic cups. We looked at the pitcher, surprised to see it already empty. I checked my phone: it was 10:38 (and no surprise, I had no text messages).

"Oh," said Logan, "I forgot to tell you guys: Will and Sarah broke up."

"WHAT?" I said. Will, like many of the guy friends we'd made during freshman year, had lived on the floor above ours, and had been quickly and collectively deemed the hottest guy on his floor and probably the whole campus. Actually, I hadn't gotten it at first: He was tall and lanky, yes, with very nice, broad shoulders, but his face—small, straight, even features—struck me as plain, and his curly brown hair unremarkable, and sometimes much too long. But then, a few weeks into the year, soon after he'd befriended Mel (and after she'd started trying to explain his appeal to me), we'd ended up in the sandwich line together in the cafeteria. We recognized each other as friends of each other's friends, and he'd said "Oh, hey!" Then he'd looked down at my tray, said, "Tuna sandwich! Nice nice," and grinned at me. And then, somehow, I'd understood. He was the most charming airhead I had ever encountered. Everyone harbored a collective, passive crush on him all fall semester—each of us bragging to the others whenever we ran into him on campus, none of us ever really making the effort to do anything more about it. He didn't seem like someone you could date, or even hook up with; he was too dopey and unfocused. Then, on Halloween, he had made out with Mel on the dance floor at Theta Chi, and when we'd all walked drunkenly home sometime around 2:00 AM, they'd trailed behind the rest of our group, holding hands while Logan and I giggled, and peered back at them, and poked each other. It had felt like a victory for humankind.

The next day Mel had modestly insisted it was no big deal, and she didn't care if that was all that happened. But when he'd started dating this girl Sarah—a pretty soccer player whose hair, we'd grudgingly noted, literally shimmered—and Mel swore she really didn't care, we didn't really believe her. Over the next two years, whenever she made out with someone at a party, she'd compare them, unfavorably, to Will.

"Where did you, uh, hear that?" she said now, visibly struggling to appear only passingly interested.

"Why didn't you tell us the second you heard??" I said. "What's wrong with you?"

"I'm telling you now!" said Logan. "I just forgot. Jamie told me in Genetics lab." Jamie was Logan's lab partner and played soccer with Sarah.

"Oh my god," I said. "Did she say what happened?" I wanted to know what had happened, of course, because it was Will, but

I was also trying to ask the questions I knew Mel wanted to ask but was trying not to.

"Ummm, I didn't really ask," said Logan.

"Jesus Christ!" I said.

"Sorry!" she said, not very apologetically. "I didn't realize I'd need to recite a timeline of events. She just mentioned it offhand, like as part of another story."

I glared at her and Mel pretended to look at her phone.

"I can try to find out more next lab..." she added.

"Good," I said. "Find out who broke up with whom, and why, and exactly when it happened, if you can." I looked at Mel, who looked up at me expectantly. "And ask if she thinks there's any chance they'll get back together," I added.

"OK, crazy," said Logan.

I blushed. "I mean, just...do your best."

"Yeah, got it," she said, nodding and leaning back to swallow the last drop of beer in her cup. "I'll get another one?" We all knew the answer, so the question was really more like a gesture. We'd thought about not drinking more; we'd just decided against it. We each handed Logan a few dollar bills and she slid out of the booth, picked up the empty pitcher, and jumped down from the platform, heading toward the bar.

Mel and I took her departure as another opportunity to survey our surroundings; I saw my poetry class friend Macey and her boyfriend at a table under one of the big TV screens, and told myself I'd go say hi later. I saw a pair of girls I recognized from Spanish Civ waiting by the bar, one of them untangling the other's many beaded necklaces from her hair while she alternated between grimacing and telling what appeared, from her hand gestures, to be a very dramatic story.

I shifted my eyes toward the front doors at the exact moment that Keith pushed one open and walked through. My face flushed, and I felt adrenaline burst through my body. He was wearing the gray knit cap that I loved and the dark green puffy jacket that I hated.

It took me as long to register these details as it did for him to get far enough through the door that I could see the person coming in behind him—*with* him, surely—was Remy.

7

Even though it took them no more than three seconds total to get in the door, I had the odd sensation that I'd predicted it—that I'd seen him, thought *Remy is going to come in that door next*, and then watched it happen. It came true so quickly, though, that it was hard to place the thought in time. Maybe my eyes had worked quicker than my brain, registering a little flash of her face or body while my brain remained focused on Keith. Then, when I'd seen her, consciously and fully, I hadn't been surprised.

Either way, there she was.

"Holy shit," I hissed, ducking down in my seat as if to avoid a bird swerving near my head.

"What??" Mel asked, turning to look where I was.

"Don't move!" I yelled. "Stop. Don't look. Shit."

"Keith?" she gasped. Her eyes were wide, her body frozen at an awkward angle, one hand hovering above the table.

I nodded upward, just once. It was really more like a head tilt. I couldn't seem to find the breath required to say the rest: that it wasn't just him. It was so much worse.

"Can I look now?" she asked. I glanced again in their direction, just long enough to see him place his hand on her back—touching her coat, cream-colored and long and wool, the kind you couldn't pull off without looking like a rich, middle-aged Protestant mother unless, apparently, you were her—gently guiding her from his side until she was in front of him, and they could squeeze through the crowd together in a two-person line. I closed my eyes and jerked my head slightly once more.

"Is that—" said Mel, cutting herself off the moment she realized she knew the answer. It was kind of her, I thought, to not say Remy's name.

"Yes," I said. "I told you. I knew it."

"What do you mean?" she said. "The Facebook post?"

"Yes!!" I was almost shrieking. "I just. I had a feeling. I knew it wasn't just friendly. I knew it."

"We still don't know anything's *really* going on," Mel said, but she didn't sound especially sure. We both turned our heads cautiously, watching them stand closely together at the bar, their backs to us. I half expected him to pick her up and set her on top of it.

"They are legitimately canoodling," I said.

"They're just standing there," said Mel. "It's crowded, there isn't much space..." She trailed off as they turned to look at each other. He was nearly a foot taller than she was—she needed to tilt her head so far back to do it.

"OK, well, now they're gazing into each other's eyes!!" I said. Mel didn't bother to argue. We sat staring at them for a few moments, finally diverted by Logan's return to our booth. She carefully placed the now-full pitcher on our table, and as soon as the beer was safe I grabbed her forearm and pulled her down next to me. I was not about to be left alone on this side of the booth, out in the open for anyone to see. I needed a shield. She tipped in beside me and I was surprised to hear myself laugh. I felt giddy, nearly feverish.

"What's . . . happening?" Logan asked, looking back and forth between us as I giggled and Mel stared. I took a few deep breaths and leaned toward Logan, and that simple movement gave me the telltale head swirls of mid-level drunkenness. I knew that when I eventually got up—although I didn't plan on it, I would never get up from this booth again, it was impossible—I would feel it even more. I poured myself another little plastic cup of beer and took a few quick gulps.

"Keith is here," explained Mel. "At the bar. And, uh. It seems like he might be with that girl from the library. Maybe."

"Not 'maybe'!" I said, setting my cup down just a little too hard. I swiped away the spilled beer with my bare hand and then looked at it. *Whatever*, I thought. *It's not like it really matters whether you have beer on your hand or not.* "Definitely. He is definitely with her. Remy."

"Her name is REMY?" said Logan, and I was momentarily soothed by her incredulousness.

"Yes," I said. "I'm pretty sure I told you that in my email."

"Yeah, but I didn't hear it out LOUD," said Logan.

"Is she like, French or something?" said Mel.

"Oh, *probably*," I said.

Logan looked over at the bar. I watched her face until it became obvious she'd spotted them and then I looked back down at my cup.

"Don't let them see you looking," I said.

"Are you trying not to move your mouth?" said Mel. "Nobody is watching us."

"GOD!" I yelled, and slumped back hard against the windowed wall. "Ouch."

"Are you OK?" said Mel.

"No, obviously," I said. I was suddenly very tired.

I looked back at Logan, who was still watching them at the bar. I looked over at them too and saw that they had just gotten their drinks. I watched Keith take his money out of his back pocket—he kept it folded together in an old brass clip, instead of using a wallet like a normal fucking human being—and place a bill on the bar. It must have been just enough for the two drinks and a tip, because he and Remy picked up their drinks and turned to walk away.

I shot down in my seat, bumping my head on the window ledge. "Ow!" I yelled. "Christ."

"You're sort of, like, giving with one hand and taking with the other, as far as trying to remain undetected goes," said Logan, who'd turned to face me.

"Yes, thank you," I said, rubbing the spot on the back of my head. "Where are they going? What direction?"

"Sort of toward the TVs," said Mel. "I think... it looks like they're meeting people who are already here."

I sat back up slowly, trying to assess whether I could safely look at their table without being seen. They were with Keith's roommates, I noticed, plus a couple girls I didn't recognize. Remy sat perpendicular to me, facing the TVs, and Keith sat immediately to her left, his back toward me once again. I felt both relieved and angry. He'd found a way to ignore me even when he didn't know I was here.

"I can't believe this," I said. Even though I'd guessed it myself two days ago, I didn't think I'd be *right*. You weren't supposed to be *right* about the frantic, crazed, Internet-stalking-based conspiracy theories you came up with to explain the disappearance of boys you liked. You were supposed to think them to yourself and say them out loud to your friends, who would vehemently deny them and tell you that you were being dramatic. And then you were supposed to find out you *were* just being dramatic. I felt, somehow, that Mel and Logan were partly to blame for taking things off that course. "I told you guys," I said. "You told me I was wrong, and I wasn't. I was CORRECT." The words felt cottony in my mouth. I swallowed the last bit of beer from my cup.

"What was there to be wrong about??" asked Mel. "You showed us her post, we said it wasn't enough information to be sure, and that was true!!"

"We're not arguing with you NOW," said Logan, gesturing toward the table where they sat, their knees surely touching underneath it. The implication was that it was now self-evident, to anyone with eyes: Keith and Remy were together. Something clamped in my chest, and I knew, if I let myself, I would cry right here. I'd known it was true from the moment they walked in, but that didn't mean I wanted my friends to acknowledge it out loud.

"Can we go?" I asked, not looking up. I pulled my phone out of my purse and checked the time: 11:02. We'd officially stayed a little over the minimum we'd required of ourselves at the start of the night.

"Are you sure?" said Logan. "Maybe it's good to kind of . . . habituate."

"Please don't turn this into a behavioral experiment," I said. "I really want to go. I don't want to be here." My chest burned; tears felt imminent. If I had to, I would walk out of here by myself to avoid the possibility of crying at Mavericks on St. Patrick's Day.

"OK," said Mel. "It's OK." She picked up our empty cups and Logan picked up the pitcher, and they scooted out of the booth. They stood at the end of it with their backs toward Keith and Remy's table, waiting for me to get out and walk the other way, and I wondered if they were shielding me on purpose. I stood up, feeling wobbly and vicious at once. *I should run over there right now and tackle their whole table*, I thought.

"You guys go," I said, waving them ahead of me, away from Keith and Remy, toward the exit at the back of the bar. Once they were past me I turned around and stood at the edge of the raised platform to look. In the ground-floor space between them and me were five or six other tables and a dozen or so little constellations of students around and among them. The distance felt massive, like I was watching them from outside a snow globe.

Just then Remy swiveled around to her left, toward me, apparently in response to a guy one table over. She looked up just slightly, and I stopped breathing, like I might chameleon myself into my background if only I didn't exhale. Was she looking at me? I couldn't tell. I couldn't move. But less than a second later she was looking away, toward the door behind her, and I felt sure (at least pretty sure) that she'd missed me.

"Harriet?" said Logan, down the platform's two stairs and waiting with Mel by the hallway to the back door.

"SHH! Shut up! Shut up!" I hissed, speed-walking toward them, partly crouched over.

"Relax!" said Logan, but when I gave her a look she grabbed my upper arm and pulled me in front of her, squeezed it, and let it go.

In the morning I woke up clammy and dry-mouthed. I opened my eyes to sunlight shining through my windows with what felt like unnatural, unprecedented force. I groaned and rolled onto my side, reaching for the travel-size Advil bottle I kept on my nightstand. I knocked it off the edge and onto the floor, where I heard it hit and then roll under the bed.

"Noooooooo," I said. I took a deep breath, closed my eyes, and tried to prepare myself to retrieve it. "OK," I said. I slid toward the edge of my bed, leaned over it, and was immediately struck with a wave of nausea. I retreated onto my back and took another few deep breaths. "You can do this," I told myself. My voice sounded like I'd been dead for three days. I slid over again, more slowly this time, and reached over the edge of my bed. I dragged my fingertips along the wooden floorboards, feeling around for the bottle. After a few moments I touched plastic. I picked it up (*slowly*) and shook out two capsules. I put them in my mouth and picked up my water glass, trying yet again to drink water on my side without pouring half of it onto my pillow. Half of it dripped onto my pillow. *Next time*, I thought.

I lay on my back and waited for the Advil to kick in. I realized I didn't totally remember getting home, or at least not what happened between getting home and falling asleep. I lifted my comforter to look at my body: I was wearing pajamas, like normal. I touched my forefinger and thumb to my eyelashes: I had taken off my mascara. I was sure I'd also brushed and flossed my teeth, though you wouldn't know it now. After heavy-drinking nights out, my roommates would collapse in their beds fully clothed with their makeup still on. I was both annoyed by and envious of their guiltless carelessness; even in the depths of total intoxication, I could not break my routines.

Without opening my eyes, I reached my right arm out toward my nightstand and picked up my phone. I brought it close to my face and opened one eye to read the time: 8:23. I lowered my arm gently onto my bed, phone in hand. Any sudden movement could undo the good work of the Advil, which was starting to numb the edges of my headache.

I closed my eyes again and pictured Keith and Remy standing together at the bar.

When had they met? Had it been that Thursday, when I texted him to come out, and he said he was staying in? Had he later that night decided to go out after all, only to a different, better party? Maybe she'd been there too, and they'd run into each other getting drink refills, and they'd "hit it off." (That would be his term, not mine—a vague, catchall guy-ism, the start and the end of the whole story.) Or maybe, worse, they, both seniors, had already known each other, and this was the culmination of three or four years of flirtatious friendship, and everyone they knew was now telling each other "God, it's about time."

I wanted to know the exact timing because I wanted to know if he'd had to decide between us. If we'd been in his head at the same time. I couldn't decide which was worse: that it was a decision and a hard one, and he'd liked both of us, and he'd thought about it a lot, and in the end chose someone else; or that it wasn't really a decision at all.

I thought again of him and Remy standing together, and then him touching her back and lining himself up behind her, replaying it over in my mind a few times to make myself feel worse.

When I finally got up, it was after ten and the house was empty, as I should have expected. There was no logical reason to feel surprised or disappointed that Mel and Logan weren't home.

I went to get a glass of juice from the refrigerator, but the bottle was gone. I checked the recycling bag under our sink and found it there. It looked so sad. *"Dammit,"* I whispered. I walked into the bathroom to wash my face, and when I leaned in to look at the mirror I noticed that a little line of zits had broken out along my jaw overnight.

"Well, I am not going to class. That's for sure," I told my reflection. Work, I couldn't skip—I needed the money from every hour I had on my schedule—but that was fine. Work (at least on Wednesdays, when I had the circulation desk to myself) did not require me to make small talk with anyone. More importantly, work did not require me to be within thirty yards of Keith. Or at least I hoped it wouldn't. If he were to come in while I was working—and the way things were going that seemed almost inevitable—I would run out the door and keep going until I hit Missouri.

With all that decided I took a bowl and a box of Cheerios with me into the living room, where I parked on the couch, turned on a *Law & Order* marathon, and remained there for four hours.

The temperature outside had taken a sharp dip since the night before. Supposedly, we were in for a spring snowstorm that weekend. Normally I would have resented the news, even my above-average enthusiasm for winter running thin by the middle of March. This time I found it fitting for my mood. I walked to the library looking at the brittle gray tree branches and half-melted islands of crusty, dirty snow around me and thought, *I hope everything stays dead forever.*

I walked into the library at three on the dot, pushed open the swinging door of the circulation desk with my thighs, and threw my bag down next to my usual chair. I stood for a second behind it, surveying the landscape: Aside from two lone freshmen in armchairs near the back wall, the place was deserted. Thank god.

I took off my coat (under which I was wearing a hooded Springfield sweatshirt I'd bought when I was an excited and team-spirited freshman and a pair of dark gray leggings I'd gotten for Christmas and later adopted as "real pants") and hung it over my chair. I was just sitting down when I noticed Remy walk in the front doors. I sank down hard the rest of the way, the cheap coiled plastic of the chair stand squeaking loudly beneath me. I swiveled quickly to look at the blank computer screen in front of me.

"You have got to be fucking kidding me," I whispered to it.

What was she doing here? I mean, yes, the library was a public resource, and she was a student who presumably had classes and didn't just spend ALL her time ruining other people's lives, but still. I'd come here, despite the worst hangover after the worst night, out of the goodness of my own heart, and also because I had to. It wasn't fair for me to have to see her again already.

I stared straight ahead, willing her to walk past me—she didn't seem the type to say hi—and up the stairs to some dingy unknown corner of our library's uppermost floors, where, ideally, she would be very cold, and a spider would drop from the ceiling and land in her hair.

But then I heard the little gate open. I turned my head slowly away from my computer and toward it, thinking, I guess, that not looking too quickly might keep anything I didn't want to happen from happening. I saw her there all the same, dropping her own bag on the ground next to a chair.

"Uh," I said. "Hi?"

"Hi," she said, looking up only momentarily from her bag (in which she was rummaging around for her things, like she'd be staying back here, which of course made no sense).

"Are you...working?" I asked. Why didn't she ever feel the need to explain herself?

"Yeah," she said, getting into her chair. "Just 'til five thirty," she added, registering my confusion.

"Oh, OK," I said. "I just always have this shift by myself, so

I wasn't expecting...anyone." I'd almost said "expecting you," which would have been truer.

"Yeah, I dropped a class, so," she said, "I thought I might as well pick up a couple shifts, get up to fifteen hours instead of ten."

But why MY shift? I thought. It just seemed weird. She certainly couldn't have picked this shift because I was working during it. After the first afternoon we spent together, she hadn't exactly seemed intent on seeking out more.

"Cool," I said anyway. "I just do ten too, but I can see doing fifteen next year."

"Yeah," she said.

Goddddddddddddddddddddddd.

Was this what Keith wanted, in a girlfriend? *No,* I thought, *that's mean.* But also: Was it? Was what he really wanted a beautiful girl who said almost nothing? Someone who would be very, very nice (to him, at least) and very, very quiet? It was certainly a type—Logan called them "Courtneys." Girls who drove boys crazy in ways other girls didn't get. The first time I'd recognized it was freshman year, in the dorm lounge, when one of our guy friends (I could no longer remember which one) announced that his number one celebrity crush was this tiny, wide-eyed, plain-pretty actress with glossy brown hair, one who starred on some TV show I hadn't seen, and every other guy in the room had just about lost it. She was the *dream,* they said. The girls had been like "Really? Her?" and "She seems boring...?" But the guys were insistent, like, "Come on, you're just jealous, she's adorable! And so funny!" I watched an episode later, trying to figure it out. Was she funny? Or was she just giggling a lot?

Remy, I decided, was a Courtney. She was a strikingly pretty one—because your typical Courtney was only pretty in an accessible, modest, natural girl-next-door sort of way—but she was a Courtney all the same.

"I think I saw you last night," she said. The sound of her voice made me jump. I looked over and she laughed. "Ha, sorry."

"No, I—apparently I was in a trance there," I said, embarrassed and forcing a smile. I was annoyed with myself for letting her spook me. *What am I*, I thought. *A horse?*

"That happens to me a lot here," she said. She smiled at me, directly, which she'd never done before. I felt a slight softening toward her and, at the same time, a wave of suspicion. I looked at her teeth, having forgotten exactly how perfect they were—so bright I couldn't look at them for too long.

"Um, at Mavericks, do you mean?" I said finally, once it became clear she wasn't going to restate her original question. Preserving what little normality this conversation had was up to me.

"Yeah," she said. "Like, across the bar. I wasn't sure if you saw me . . ."

If she had seen me, and was now willing to admit to seeing me, then why hadn't she waved or anything?

"Oh, I didn't!" I lied. "I was super drunk," I added, then regretted it immediately.

"Ah, well," she said, laughing a little in a way that struck me as sanctimonious. Well, good for her. A year older than me and already SO over getting drunk on St. Patrick's Day. She had probably had her one gin and tonic, and then a glass of water, and then held hands with Keith the whole way home, the two of them walking together in a perfectly straight line.

"On St. Patrick's Day two years ago, I threw up in the bathroom at Butler's, and this girl I'd never even met held my hair back. She was really nice about it, considering, but I was so embarrassed that I cut it all off the next day," said Remy, gesturing at her short cut with a flourish of her hand, which she then tucked with the other between her crossed knees.

"Wait, really?" I asked.

"Yes," she said, and laughed. In spite of myself, I laughed, too.

"That's sweet," I said. "I have had so much good drunken bonding in bar bathrooms. A lot of tampon lending."

"Really?" said Remy.

"Yeah," I said, self-conscious again. "I mean, not all the time or anything, I have my own, uh...feminine products. Usually."

"No, um," she said. "I just meant, that was the only time anything like that has happened to me. Bathroom bonding."

"Oh," I said. "I guess that probably just means you're responsible."

"I think it's more that I just don't have that easy a time talking to girls," she said.

OH, I thought. *There it was.* So that's the type of girl she was: not like the other ones.

I didn't know how to respond directly to this, nor did I really care to. So I pretended it hadn't been said.

"So," I said. "That's why you have short hair, then?"

"Oh, well, I mean, it kind of was at first," she said. "But then it grew out a little and I just kept it. It's not *still* a security measure."

"Well," I said. "It's really cute." It was; it suited her features perfectly.

"Oh, ha, I wasn't—"

"I know!" I said. "I already thought so, I just. Hadn't said."

"Thaaaaaanks," she said. As she did so she sort of tucked her face back into her neck and widened her eyes, looking off to the side. So Remy wasn't great at getting compliments, it seemed;

you'd think someone that pretty would have had lots of practice. She swiveled her chair back toward the stack of notebooks and folders she'd placed to the side of the keyboard.

Then our chat was over, and with two brief exceptions—once when a group of super-loud, super-showily hungover freshmen girls staggered through the front lobby on their way upstairs, and we were like "Okay" and "We get it" to each other; another when some guy came up to ask where he could find some religious mysticism textbook, and it seemed clear that this was a) very far out of his typical field of study and b) his first time setting foot in the library—we didn't talk until Remy's shift was done at five thirty.

"See you Sunday?" she said.

"Oh, right!" I said. *Oh, right*.

I'd never forgotten, really, but it was only once Remy walked out of the library that I was hit with the feeling I'd had upon seeing her walk into the bar last night. She'd been marginally nicer to me today, and why shouldn't she? To her I was just some junior she worked with at the library. And even though I was so hurt, and angry, and considered her on some level to be my sworn enemy, because she talked to me, I talked back. Against my will. It felt like just one more thing she took from me. I wondered if Remy Roy had ever not gotten what she wanted.

When I got home I walked right into my room, straight to the whiteboard I kept hanging on the inside of my closet door. With the palm of my hand I erased its contents: New Year's Resolutions: 1) exercise, 2) ~~no~~ fewer Pop-Tarts, 3) develop good 5-year-plan, 4) 1 glass of water with every alcoholic beverage, 5*) [added just days earlier] Ruin Keith's life. I wiped my hand on my jeans and unclipped the marker from the top of the board, and then I wrote "Reasons Remy Is The Worst" at the top of it.

1. Courtney
2. Guy's girl
3. Unself-aware (see: florals, thinking anyone can wear them)
4. Too pretty
5. ~~Took Keith~~

This last one I crossed out, then erased, because I knew, technically, that it was wrong. She didn't take him. He chose her. She had no obligation to me—she didn't even know me. It was him I should be mad at if I was going to be mad at anyone. And I *was* mad at him. I was furious. I just hated her, too. Even though I wasn't supposed to, and I knew it.

I paused, putting the cap back on the marker while I thought so the ink wouldn't dry out. After chewing on the end of it for a few seconds I uncapped it again and wrote:

5. Is going to make Keith very happy, I AM SURE.

8

"Will texted me last night."

We were halfway through the sandwiches we'd made for our Friday lunch, which we often made and ate together after our classes and labs and seminars were done for the week. In the afternoons, Mel would return to the library, and Logan would do something annoying like go for a run, and I had a shift at the library from three to five thirty. (With established coworker David, a freshman I did not particularly like, but who got high marks, at least, in being Not Remy.)

"And you're only telling us now??" I asked.

"I don't know," said Mel. "It wasn't a big deal."

"Of course it's a big deal!" I shrieked. "What did it say?"

Mel looked down at the ham sandwich she still held in her hands and, trying (and failing) not to smile, set it down on the paper towel she insisted upon using as a plate.

"It was so stupid," she said. "It, like, didn't even make sense."

"Of course it didn't! Say it!!"

She turned around in her chair to pick up her phone, which was charging on the kitchen counter behind her. We waited patiently for a few moments while she unlocked the screen and paged through her texts to find the right entry.

"Where . . . is it?" she said.

"COME ON," I said.

"OK, OK, here," she said. "It was at 1:23 so I was asleep—"

"Of course."

"God, they're like bats or something," said Logan.

"What, guys?" I asked.

"Yes. Blind, for example. No endurance. Acting like it's day-time when everyone else knows it's night," said Logan, ticking off points on her fingers. "Whiny."

"They're not *whiny*," said Mel.

"Bats or guys?"

"Mel!" I said. "Read!"

"OK," she said. "So, 1:23—"

"Right—"

"He writes, 'Wats up Alves,'" said Mel, reading the message in a deep voice she produced from the back of her throat.

"Was that supposed to be him?" asked Logan.

"What's like w-a-t-s?" I asked.

"Yes," said Mel. "Should I go on?"

"You wrote back to that?" I asked.

"Yeah, when I woke up. I wrote, 'Hey Will, just woke up, how are you?'"

"OK," I said. "Great." As I had often pointed out to her over the course of our friendship, Mel's texting style was strangely dry and formal, especially compared to how fun she was to talk to in person. Sometimes she'd have me write a second draft to casualize a message, but the three of us had mostly come to accept that her MO was to sound like she was corresponding with a great-aunt who she hoped would one day leave her a large inheritance.

"Then what?" asked Logan.

"THEN he didn't write back," said Mel, setting her phone down just a little too hard on the table.

"Careful!" said Logan and I.

"He is SUCH a beautiful, stupid freak," said Mel. "He always does this! It's, like, why did you text me in the first place then?"

"Doesn't he always respond like, two days later?" asked Logan.

"Yes, he does," I said. "He'll probably write back tonight at four AM or something."

"Eh," said Mel. "I don't know. Maybe. He was probably just drunk."

"Do you want him to text back?" I asked. I knew the answer, obviously; it was more the type of question you ask your friend to see whether she's being honest with herself or not.

"I don't know," she sighed. "It'd be fun to make out, I guess, but . . . it's just never going to be any more than that with him."

"I don't know that that's true," I said, because I didn't, and because it would have been nice if it didn't have to be. Will was flighty, and only recently single again, and part of me thought if it was going to happen it would have by now, but he really was a nice guy, all things considered. Also, he was hot.

"Well, I think so," said Mel. "But, whatever, it's fine. I'll just probably get these pointless three-word texts from him for the rest of my life!"

"We should be able to monetize useless texts from men," said Logan. "A dollar per word or something. It's like a refund from the patriarchy."

"Two dollars per emoticon, I think," I said.

"Five for calling me by my last name," said Mel, and Logan and I nodded in agreement.

*　　*　　*

When I got to the library, I waved to David, who was wearing headphones. He looked up to give me an obligatory close-mouthed smile and quickly looked back at his computer screen. We weren't really supposed to wear headphones at the desk, because, according to Deb, the staff librarian, it made us look unavailable to other students. But she wasn't physically present at the library from 12:01 PM Friday through 6:59 AM each Monday, so on the weekends, much of the work-study staff overruled that particular policy. Publicly, I pretended to support the lawless mutiny, but privately, I wished David would just follow the stupid rule. Instead, when someone approached him at the desk, he would look at them and just wait, silently daring them to go away. Then, after this several-seconds-long staring contest, he would slowly remove just one of the earbuds and hold it aloft between his fingers while they talked to him. It made every interaction with him feel timed and falsely grave. Early on in the semester I'd tried to make friends with him, or at least acquaintances, but whenever I'd tried to talk to him he looked over but kept his headphones in. Since then we had communicated almost exclusively in shrugs and waves.

As I often did on Fridays, I decided to take the book cart for a trip around the library's five floors. There was no real need for it—unless there was an unusually large wave of returns, the job was typically left to students working at night, just before closing—but the cart was a prop I used to legitimize what I really wanted to do, which was to walk around spying on people, to find and talk to Mel for a few minutes, and to see whether I could find anyone reading the paper, which was posted online and delivered around campus on Friday mornings. I had this idea that one day I'd come across a group of girls reading and talking about my column. While Mel and Logan complimented me on it once in a while, I never knew what anyone else thought; earlier editors had decided a long time before I started writing for the paper that allowing students to post comments had been a grave mistake and had subsequently disabled them altogether.

I pushed the unwieldy cart across the carpeting and bumped open the circulation gate. I looked back at David to give him an I'm-just-gonna-go-do-this-now–type hand gesture (a point and a head tilt, I thought), but his eyes remained glued to his computer screen. I knew he could see me from the corner of his eye.

The cart jangled loudly as I pushed it, and once I'd hit the tile part of the floor, it legitimately clanged. I suspected that it had been with the library since the '80s, when the building went up. One of the wheels was rusty, and on top of that the whole thing seemed uneven, rolling along as if with a limp. It was likely that the fact that anyone (whether they were wearing headphones or not) could hear the book cart coming from fifty yards away undercut whatever reconnaissance I might have been able to do.

I pushed the cart into the elevator and pressed "3," bypassing the second floor, which was always entirely taken over by stressed-out, wan-looking freshmen.

The doors opened to the third floor and I remembered telling Keith I thought the lights on 3 gave people a jaundiced look. It wasn't really true. It had just been a sort-of clever thing to say. I'd thought it would turn into a little round of half-mean flirting, but then he hadn't responded. I wondered if I should have known right then. I pictured a scene: me walking into class, a few minutes later than him, and sitting down next to him as if nothing had ever happened. "You didn't come study!" he might have said. And I'd have looked at him all pitying and said, "Oh, were you serious?" Then I'd have laughed to myself and shook my head, and he would have shriveled away on the spot, literally shrinking into his chair, until he stood three inches tall. I smiled.

The elevator dinged as the doors started to close and I jumped, realizing I was still standing inside it.

I quickly pushed the cart through the remaining open space, heading toward the back desks Mel frequented. I walked between several rows in the History section, past an open group-table area, and alongside the east wall, where several glass-windowed whiteboard rooms sat dark and empty. These were normally prized spots, but it was a Friday afternoon, so the building was almost entirely deserted.

I reached the wall and turned the corner with it, bumping the cart into the row of books on my left. The cart made a loud screeching noise, and a few books leapt off it, as if it were a sinking ship. On any other day I would have been mortified, but there was nobody really around, and I didn't have the energy to care if the few that were noticed or not. "Idiot," I whispered, leaning over to pick up the books. Even I was not sure if I meant them, or me.

When I got closer to the desks, I spotted Mel right away. She was the only one there—facing away from me, hunched over, pressing down the pages of a book with one hand and using the other to pull out her hair. She nearly always wore it back, in a ponytail she'd unconsciously twist around and around when stressed. She'd move inward on it, singling out a smaller chunk of six or eight hairs, twisting them and pulling on them until a few fell out into her hand. At that point she'd realize what she'd been doing and slide the offending hand under her thigh, where it could do no further harm. But then she'd need to make a note, and she'd take the trapped hand out to turn a page in her book, and it would be free to creep toward her head yet again. It was only because she had so much hair to begin with that she had a relatively normal amount left on her head.

Mel turned around as I rolled my way over to her and I saw her phone sitting on top of her open notebook. She smiled, waving with the hand that had, seconds earlier, been in her hair.

"Hi," I said, leaving the cart to the side of the carpeted path and sitting down in the chair next to hers.

"Hey," she said. "How's it going?"

"Oh, you know," I said. "Terrible."

"Same," she said, pushing her phone aside to gesture at her notebook, which appeared to have just a single note written down in it so far.

"Well, it's a Friday," I said.

"Yeah, but I have a Genetics exam next Wednesday."

"You have plenty of time."

"I got a C on the last one."

"C plus."

"That is very much still a C." I watched her hand move back toward her ponytail.

"Don't!" I said, and she took it away.

"It'll probably be fine," she said. "I just can't go out this weekend." Mel liked to announce on Fridays that she was definitely, absolutely not drinking that weekend. Not at all. Out of the question. At least not Friday night. Maybe on Saturday she would, if she stayed in and studied on Friday. Because it's not like you could really get that much done at 10:00 PM on a Saturday, anyway. Everyone knew it.

Normally Logan and I would help her to that conclusion, but this time I had no desire.

"I don't want to, either," I said. "I'm still recovering from Tuesday, I think."

"Physically, or emotionally?"

"Both." I saw them again, at the bar, in my head. How is it that it was still true, three whole days later? "Do you...think she's prettier than me?" I directed the question at my feet. It was too embarrassing a question to ask Mel directly, so instead I said it in her vicinity. If she wanted to interpret it as a question meant for her, that was her choice.

"You can't do that," said Mel.

"Ask you?"

"Ask yourself."

"I know," I said. "I know that beauty is subjective, kind of, even though sometimes it's, like, not really, that person is just actually really beautiful. But, whatever. I know it doesn't do me any good to compare myself to her, because he wanted her and not me, and the reasons don't really matter. I just think I would feel a LITTLE bit better about it if she were...a troll."

"Harriet," said Mel, scolding me but also laughing.

"Imagine if he had come out on St. Patrick's with an actual troll," I said. "Like, 'This is my new girlfriend, Gort.'"

We leaned in toward each other in a huddle, keeping our laughter to a somewhat respectful volume, until Mel snorted.

"And she's like, drooling," said Mel.

"There's, like, flies swarming around her head."

"Stopppp," said Mel. We both wiped at our eyes.

"I just don't get what happened," I said. "I know I keep saying that."

"It's OK. I know," she said. "Nobody does. Probably not even him, really."

"She's just so *dull*," I said.

"Remy?"

"Yeah," I said. "And not very friendly," I added, picturing her turning quickly back to her notebooks every time she gave a one-word answer to my questions. "And she basically told me she's not really friends with other girls."

"Uh, rude," said Mel.

"I know."

"Well, whatever," said Mel. "At least if she sucks, and they stay together, you will know he actually wanted to be with someone who sucks. Which you don't!"

"Thank you," I said.

"It'll get better soon."

"Yeah," I said. "I know."

"I should probably get back to work," she said. "Unless there's something else."

"Oh," I said. "No. I'm just wasting time."

"I mean, I would much rather hang out, but I need to get through two chapters today, and I've barely started the first," she said. She did look sorry.

"No, it's OK," I said. "Maybe we can all watch a movie or something tonight though."

"Yeah, that should be good," she said.

"See you later," I said, and she nodded. I got up and walked back to the cart, and when I looked over at Mel as I rolled it away, her hand was back in her hair.

After I'd slowly put all fourteen books back on their proper shelves, I took the cart downstairs and wheeled it back into its spot behind the desk. I sat back down in my chair and glanced over toward David, just to see if he'd acknowledge my return. (He did not.) I followed his gaze to the stack of books he'd placed on the desk to his left, the side closer to me. On top of it was a copy of the school paper, turned to the page my column was on.

I could see the little DEAR EMMA banner at the top and everything. Involuntarily, I gasped.

"David," I hissed. He didn't move. "David."

I waited.

"David. Daaaaaaavid. David!!!" The last one came out shrill, and I looked around to see if anyone had looked up. I briefly met eyes with a girl holding a German textbook pressed against the edge of her table. Normally I would have just looked away, but I held eye contact until she looked back down at her book. *That's right*, I thought. And then: *Actually, sorry, that was unnecessarily aggressive.*

David still didn't look up. I slid off my chair, crossed the four feet between us, and poked him on the shoulder.

He jumped, yanking both earbuds out at once. He flung them down to his sides, his hands hovering above the table as if prepared to defend himself from a physical attack.

"Jesus!" he said.

"It's just me, Harriet," I said. "We work together here in the library."

"Yeah, I see that now, thanks."

"What were you listening to?" I asked. I looked at David's oversized black sweatshirt and skinny neck and, inwardly, I guessed: EDM.

"Miley Cyrus."

"Is that a joke?"

"No." It was impossible to tell whether he was joking about the fact that he wasn't joking.

"Oh, OK," I said. "Cool."

"Did you...need something?" he asked.

"Oh! Yes," I said. "I was...well, I just saw you were reading 'Dear Emma.'"

"Yeah," he said. "Do you want it after I'm done?"

There was an entire stack of papers standing about six feet from us in the entryway.

"No, that's OK, I read it earlier," I said. "I was just wondering what you thought about it. This week's column, I mean." I blushed. Surely I was completely transparent, and he could see that I was Emma, and, more embarrassing still, that I was asking him, a mere acquaintance and a freshman, to tell me what he thought of me.

"Oh, I haven't finished," he said.

"Ah, never mind then, that's fine," I said.

"No, let me finish it, just a sec," he said. He looked back at the paper and put his earbuds back in. I stood there uncomfortably for a moment, wondering how long he thought this was going to take that he needed a soundtrack for it. I backed up a few steps and eased myself back into my chair. While I waited, I swiveled.

After what felt like four hours but was probably closer to ninety seconds, David removed his headphones and looked over at me.

"OK," he said.

"OK... what did you think?" I asked.

"I mean, I agree that that guy sounds like a dick," he said.

"Well, *obviously*," I said. "Literally everyone would agree with that."

"Ehhh, maybe not everyone," he said. "Some guys might think, you know, maybe he's not the best guy in the world, but he did his best in a tricky situation."

"'TRICKY SITUATION'?" I said, several octaves up from my normal pitch. I could feel the German-book girl looking up into the back of my head. "What do you mean, 'tricky situation'? He completely like, pulled the rug out from under this girl. All he had to do was tell his ex no, he can't go to the dance with her, because she is his ex, and he couldn't do it. Because he's a cowardly piece of shit."

My heart was racing, like it did whenever I started an argument.

"Sure," he said. "I just think some guys might view it differently."

"Oh, okaaaaay, so you're like the boy-whisperer or something?"

"Like I said, I basically agree with Emma. I'm just, like, playing devil's advocate here."

"Oh, of course. 'Devil's advocate,'" I said, raising my arms up to make mocking air quotes. Playing devil's advocate, every nineteen-year-old boy's favorite pastime.

"You have to admit she was kinda harsh this week," he said.

"Was she?" I asked. Where I had moments earlier felt only righteous indignation, I was now curious, and a little anxious. I would never admit that I worried about offending anyone with Dear Emma. I liked being considered blunt, and I even liked the idea of being somewhat polarizing. Especially because nobody (or, almost nobody) knew Emma was me. But still, I wanted most people to like her. Respect her, at least.

"Yeah," David said. "The sense I got was like, 'Damn, did she just get dumped or something?'"

"That's so...so...*typical*," I said. Flustered, I reached down for my bag and pulled it up into my lap. For a few seconds I pretended like I was looking for a pen or something, and then I just sort of rested my hands in the bottom.

"Typical of what?" he asked.

"Just. Guys," I said. I pushed the bag off my lap. We both watched it slide to the floor.

"Well, I'm just telling you what I thought."

"I didn't *ask* what you thought, David."

"You literally did," said David.

"Well," I said. "I regret it."

"OK," he said. "I'm gonna just..." And he trailed off, pointing vaguely in a way I took to mean *do anything except this*.

David turned away and put his headphones back in, and I turned back to my computer, where for the next hour and a half I alternated between looking at Facebook and creating revenge fantasies. At five thirty I texted Mel to tell her I was going straight home and that I'd see her there later. I put my untouched books back into my bag, got up from my chair, and walked quickly through the gate and out into the vestibule without another look in David's direction.

In the library entryway, once out of the circulation desk's eyeline, I picked up a copy of the newspaper from the stand near the door. On the walk home I reread Jess's question and my answer. It wasn't that harsh, I decided. I could have been even harsher, if I'd had the space. I carefully folded the paper back up and put it into my bag.

9

When I walked in the library's front doors on Sunday afternoon, I was still in a daze, having spent the vast majority of the weekend horizontal, watching *Law & Order* on the couch and feeling sorry for myself. It was weird just to be standing again. So when I saw that Remy was already at the desk, I didn't have enough mental clarity to feel any particular way about it. Apparently, this was just how it was going to be from now on.

"Hey," I said. Remy looked up and smiled.

"Hi," she said. Then she looked back down at the paperback she was reading. I tried to make out the cover, but she was holding it so close to the keyboard that I couldn't.

As I sat down and arranged my things around me on the table, I glanced over a few times to take stock of Remy's outfit: black boots; ripped jean shorts over black tights; a wrist full of thin metal bracelets; a gray sweatshirt with a maroon ring around the neck. How was it possible for one girl to have so many cool sweatshirts? None of it was even identifiable to me as having come from the three or four stores where everyone else at our school shopped. I wondered where she got it all. Most likely, it was vintage.

I looked into my own lap at the near hole in the jeans I had, for some reason, decided to wear today: It was along the inside of my upper left leg, where the denim had worn thin from my thighs brushing past each other when I walked. I pressed my legs closed and sat up straighter in my chair, looking over the top of the desktop computer at the tables. Most were occupied by groups of two to four students. I counted nine pairs of sweatpants and six visible bottles of partially drunk neon Gatorade. Every person I could see was sitting in various degrees of slump; I figured most of them had to be freshmen. Only freshmen had the vitality and the misplaced optimism needed to go out again so soon after St. Patrick's Day.

For a few minutes I watched a group of boys with unwashed hair flip through their accounting textbooks, punch keys on their calculators, and write things down. They moved so much while they studied: leaning over to rest their jaws in their palms, folding their arms in closer to their chests, then twisting around to assess whether they could rest their chairs against the four-foot-tall metal racks of science journals behind them without falling. Lean back, lean forward, hood up, hood down. Even hungover, they could not be still.

"Hey, umm," said a voice. A younger girl with French braids in her hair had approached Remy's side of the desk and stopped to speak from about four feet away. She seemed afraid of getting too close to Remy, for which I did not blame her. "I think the copier's out of paper?"

"Oh, OK," said Remy. She slid out of her seat and went behind me to the kitchen area, which was also the supply room. I pretended to take sudden interest in my day planner, open next to me on the desk, but when she emerged seconds later with a thick packet of printer paper, I watched her follow the girl toward the printers and copier, which sat across the entryway and around the corner. With her back to me I was free to stare at her real-life person: She was shorter than she seemed in pictures, and walked cautiously, her toes pointed in. I was still staring at the spot where she'd rounded the corner when she shuffled back around it, now empty-handed and alone. She wasn't looking at me but still I turned sharply back to my screen, just in case.

"She was printing, like, an entire book," said Remy.

"Oh, I hate that," I said, and I did. There were three laminated paper signs hung above the row of printers which advised students to *Please help us conserve paper—print only what you absolutely must!* The request was followed by a string of Microsoft Word clip art pictures meant to induce students' vague environmentalist guilt: a recycling symbol, the planet Earth, a fan (presumably meant to recall wind energy), and, for some reason, a little boy holding an ice-cream cone. It was hard to know how well these signs worked, but the consensus among library staff was: not very well. Hating students' overconsumption of printer paper was one of the four or five context-specific political causes that united Us against Them, along with late returns, the repeated theft of library highlighters, and the misuse of the basement microwave.

"If you need that many pages from a book, you should have to buy it," said Remy. "Like, just get a used copy for two dollars."

"I know," I said. "It's kind of the professors' fault, too. Like it's 'nice' to provide files of the required pages, but. They're just encouraging waste."

"I know," said Remy.

We paused to look at the patch of carpeted floor between us. It was a tight geometric print: tiny beige and burgundy right angles that looked like Tetris pieces.

"I printed a lot when I was a freshman, though," said Remy.

"Yeah, I mean, same," I said. "But that doesn't mean *they* should."

"Right," said Remy. "Learn from your elders." She laughed for a moment—a short *ha* followed by a few silent shakes of her shoulders—but when she stopped she didn't turn back to her things like she usually did.

I smiled back. This was a goddamn disaster. I had come to rely on Remy's lack of interest in talking to me.

"Anywayyyy," I said. *Anyway WHAT?* God. What else do people talk about? I couldn't remember a thing. I tried looking casually to my right for potential topics, scanning the archives, the return rack, the fire safety placard on the wall. I sighed.

"Have you ever been in here when the fire alarm went off?" I asked. I wondered if there was any poison in any of the desk drawers with which I might kill myself.

"Ha, ummmmm," she said. "I don't think so. I don't remember for sure, but I don't think so." *OK*, I thought. *Wonderful.*

"I only have once," I said. There was no turning back now. It had become Share Your Personal Experience with Library Fire Alarms time. "Someone put a wrapped chocolate bar in the microwave for four minutes."

"Four minutes??"

"Yeah," I said. "I think she meant to do it for forty seconds? I don't know."

"Did it actually catch on fire?"

"I think it just kind of sparked—from the metal-y part of the wrapping, which she left on—and then it smoked a lot? I remember it being very hazy down there."

"Wasn't she standing right there? Didn't she notice something seemed . . . off?"

"You know, I asked myself a lot of the same questions, and I just don't know," I said.

"She must have gone to the bathroom or something," said Remy, shaking her head.

I was pleased to note that she seemed genuinely perturbed. "Yeah, maybe," I said. "She didn't really have an explanation."

"Did everyone have to evacuate?"

"Yes!!" I said. "I mean, at first, when the alarms started, everyone just kind of looked at each other, like, 'Is this real?' It was November, so it was really cold, and nobody wanted to move unless they had to."

"Ugh, right."

"But then it kept going, and it started to smell like smoke. And I was at the desk, so I sort of felt like I needed to take charge in some way? Like I was a ship captain? But in my head I was like, 'I'm only a sophomore! I'm not ready to lead!'"

Remy started shake-laughing again. She held one hand in a curl a few inches in front of her face, partially obscuring her mouth.

"But then I was like, 'You have to do this,'" I continued. "I don't know why. Like, everyone knows where the exits are. You just walk outside. But I was like, '*No. Get them out of here.*' And I stood up from my chair and shouted, 'Please clear out the premises.' Which was confusing. And everyone looked at me like, 'What?'"

"Did you call 911?"

"No! That never even crossed my mind!"

"You do always think someone else will do it."

"Right! And I kind of just thought . . . the alarms would summon them? Or something? I mean, no, I just didn't think about it. At all. My first instinct was just *run*," I said.

"So what happened?"

"Everyone kind of picked up their coats very slowly. Like, super casual, like, 'I GUESS I'll go outside?' And then when I was sure they were heading outside, I ran upstairs to tell people they had to evacuate, but people were already coming down. I ran into another girl on staff—from IT—and she was like, 'Fire department's on the way!' And I was like . . . Oh my god."

"It worked out though," said Remy. "Nobody was in any real danger."

"Yeah, but I didn't know that!" I said. "I could have stood outside with everyone and watched the library burn to the ground before thinking, like, 'Is there anyone I should maybe call, or?'"

"You would've remembered eventually," said Remy.

"Yeah, maybe," I said. I felt self-conscious then, reassured by my enemy that I, like an average elementary school student, could remember 911 in an emergency. I reached over to the computer and shook the mouse around until the screen brightened. I looked at the clock: 2:32.

"Well, now I feel like my time in the library has been super boring," said Remy. She paused, evidently trying to recall any dramatic events she might be overlooking. "Although! A guy puked on the stairs once."

I grimaced. "Going up or coming down?" I asked. I pictured a version of each. "I don't know why that matters, but I feel like it does."

"Going up," she said. "Which I think is worse."

"It's definitely worse," I said. "Because it's like, he was still going for it. He was trying to push through, get that paper written, and he was so, so wrong."

Just then, over Remy's shoulder, I saw Mel. She pushed open

the building's outer doors and paused in the vestibule, dropping her backpack to the ground and redoing her ponytail.

"Exactly," said Remy, calling my attention back to her. "He puked against gravity."

"Horrible," I said. I looked back toward Mel and popped up in my seat, craning to get her attention. Was she really only getting here now, after two? That didn't make sense. Midterms started in three days. She hadn't been home this morning, had she? I tried to visualize the way the kitchen had looked when I ate breakfast: Had her door been open, or closed? Open, I thought. I was almost certain. She must just be coming back after taking a break for lunch.

As soon as she pushed open the second set of doors, I hissed: "*Mel!*"

Remy looked over her shoulder, following my call. Mel stopped abruptly and looked over, seeming startled at first and then, quickly, normal. She smiled and headed toward the desk.

"Hey," she said, dropping her bag to the floor at her side. Her bag was always Mary Poppins–level stuffed, and so heavy I was sure she'd be hunchbacked by thirty. She unzipped her black fleece jacket and dropped it, too.

"Are you wearing the same thing as yesterday?" I asked. It was something of a rhetorical question, because I could see that yes, she was. When she'd left for the library yesterday morning, she'd been wearing those same exact jeans and that same exact off-white and navy striped sweater.

"Oh, um, I guess," she said, looking down at herself and shrugging, as if to say there was simply no way to know for certain.

"What's going on?" I asked.

"Nothing," said Mel. "I'm just really behind schedule for my midterm study plan." So maybe she was just starting now. She pressed each hand against the sides of her head, smoothing her ponytail so severely that the corners of her eyes were pulled up and out. Despite the gesture, she seemed atypically unstressed, given the situation.

"You'll be fine," I said. "You still have four days."

"Yeah," she said. "That's true."

WHAT? I nearly screamed. Something mysterious was going on, and now I was certain. Mel never admitted to having enough time for anything.

"G . . . ood," I said. I wanted to interrogate her, obviously, but I didn't want to get into anything below the surface in front of Remy, whose observant presence vibrated at the outer edges of my attention. And anyway, I didn't know what I'd ask. "Why aren't you more worried?" would sound accusatory, and probably a little rude.

"OK," said Mel. "I guess I better go start." She leaned over and picked her backpack and jacket up from off the floor. She shifted them around on her body until she was steady, pulled at a piece of hair that had fallen forward, and smoothed it back behind her ear.

"OK," I said. "Maybe I'll come visit when I'm done, if you need a break by then."

"Um," she said. "Maybe. I should probably just stick it out. But I'll see you at home later!" She waved, and turned to walk toward the elevator.

I glanced over at Remy, embarrassed. We made eye contact and smiled at each other, unsure what to say after being interrupted by the appearance of someone only one of us knew. Should I have introduced them? I wondered. Probably that would have been weird. I wouldn't have introduced Mel to any other co-worker. Especially not David.

"I know you don't know her, but that was very weird," I said.

"The clothes?" she said, and I thought, *Eavesdropper.*

"Yeah," I said. "And she's usually a lot more stressed about exams."

"Is she—" said Remy. She paused, closed her mouth, sank slightly into her chair.

"What?" I said.

"Sorry, I just realized I was about to be nosy," said Remy. She smiled, waving away the rest of what it was she'd wanted to ask. Of course, now I had to know.

"No, it's OK, I'm like, the nosiest," I said. "What were you going to ask?"

"OK, I was going to say, is she dating someone?" she asked.

"Oh! No," I said. I felt relieved, and laughed. (What had I thought she was going to ask?) Mel may have thought at least three-quarters of the boys at our school were hot, but for her to devote time that could be spent studying to hanging out with any of them regularly would require truly remarkable circumstances. Boys always liked her, but only two since Jacob had succeeded in winning her over, and only then very temporarily—she called off each one after just about a week. There was nobody she'd liked well enough to make it past the first exam. At least, not before.

"Oh, OK," said Remy. "Never mind, then."

"No, what?" I said. "Tell me anyway."

"I was just gonna say, that would account for the repeat outfit," she said. "Like, sometimes I come to the library in the same thing if I slept over at my boyfriend's house."

Oh, I thought, I might throw up. Boyfriend. I heard the sentence in pieces, in reverse. Slept over. Sometimes. Sometimes, lately, when I was talking to her, I forgot who she was.

"See??" said Remy. "Nosy."

I forced a smile, shook my head.

"No," I said. "I mean, I brought it up."

"Anyway," she said. "It's irrelevant, because she's not dating anyone." There was no reason for her to think she could know something about Mel that I did not—but there was something in the way she said it that made me wonder if she did.

"Right," I said. The weird fake smile again. Maybe, if I got enough practice here in the library, with Remy, I'd get really good at it.

"Are you?" she said.

"What?" I said. I'd heard her, just in delay. I thought: *I will burn this library to the ground myself.*

"Are you—" she started.

"Oh, no," I said. "Nope!"

"Oh, cool," she said, and I hated her for it, even as I knew full well there was no good way to respond to that response to that question, apart from "Me, neither." But that wasn't true, so she couldn't say it.

"Yep!" I said, and laughed a weird, small, bark-sounding laugh. It was almost funny, or would've been if a portal to hell had, right then, opened beneath my chair and sucked me down into the earth's burning core. Instead, I swiveled my chair away from Remy and toward my computer, where I opened a new document and tried to feel—or at least appear—determined to work.

It wasn't cool, really. But it was, or would be, fine.

*   *   *

Dear Emma,

For the past few months, ever since spring semester started, I've been wondering if I should transfer. I had an OK first semester (I was excited to move away from home, anyway) and made a couple buddies on my floor. But by the end of the year, I'd figured out we were pretty different. And I kind of feel that way about every new person I meet. (I don't really drink, which seems maybe important for you to know about, as that seems to get in the way of a fair amount of bonding.) But, on the other hand, sometimes it takes me a long time to get to know people. I don't want to be impatient, but it's hard knowing whether to try hard at a friendship with someone when in 4 months I'll probably realize we're never going to be that close. My classes have been OK, and everyone says they get better later, when you're done with gen. eds and prereqs and everything mandatory. But I guess I just feel like everyone else is having a much better time here, and that makes me wonder if I should be somewhere else. Maybe someplace out west, where a few of my high school buddies go. (I came here partly for a football scholarship.) I guess I'm rambling so I'll get to my question: how do you know whether to stick something out in hopes it gets better, or to move on?

Sincerely,
Fear of Missing Out

Dear FOMO,

When I was a freshman (I won't say when that was), I made best friends with every girl on my floor. (Or, perhaps more accurately, all of them made best friends with each other, and went everywhere together, and nobody minded if I happened to be there, too.) I tell you this not to make you feel badly about your own experience, but rather because 90 percent of those friendships fell apart by spring break, and another 5 percent were dead by summer. It is, perhaps, more typical for a new freshman to feel ecstatic and hopeful about everyone he or she meets when he or she first meets them. It is (or can be) very exciting just to live around so many people who aren't part of your immediate family. But I promise you that you're not the only one who feels confused, like you were sold on an experience that doesn't match what you're living. College is not the best four years of *everyone's* life. It's just that the people who do feel that way are the loudest.

Here's something that most freshmen (including me, when I was one) don't know: The novelty of campus life coupled with an interest in heavy drinking can only carry relationships so far. Freshman year is probably the easiest time to make lots and lots of low-stress, low-commitment friends, and you could do that too, if you wanted. But it sounds to me like what you want is a smaller, closer group, which, you're right, does take more patience.

My friend group was winnowed by the spaces between parties—who was semi-productive and, more importantly, fun to study with? Who was interested in (and good at) lunchtime gossip in the cafeteria? Whom did we find ourselves staying up past one AM to talk to, even though we had class at eight the next morning? Who wanted to watch the same TV shows late on Wednesday nights when we couldn't study anymore? Who was there when someone had a problem bigger than a hangover or a class they slept through or an exam they failed? I don't think the answer is ever more than a very few people.

That's the bad news: It can be hard to find your two or three or four people in our crowd of a little over 5000. The good news is they're there. Whether or not they end up being the best friends you make in your entire lifetime, I can't say. But there are people here you'll be happy to know, for a year, or two or three, if not more. I think you, like many people, are most likely to find them next year, as a sophomore, once you start specializing your classes a bit more. Freshman dorm friends are mostly a matter of luck; from then on, it has more to do with choice. I would also recommend getting involved in at least one more extracurricular outside your main sport. (One of the politics clubs, maybe, or intramural racquetball, or PRIDE, or even those kids who set up tightropes between trees on the quad. What are they up to?) Here you will meet, at the very least, people you're fine with seeing once or twice a week.

As far as transferring goes: Know that if you do, it will not be easy. If you switch schools to enroll at the school where your high school friends are, know that those friends will struggle to balance their new lives with you—not because they don't still care about you, but because they had to start over without you. You may fit in seamlessly, but more likely than not, it will be an adjustment that takes time. You may even find that you're not so interested in your high school friends as you were when you were actually in high school. Context changes things. There is no shortcut here. Going into any new school as a sophomore will require you to insert yourself in patterns that have already formed. You'll be playing catch-up, so only go if the school in question is offering you enough to make it sensible for you, independent of the friendship question. Change of place can't fill you up by itself. Anywhere you go will leave you feeling alone and hurt sometimes.

One last thing to remember: It won't always take four months to decide a friendship is meaningful to you. Many times it will take much less. But sometimes it'll take more.

Most humbly yours,
Emma

10

Later that night, feeling restless, with neither Mel nor Logan home and nothing better to do that I could think of, I decided to go to the gym. Pushing open the Clark Center doors, I was immediately struck with the usual rush of humid, chlorine-scented air. I walked over to look at the pool through the pair of large viewing windows, but it was empty, and the water was still.

I walked downstairs to the check-in desk, where I swiped my student ID and smiled at the girl sitting behind it. Most of the students with work-study jobs at Clark were athletes, and guarded the building's various desks while impressively wearing their warm-up uniforms. I knew the vestments particular to each team—the soccer girls' swishy black pants, the volleyball team's tight red track jackets, the tennis team's heather-gray hoodies with the little green ball patch sewed onto the back. It all looked so luxuriously comfortable, and well earned. And while I did not believe that this girl, a basketball player (black T-shirt, thick gray sweatpants, slick ponytail held in place by a black elastic headband), mistook me for an athletic equal, I did hope, as I did every time I went to the gym after many weeks of not going to the gym, that if I smiled at her hard enough, she would think I came here all the time. "Who, me?" the smile said. "Just making my daily trip to my favorite place on campus, the Clark Memorial Athletic Center."

After taking a minute to look at the few people running around the indoor track as if considering whether or not to join them, I walked over to the gym area and carefully pushed open one of its creaky doors, hoping that half the room wouldn't look over when I walked in. Fortunately, because it was the evening, the gym was very full and loud, and my entrance wasn't as noticeable as it might have been. I was relieved to see that my preferred machine, the left-most elliptical in the second row (aka the least conspicuous one), was open. Staring at the floor, I sped over to it, placing my water bottle in the holder, my Spanish Civ. reading packet over the screen, my headphones into my ears, and my phone on the ledge.

I was no more than a minute or two into my workout—push left leg slightly forward, then right, then repeat—when I saw him. Keith approached a treadmill in the row in front of me, on the far end, fifteen or so machines down the line.

Fuck, I thought. *Goddammit! What the fuck!* Instinctively I stopped swinging my legs, the sudden halt in my body causing my earbuds to pull my phone off its delicate perch. "No!" I hissed, managing, just barely, to catch it in my left hand before it could clatter to the ground. I put it back and tried to look over at Keith without moving my head. When my peripheral vision refused to stretch that far, I tilted my head very slowly, very slightly up and to the right. Were I being filmed, for a daytime movie for women, this would be the scene in which the viewer realized, *oh*, that bedraggled-looking lady is going to kill that handsome man.

He was wearing a royal-blue T-shirt (which I recognized) that clashed with his navy gym shorts (which I did not). The effect suggested someone who either mistakenly believed he knew what colors made sense together, or someone who didn't care. Keith was the latter, or at least pretended to be. He only managed to be convincing half the time: To class he alternated between wearing T-shirts and jeans and a small rotation of cuter, coordinated outfits. These he repeated without variation, each particular combination of shirt and sweater or jacket worn so relentlessly and so precisely that they had to have once been arranged that way by someone else.

Keith started to jog and my eyes were drawn to his arms, and then his back. His broad, sharp shoulders pulled at the seams of the shirt, which he'd probably gotten years ago. It was surprising to watch him work out, though I didn't know why—it's not like we'd ever discussed his exercise regimen, or even whether he had one.

My playlist switched over to a new song, and I realized that I had, once again, essentially stopped moving. The screen on my machine was paused, no longer able to tell if there was still a living human standing on top of it. "Do you wish to resume?" it asked. I looked back over at Keith, cluelessly jogging away. I didn't want to be near him, but neither did I want to leave and grant him implicit custody of the gym, or any other place on campus. I would do the mature thing: stay out of stubbornness, and ignore him completely.

For twenty-five (okay, 22.5) more minutes I pushed and pulled at the machine's levers, my legs flying forward and back at what was, for me, an unprecedented speed. I stared straight ahead for nearly the entire time, except once, about eighteen minutes in, when I noticed Keith get off the treadmill and walk over to a stationary bike. This took him about seven feet farther away from me, and I quickly prayed that he had no plans to lift weights, since they were on what I had come to consider my half of the gym.

But then I was done, and a glance in the direction of the bikes revealed that Keith was still on one. I hopped off the elliptical and hustled over to the nearest pole with a paper towel dispenser attached. I ripped off a piece, sprayed it with disinfectant from the bottle on top, and returned to my machine to wipe it down. My face—particularly, unfairly, my upper lip— was dripping with sweat, and as I made my way over to the doors, I pulled my shirt up by the collar to wipe it off.

Now that I had made it through, and it was certain I could escape without notice, I didn't want to move. If there had been a scene of some kind, and I had stormed up to him, tapped him on the shoulder, and yelled at him while he ran, it would have, I knew, been more embarrassing for me than for him. But later, after (most) everyone stopped talking about the crazy girl who screamed at some guy while he was just trying to jog, would it have been satisfying, too? Would it be more satisfying, at least, than walking out these doors, knowing I had succeeded in going totally unnoticed?

But the truth was I didn't want to yell at him—I didn't even want to talk to him. I wanted to be someone who would or at least could flip out, demand answers, but I wasn't. I didn't want to risk giving him the satisfaction of thinking I still or ever cared. And I had nothing to say, and no desire to see what his stupid face looked like when I said it, so when some guy came up behind me, and I realized I'd already been hovering there too long, I pushed through the doors and left the building.

The shock of seeing Keith was replaced by irritation as soon as he was no longer in sight, and I walked toward home with a speed made possible by the growing sense that I had been deeply wronged. I crossed Emerson Street and turned onto Randall, which took me between the languages building and a pair of freshman dorms. There were little pockets of human activity—it wasn't yet 9:00 PM, and it was getting warmer—but the campus was largely quiet, draped in dampness, the yellow-bulb lamps barely brightening the piles of wet leaves that covered most of the ground.

How *dare* he show up at the gym tonight, at this time, of all the possible days and times, especially when he was already so skinny? Why didn't *he* ever worry about running into *me*?

I turned sharply left, heading onto one of the quad's several intertwining pathways.

Or—wait, OR, DID he worry about running into me and, in evaluating all the places on campus I could possibly be, decided the gym was the safest of them all?

"*Dick!*" I hissed. Two guys walking about fifteen yards or so ahead of me paused their conversation, turning their heads slightly. A moment passed in which they recognized that this was not about them, and they started talking again.

I modified my pace so I wouldn't catch up.

This was annoying, of course, because I needed to get home as quickly as possible, and at this rate, it could take up to thirteen minutes to get there. I dragged along for half a minute— how was it possible for living creatures to move *this* slowly, were they *ill* or something—before I decided I could not withstand twelve and a half minutes more of having the only person who knew what had just happened to me be me. I pulled my phone out of my bag and opened my text messages. The name at the top of the list was Mel's, and it was at the same time that I realized she was the person I'd been planning to text that I remembered she was the one person I probably shouldn't. Because something was going on with her, and she wasn't telling me.

The boys ahead turned right at the next sidewalk intersection, heading in the direction of fraternity row. I dropped my phone back into my bag and resumed full, concentrated speed. When I cleared the quad, I jogged across John Street.

What could I possibly have done to make Mel keep something from me? Was she upset with me? I couldn't think of a single thing that made sense. Whatever it was, it was sure to be unmemorable and small, a throwaway comment I'd made that anyone else would have let go. Mel always had to let things build up. Logan would call you a bitch to your face, but at least you'd know she thought so right away.

All I wanted to do was to tell Mel about the gym, how powerless and tiny and embarrassingly afraid I'd felt, and to then feel her firmly on my side. Instead, first, we would have to dance around the fact that she was, apparently, mad at me, and refused to tell me why.

So in the space of the last block, just before I turned onto Locust, I got livid.

I banged open our house's side door, dropped my bag on the kitchen table, and found Logan in the living room watching the Food Network and eating a bowl of fruit.

"Did you go to the gym?" she asked, assessing my outfit.

"Yes!" I said. "I go to the gym sometimes!"

"I don't know if it's often enough to qualify as 'sometimes'..."

"'Sometimes' just means SOME of all of the times that there are," I said. "I go. Some. Times." I was still standing there in the entryway between the kitchen and the living room, and as Logan shrugged and popped a strawberry into her mouth, I realized how hungry I was.

"Is Mel home?" I asked, turning to look at her door at the same time. It stood a few inches open, the lights off inside. "No," I answered myself.

"She said she thought she'd be home by ten," said Logan.

"She texted you that?" I asked. So she was fine taking time out of studying to communicate with Logan, then?

"No," said Logan. (Oh.) "That was just her guess when she left for the library."

I opened the refrigerator, scanning the various bags of grapes, strawberries, blueberries, celery, and baby carrots, thought better of it, and grabbed my cereal box from off the top of the fridge, a spoon from the silverware door and, hands now full, pushed the drawer closed with my hip.

"I think she's mad at me," I said as I dropped onto the open end of the couch.

"Who?" said Logan.

"Mel!!" I said.

"Oh," said Logan. "Why?"

"I don't know! I can't think of a single reason!"

"How do you know she's mad?"

"Well," I said, "she did *not* want me to come talk to her at the library this afternoon."

"Because she's stressed about midterms…"

"Yeah, but it was like, weird," I said. "She wasn't actually that stressed. And she didn't even want to look at me."

"That doesn't seem like very much evidence to me," said Logan, through open-mouthed bites of fruit. "She's always weird around exams."

"Well, you weren't there," I said. "It was strained."

Logan said nothing and looked back at the TV, where some kind of judgment was taking place. A chef was eliminated, and Logan smiled, evidently pleased with the decision. "That guy was sooo condescending to the woman contestant," she explained. "It's like, we get it, you think your restaurant is a metaphor for your dick."

"Ugh," I said. "Oh! Wait!" I dropped my spoon into the box and grabbed Logan's arm. "I remembered the other weird thing—Mel was wearing the *same exact outfit she wore yesterday*."

"So?" said Logan. "I do that all the time."

I let go of her arm and sighed. She had me there.

We'd watched the rest of the episode and gotten a third of the way into another when I heard the door open. I forced myself not to look, waiting for Mel to engage me or Logan. Instead, I heard her push open her door and drop her bag on the floor by her desk. I heard her pull open a drawer in her dresser. I couldn't think of a time she'd walked into our house after studying and not gone immediately to her room and changed into sweatpants.

Aaaaand *now*, I thought. Now was the moment of truth: Either she'd emerge, get food, and join us, or she'd emerge, get food, and retreat back into her room. I listened, still refusing to turn my head even a little. There was the cabinet, the fridge, general food preparation sounds, then the sounds of putting things away. And then, finally her door: pushed open from the outside, pushed closed from within. Not hard—Mel was not a slammer—but intentional all the same.

"Wow," I whispered.

"I know!" said Logan, thinking I meant something on the show.

When the show ended I got up, picked up my cereal box, and went into the kitchen. I wiped my hands on one of the garish pink dishtowels Mel's mom had found for us at a garage sale, and decided I couldn't go to bed without talking to her. I crossed the few feet to her door and knocked softly, once, twice.

"Yeah," she said.

I opened the door to find her sitting at her desk, hand in hair. "Hey," she said.

"Hey," I said. "Are you busy?"

"No, it's fine," she said. She put down the pen she'd been holding, scribbling study plans into her notebook, and gestured toward her bed.

Whenever we talked in her room, she would sit at her desk, and I would sit on her twin bed, mostly because there wasn't a second option. The bed was small and unusually girlish for her—white headboard, purple comforter; it had belonged to her older sister, now graduated and living in an apartment in the city. Her dad kept offering to buy her a new one but each year she refused.

"Do you feel better about your first midterm?" I asked.

"Um, maybe slightly," she said. "At this point I don't think I'm going to absorb a whole lot more."

"You should come watch a show with us then."

"Yeah," she said, to her lap, in the way of hers that really meant "no."

"Are you mad at me or something?" I asked.

"No?"

"Then why are you acting so weird?"

"I'm not acting weird," she said. "I'm acting stressed. Because I am."

"Mel," I said. "Don't patronize me. You're always stressed. I can tell the difference."

"OK, well, I'm not mad. Me being stressed about midterms

doesn't necessarily have to have anything to do with you," she said. She flushed.

"What is that supposed to mean?" I asked, though I was pretty sure I knew what it was supposed to mean.

"Just, if someone's acting in a way that you think is odd around you, you always think it has something to do with you," she said.

"I don't *always* do that," I said. "And besides, it's not, like, crazily self-absorbed to think that if someone's being weird to me, it's because of me! That is a normal conclusion to make!"

"But I'm not actually being weird."

"Yes, you are," I said.

"How? In what way?"

"You barely looked at me at the library," I said. "You're wearing the same thing as you were yesterday. And you didn't even want a five-minute break from studying to talk to me at the library."

"Those are all just examples of things that *a busy person would do*," said Mel, the last few words pushed out through gritted teeth. "I'm sorry that I can't just breeze through all my schoolwork in two hours like you can."

"I know you think my major is easy—"

"No I don't. I'd never say that—"

"Because you'd never say lots of things that you feel! That's the whole problem!!" My voice sounded shrill. Mel was silent. I listened for Logan on the other side of the door, but all I heard were the muted voices of the TV. Mel took a deep breath and began again.

"I know I sometimes keep things in for too long," she said. "But in the past, whenever I've been like, sitting on something that's bothering me, and you've asked me if I'm mad, or upset with you in some way, I've told you right then."

"Maybe," I said. "Not every time, I don't think."

"Well, OK. All I'm trying to say is that if I were mad at you, which I'm not, I would tell you right now." Mel's face assumed her best "You know I'm right, but I will be patient while you figure that out" look, which made me mad on at least 60 percent of the occasions she gave it to me. We sat in silence for a moment, looking at each other. Finally she looked down, pulled her legs up onto her chair, and reached a hand back into her ponytail.

"I just don't believe you," I said. "Something is going on."

Mel opened her mouth but said nothing. She twisted her hair and slowly raised her shoulders up into a shrug.

"Why are you wearing the same clothes?" I said.

"I wasn't—" Mel cut herself off.

"You weren't what?"

She paused, took her hand out of her hair, and held it with the other in her lap. And then, shockingly, and seemingly against her will, she smiled a little.

"Mel!! You weren't what!"

She looked back at me and stopped smiling. "I wasn't going to say anything yet, because..." She trailed off.

"Say anything about what?? This is torture!!"

"I slept over at Will's last night," she said.

I felt several emotions all at once, or in very rapid succession. First, a searing flash of jealousy or something very close; something that mixed up feeling shocked with a mental picture of Will's face, and that smile just before she told me. Then I was excited for her. (Will!!) And that subsided very quickly into frustration that she hadn't told me right away, and wouldn't have even told me now if I hadn't more or less forced her to. Then, embarrassment: because I hadn't thought anything like this was a realistic explanation.

And last: *How had Remy guessed?*

"Harriet," she said.

"I don't know what to say!" I said, which was true.

"Well, it probably doesn't even mean anything, so," she said, "whatever you're thinking, don't think it too much."

"Why didn't you tell me sooner?" I asked.

"It was just last night!" she said.

"You should have told me on your way over there," I said. "You should have texted me, 'Hey, FYI, I am currently en route to see my longtime love, Will Reid, for a romantic sleepover.'"

"Well, I didn't know what was going to happen for sure," she said. "And he's not my 'longtime love.'"

"No," I said. "You didn't want to tell me, period. And that's why you were acting weird at the library."

"That's not true," said Mel. "I did, I just..."

"What?"

"I thought that if you came up to my table after work, you'd probably say something about Keith, and then because we'd be talking about boys I'd accidentally just tell you my boy news, but my boy news is good, so...I didn't want you to feel bad," said Mel.

Another feeling, fifth or sixth: the mortifying realization that I was being pitied.

"So you were protecting my feelings," I said.

"I mean, kind of!"

"Because I've been such a miserable sad sack."

"Have you not been miserable??"

"I have had very good reason to be upset!" I said. "It's not like I've been moping around for months! It's been like a week!"

Mel paused.

"Are you counting days right now?" I asked.

"No," she lied.

"And even if it had been four weeks, or twelve, so what? Not everyone is a no-nonsense ice fortress like you, Mel."

"I'm not an *ice fortress*," she said. I could tell that she was starting to get mad, and because she was so hard to rile up about anything nonacademic, I felt almost proud.

"I know that," I said. "But you act like you are."

"Don't make this all about me."

"You just TOLD me not to make this about ME!" I said. "Who else is left to make this about??"

Mel groaned slightly and pressed her fingers into her temples.

"OK," she said. "I think those were separate things, but whatever. What I'm trying to say is that I was nervous to tell you, because I thought you'd be upset with me, and now . . . you're upset with me."

"BECAUSE you didn't tell me," I said. "Not, like, because I can't possibly stand the thought of you being happy about a boy. I'm not a psychopath."

"It's not like I thought you'd never be happy for me," said Mel. "Just maybe not now. And, anyway, like I said, this might be all it is! In which case this fight is pointless!"

"OF COURSE I'm happy now!" I said angrily. "You've liked him for years! It's great news!! He's very hot!!!"

"OK," said Mel. "I can tell you really mean that. It's obvious now."

We sat and looked at the floor, which was covered in a shaggy lime-green rug. Another garage sale find from her mom.

Maybe I didn't mean it. I was probably lying aspirationally. I wasn't completely happy for her right now, today. But I wanted to be, and didn't that count for something? If things went somewhere with Will, he'd be the first person she'd actually, officially dated since she was eighteen, and I knew that was big. But Jacob was from the life she had before I knew her, and in the time since, I guess I'd just started counting on us staying the same: perennially single, only half intentionally. But that was a trick I played on myself. She'd always been so much more experienced. And it had always been true that Mel could get almost anyone she wanted. There had always been people who wanted her; she just hadn't come across anyone she wanted enough since Jacob. Except for Will. And now it was happening, and she was probably so excited, and still, she hadn't wanted to talk about it. Not with me.

"I just wish you'd told me," I said.

"Well, now I did," said Mel.

"Yeah," I said. "Great."

"I should probably go to bed," she said. She pulled her knees into her chest and clasped her arms around them, forming a tight ball. "I'm exhausted, and I don't want to fail the rest of my midterms."

"OK," I said. "Good luck."

"Thanks," she said. She watched me and I watched her, each of us daring ourselves to remain silent and the other to apologize.

"OK," I said finally. I stood up from her bed and smoothed out the crater my body had left in her comforter. "Night."

"Night," she said, her legs sliding off the chair as she swiveled around to face her desk, at least until I left the room.

I pulled her door closed slowly behind me. I knew as soon as I heard it shut that I was going to cry. I noticed that the living room was now dark; a soft light peeked out through the bottom of Logan's door. I wondered how much, if anything, she'd heard.

I stood there in the kitchen (why did I keep finding myself hovering in this same stupid spot?) and thought about knocking on Mel's door and going back in, trying to undo whatever the past half hour or hour or whatever it was had done. I always felt this little panic immediately after a fight. I was good at starting an argument; it was possible I was less great at allowing them to end. Was it regret for saying things I meant, or regret for meaning them? Either way, I wanted to inhale every word back into my mouth.

*   *   *

Dear Emma,

It has semi-recently come to my attention that everyone else in my group of friends has more money than I do. I mean, I had an idea pretty early on that something was up—some jeans just LOOK expensive, you know? You can see it in the stitching— but it didn't matter so much when we were just freshmen, and all we did was hang around campus and drink whatever Smirnoff leftovers we could leech off other people. But every semester it just gets more and more noticeable. First a couple of them came back from summer break with cars, and then they went on their semester-long trips to London and Rome and Paris, and in between all that, there are bars. I love the weekdays with them, because weekdays just mean studying and watching TV and cooking together. But I dread every Friday and Saturday (and sometimes Thursday), because that's when everyone goes out to the bars, where I can never afford to get more than one drink. My friends offer to pick up my tab all the time, especially once they're drunk, but I feel too weird about letting them. Sometimes I say I have too much work to do just so I can stay home and avoid the whole thing. I try not to hold it against them—going out is fun! I'd spend more on it if I could, too—but it's hard not to feel left behind. Besides winning the lottery, what can I do?

Sincerely,
Broke As Hell

Dear BAH,

I know exactly what you mean about the jeans. They look so good and crisp!

So: Yes, if winning the lottery were an available, guaranteed option, I would definitely suggest you do that. There is really only one way to completely solve this problem of yours, and that is with money. For reasons unknown to myself, I read dumb DIY blogs constantly, and once I came across this post about "Thrift-Tacular Activities" to do with your friends when you're feeling broke. The author suggested inviting your friends over for a relaxing midafternoon hangout (so you don't have to provide food) and making flower arrangements out of tissue paper and pipe cleaners. I started screaming and I haven't stopped since.

For the foreseeable future, the main thing you and your friends are going to want to do with your money and free time is buy booze and drink it. So what can you do about that? It sounds like you're a junior, so when the career center listings go up online this August, apply for every TA and research position in your major/minor/interest area. It might not work out, but it's well worth trying—they pay at least $4 more an hour than any other part-time job you could find in town or on campus. If there's a professor you're close to, ask him/her if s/he needs a research assistant next year. Sometimes they'll create a position for you.

In the short term, sell any clothing you haven't worn in six months and any books you won't read again. If you drink coffee, don't buy it at the campus shop. Take it from the free pots they keep going in the welcome center and the humanities building. (It's the same coffee, I promise.) Look at the students' board in NSC for "experiment subjects wanted" postings. (Ha, I KNOW, but it's not like you're trying weird pills. Usually it's like, you go in and click through stock photo faces on a computer screen for half an hour so they can see if pupil size affects perceived attractiveness or something.) I know both of these options involve a max return of maybe $15 or $20 a pop, but that's enough to go nuts (responsibly, of course) for one night. I'd also try getting your friends into the idea of going to one of the cheaper bars, at least some of the time. Make Van Ruin your new Thursday bar—they have a special for $1 tap beers before 10. It's a block off the main strip, I know, and it's definitely kind of a weird townie scene, but it's fun, and cozy, and it should really be more popular than it is.

And finally: Consider letting your friends pay for your drinks. Even just once in a while! Save it for the big nights if you want—St. Patrick's Day, for instance—but if you guys are out having fun, and one of them offers to get you a drink (or all your drinks), just say, "Sure, yes, thank you so much." It doesn't mean you owe them anything, or that you can't take care of yourself, or that they're better or more adult than you. It just means you both know that their parents have given them more money than yours have, in one way or another, and you both want you to have another drink, and stay out later, and have fun. I know it's not easy! It's a vulnerable thing to accept anything from other people, let alone money, but you can do it. You certainly don't have to, but you can.

Minor point, but, isn't it funny how all the rich kids go to the same three cities for study abroad every year? It's like, have some imagination.

Most humbly yours,
Emma

11

Half a week passed, and Mel and I hardly saw each other. This happened, sometimes, particularly near the middle of a semester and again toward the end. We had a couple of brief run-ins in the kitchen, but on a few of the days, the timing worked out so neatly that we missed each other altogether. Usually, if this happened, I'd text her, but this time I didn't. At first I felt bad. I was being stubborn, and possibly petty. Then Monday came and went, midterms started, and I stopped feeling bad. I was always the one to reach out to *her*, to ask her to hang out, to see how she was doing. Well, I thought, standing over the kitchen sink on Tuesday evening and squinting out the window into the dark driveway like a madwoman, *enough*.

"Mel's mad at me," I said. Logan sat behind me at the table, eating dinner. "Well, technically I am also mad at Mel."

"I know," said Logan.

"What??" I asked, turning around. "She told you?"

"We spend a lot of time together," said Logan. "Things come up."

"OK," I said. "Yeah. I know."

I paused. When it became clear Logan wasn't going to volunteer more information in a reasonable time frame, I asked, "What did she say?"

"She said that she'd told you about Will, and you got upset, which was what she'd been afraid of, because you've been emotionally delicate," said Logan.

"Are those her words??"

"I'm paraphrasing," she said.

"'Emotionally delicate' is your phrase, though, right?"

"Yes."

"OK," I said. "Go on."

"What do you want me to say? She was upset that you were upset."

"Ugh," I said. "Why doesn't she understand that I basically only got upset because she told me she didn't want to tell me because she thought I would be upset?"

"What?"

"I don't know."

"I mean," said Logan, "you have to know you've never reacted particularly positively to anyone's new boyfriend, at first."

"That is not true!" I said. I paused. "'Boyfriend'?"

"It is true," she said, ignoring the question. "Not that I think you're wrong, necessarily. Everyone's new boyfriend blows."

"I like Will fine!" I said.

"I know. It's not about Will the individual," she said. "It's about what he represents."

"Oh," I said. "Obviously. DO TELL."

"He represents male mediocrity."

"Ugh, Logan," I said. I sat down across from her. "What are you talking about? Ever?"

"Every time one of my friends starts dating a guy, it's like, 'This one? Are you sure? Is this really as good as it gets?'"

I laughed. "OK, sure. Fair. But, my point is, I'm upset because Mel wasn't going to tell me about Will because she thinks I'm sad and pathetic. She was fine telling you, right?"

"Well, I wasn't recently rejected," said Logan.

I stared at her. I knew she was not trying to be mean. It was just that the words that came out of her mouth sounded horrible.

"You didn't need to say it like that," I said.

"I'm sorry," she said. "I knew it was bad as soon as I said it."

"It's OK," I said. "You're not wrong!"

"Anyway, she's not mad," said Logan. "Just frustrated and unsure what to do about it."

"I don't feel like I'm getting a sense of which one of us you think is wrong in this situation," I said.

"Harriet," she said, setting down the knife she'd been using to spread peanut butter on her already-peanut-buttered toast, "it's not always the case that only one person is wrong."

The next day, I arrived purposefully early for my Spanish Civil War midterm, wanting to be free to walk up the stairs to the back row of the class without feeling looked at and without feeling like I was avoiding looking at anyone else. I read over my note cards, ignoring everyone who came in after me, until Professor Ferrer announced his arrival. "*Hola, clase*," he said, "I've got a lovely surprise for you today!

"No midterm!!!" he said, holding his arms in the air, waiting a moment. "Only kidding."

I put my cards away very slowly, trying to scan them one last time, hoping that touching them for even a second longer would implant some meaningful piece of information into my memory. I really wanted to do well, and mostly for my own benefit. But there was a small part of me that wanted to do well to do better than Keith, even if I knew I wouldn't get to compare scores with him anyway.

I took out my best pen, which I'd found in the library last year. According to the writing on the side of its barrel, it was from the La Quinta Inn in Irving, Texas, and I tried to use it sparingly. I wrote my name on the top of the quiz, admiring how it looked. I had never cared much for my name, but in this pen's slightly smeary almost-navy-blue ink, it looked almost elegant. Nobody was sitting to my left, so I glanced over to my right to see if the girl sitting next to me noticed how beautiful my handwriting looked. Her face was pressed so close to her desk that I watched her for a second, trying to understand how she could even see what she was writing. She jerked her head in my direction, whipping her long, straight ponytail around as she did. I jumped.

"Eyes on your own paper!" she hissed, peering at me over the top of her unrimmed glasses. Clearly, she was a freshman.

"I wasn't looking at your paper," I whispered. She rolled her eyes and returned to her quiz, hunching even lower to the desk. *Honestly.*

I returned to the piece of paper on my own desk, gripped my pen, and began to do the best I could do. I knew the answer to the very first question (How did the War of the North affect public perception of the larger conflict?), and most of the middle section and the end, and those I did not know exactly I wrote my way through until something reasonable-sounding came together. I wasn't sure whether I'd gotten an A, but when I turned over my quiz I looked over at Keith, who was shifting around in his seat with his quiz still facing up, and I smiled to myself, because at least I got to walk out first.

*　　*　　*

When I left the humanities building, it had started to rain. It was only slightly too warm for snow, still cold enough that those small, grayish, crusty piles of ice that were already (or rather, still) on the ground had not yet melted away. My cheer was erased immediately; there were few nonthreatening weather events more dispiriting than the kind of rain that fell from the sky in the Midwest in March. It was like a warning meant to manage one's expectations: maybe someday it would feel mild and pleasant outside once again, but not for a very, very long time.

I decided to duck into the science building in order to make use of our campus's partial provision of indoor tunneling—from there I could walk down a brick hall (unheated, but dry) past the entrances of the twin freshman dorms, through the double doors into the heated linoleum hall, and into the area containing the sandwich shop, coffee-and-smoothie shop, and club meeting room that sat in the semi-basement of the Evans-Caskill building. There was also a fruit stand, but as a student body we'd established an unspoken agreement to ignore it for the most part. The only people I ever saw using their campus cash to buy fruit were boys who ran cross-country, and there was a lot about their way of life I didn't understand.

As I got closer to the carpeted area that held the dugout's six or seven large circular tables, I slowed my pace. I scanned the tables, looking for anyone I knew so that I could immediately look away and pretend I hadn't seen them. I hated running into people during exams, when everyone would just ask you how studying was going, and soon you'd find yourselves attempting to out-despair each other. They'd be like, "Oh my god, I really think I'm going to fail," and you'd find yourself telling them, "You won't. You'll be fine. *I* am going to fail. I am going to fail so badly on every single one of mine that I would probably do better if I didn't even go." There was nothing productive about it.

I grabbed a small hot chocolate to go from the coffee counter, and on the way out of the building I checked my phone, realizing that I was probably running a few minutes late for my shift. And sure enough, it was 2:59. I hesitated by the glass doors—I didn't have an umbrella, and the rain seemed to have picked up since I'd escaped into the tunnel-way. I set my hot chocolate onto the window ledge and pulled my bag up into a makeshift hat. It seemed light enough that I could support it with one hand and hold my cup in the other, tucked in close to my chest to keep rain from sneaking into the hole on top. In this position I pushed my way through the double set of doors and took off in a trot toward the library.

When I reached the covered library doors, having fully run up the stone steps, I paused to catch my breath and adjust myself. I let go of my bag, which swung around the front of my neck toward the hand that was holding my cup. I jerked that hand up and out of the way, and hot chocolate poured straight out of the cup, directly onto the front flap of my bag, like that had been my plan all along.

"Are you *kidding* me?" I said aloud. I wiped at the bag's blue canvas with the drier of my two sleeves, which did not do much apart from transferring a light brown wet patch onto my light gray sweatshirt. I used the other side of the same sleeve to wipe off the rain that had dripped from my hair onto my forehead, collected myself, and sank my body into the revolving door.

Because I was late, I was prepared for Remy to be already sitting at the desk when I arrived, but mercifully, she wasn't, and I could collect myself. I sat down, set my cup to the side of my computer, and began taking care of the aftermath of my spill.

I pulled my books out of my bag and found them wetter than I'd feared. I opened each of them and laid them all facedown on the desk around me, hoping to dry them out. I went to the kitchen for paper towels, dampened a few, and brought the rest of the roll back to the desk. I had finished jabbing at the brown spots with the damp towels and was attempting to squeeze the color out with dry ones when I heard the desk gate swing open. I looked up to find Remy, who appeared equally soaked as me. Maybe more so.

"Heyyyy." I laughed. She gave a dispirited wave, leaning over to the side to let her backpack slide off her body to the floor. She took stock of my situation: the sea of spread-eagle school materials, the one fistful of paper towels on the desk and the other in my hand.

"Oh no," she said. "What happened?"

"I spilled hot chocolate into my bag," I said, pointing at the cup. "Well, that and the rain."

"I'm afraid to even look at my books," she said, looking down at her backpack.

"You have to!" I said. "It's only going to get worse every second you wait!"

"You're right," she said, and she crouched down to the floor.

"Here, hand them to me," I said. She took out the first book—*Themes of Contemporary Art*—and held it out tentatively. I saw that it was wetter than any of mine, so I placed it open, cover down, on the stretch of desk between our chairs. I took the roll of paper towels and quickly ripped off a bunch of sheets, which I placed between the most waterlogged pages.

"Does that work?" asked Remy.

"I have no idea," I said. "I've never tried it before."

Remy laughed and reached into her bag for another book. "Oh

nooooo," she wailed, taking it out and opening it to reveal huge clumps of stuck-together pages. "This one is even worse."

"You could hold it under one of the hand dryers in the bathroom?" I suggested.

"Oh, that's a good idea," she said. "I'll be right back."

Remy stood up and slipped her phone out of her front jeans pocket. She placed it on the desk between our computers. I noticed that it was completely uncovered, the silver sides marked up with scratches. A crack stretched across the bottom quarter of the screen.

"Did that just happen?" I asked.

"What?" she said. Remy looked at the phone, following my finger, but even looking right at it, she took a moment to understand what I meant. "Oh! Ha, no, it's been like that for ages." She shrugged, like, *what are you going to do?* But there was something she could do. She could immediately take it to the store and exchange it for a new one. And buy a case for it.

"Be right back!" she said, and turned to take her book to the bathroom.

I stood there placing paper towels between pages of Remy's art book and watching the crowd of students in front of me. Every seat was taken. Two of the four inhabitants of the circle of armchairs at the center of the room were asleep. One of them seemed to have planned for it—her books closed on the little table in the middle and her phone resting on the chair's arm, presumably set to wake her up in fifteen or twenty minutes—and the other had not. His book was open in his lap and his head was slumped back, his mouth wide open. I watched him slide down the seat, be shaken awake by gravity, close his mouth, and nod off again. This, I knew, could go on for hours, and he would never commit to the idea that he was asleep.

I heard a loud buzz and looked to my phone, but the screen was dark. I looked at Remy's as it buzzed again. Against the wood desk it sounded almost jackhammer-like, so I reached over to silence it, and that's when I saw the little green square of a text message, and the name Keith next to it. Actually, it was written "Keith <3." I saw a glimpse of text before it disappeared into the top of the screen. It said "Sorry."

Before I realized what I was doing, I had pushed the phone away. I watched it slide across the desk until it bumped into Remy's keyboard. I looked at it for a moment and realized that I couldn't leave it there; it was so far from where Remy had left it that surely she would notice and would therefore know I had looked at her phone. I looked toward the bathroom to make sure she hadn't yet come back out and slid the phone back into place.

In a state of panic, I tried to evaluate what just happened. Did it count as looking at her phone if I hadn't been actively trying to do it? My brain's comprehension of the text was passive, done without my full participation. I didn't ask for this. If you really thought about it, in fact, I had been forced into it by Keith. Which just figured.

I sat down in my chair, pulling Remy's books and the paper towels closer so I could finish my project there, farther from the scene of the crime. I glanced at the phone again. Had it been a little closer to her computer before? I stood up, moved it half an inch, tilted it to a jauntier, more natural-looking angle—the way it might look if someone had just set it down without thinking too much about it, like, "I'll just set this down wherever"—and sat down again. It still looked wrong. But it was too late to do anything more about it now, because when I looked up again, Remy was heading back to the desk, smiling.

"I don't know if that really helped much or not," she said of her book, holding it up for me to see. "There are still clumps, but maybe they'll come apart more easily now?"

"I think they will," I said. "Maybe if it's sunny tomorrow, leave it open by a window or something." Who was I, Dr. Wet Textbook Expert all of a sudden?

"Yeah," said Remy. "I will." She laid the book open and facedown on the desk and sat down, at which point I felt myself inhale. She picked up her phone and I held my breath—I didn't think it looked like she was wondering why the fuck it was in a different spot than where she'd left it, but it was hard to say. She swiped at the screen, presumably reading the text from Keith. I couldn't look at her.

"Ugh," she said, and let the phone drop and clatter on the desk. In any other situation, I knew, I would have said "What?" But I couldn't. She might know.

"How are your midterms?" I asked instead.

"Oh, fine," she said. "I actually only have two. For the other two classes I just have final papers."

"Me, too! Just a couple, I mean."

"Oh, OK!" she said. "That makes me feel better. I've felt bad every time anyone's asked me about midterms. I've been, like, apologizing for not having more of them."

"Me, too," I said. "I just want it to be over with. Even though I have like nothing."

"This is a safe space for complaining," said Remy. "We're allowed."

"OK, good," I said. I turned to the roll of paper towels and realized that only one remained on the tube. "Oops. Well, I guess this is as good as it's going to get," I said, and pushed the book a little ways down the desk toward Remy.

"Thank you." She laughed. "No matter what, it'll be better off than it would have had it been left to me."

We turned to our computers, and I opened my email, Facebook, and the draft of my literature review. I opened the library site's journal search page and, feeling like this constituted a good and meaningful start, clicked back over to Facebook.

I scrolled down the main page, where people were logging their progress. "How many hours can I survive without sleeping? Let's find out..." said Jordan Harrington. Maya Berg: "Two exams down...three to go. Lol #premed #killme." I came upon Mel's name, not in the form of a status but tagged in a picture of a Tri-Beta meeting the past week. It had been someone's birthday, it looked like, so they were eating sheet cake from the grocery store and Mel was mid-bite. Not a cutesy make-believe mid-bite; an unposed, real mid-bite. Anyone else would have untagged the picture by now.

"You were right, by the way." I turned to look at Remy. "About my friend Mel."

"Oh really?" she said. "You mean about her dating someone??"

"Apparently!" I said.

"Huh," she said. "Did it, like, start up very suddenly? Who is it?"

"Will Reid?" I said. I waited a moment for possible recognition, but Remy just shrugged. "He's a junior," I explained. "Anyway, they had a little thing freshman year but nothing really came of it, and she's sort of liked him ever since."

"Aw!" said Remy.

"Um, yeah. So, he'd been dating this girl Sarah, but they broke up a few weeks ago I think, and he texted Mel a few nights ago. Which I did know about. But I didn't really think anything else was going to happen," I said.

"Why not?"

"Well," I said. "I don't know. He's really flakey."

"Ohhh," said Remy. "Aren't they all."

"Well, right. But he's like. EXTRA flakey."

"Oh, OK," said Remy.

"So I thought the one text was kind of it, but then I found out last Sunday that she'd hooked up with him on Saturday night and wasn't even planning to tell me about it," I said. I hadn't been planning to tell her that much of the story. It just came out.

"Whoa," she said. "How did you find out?"

"Well, she finally told me because I confronted her Sunday night, because, like you saw, she was acting weird. I thought she was mad at me, and she insisted she wasn't, but she wouldn't say what was going on. But then she finally told me," I said.

"Why didn't she want to tell you?"

"She said she didn't want me to feel bad."

"What? Why would you feel bad?" she asked.

Shit. I hadn't really thought this through. I couldn't very well tell her the real answer. At least not specifically.

"Oh, um," I said. "Just, like...I guess, she just thought I would feel jealous."

"What??" she said. "I mean, I don't know her, obviously, so I don't want to...I don't know, I think that seems like a harsh assumption to make. I would be annoyed, too."

"Yeah! Right? And then she was annoyed with *me* for being annoyed at *her*, and that made me even more annoyed," I said. We both laughed. "So anyway, as you can tell," I continued, "it's a very logical and mature conflict."

"Don't do that," said Remy.

I stopped smiling, stunned.

"I mean," she said, "it's not illogical or stupid. She hurt your feelings. You don't have to make fun of yourself for being upset about it."

I paused. I felt hot, and I was sure I was blushing.

"Are your parents therapists or something?" I asked.

She laughed. "No. I've just spent a fair amount of time seeing them myself," she said. I tried not to react to this in any visible way. "I'm sorry," she added, "sometimes I end up sounding bossy. Really I'm just trying to remind myself of these things as much as I am telling anyone else."

"No," I said, "don't apologize."

"OK," she said. "I take it back!" She smiled.

"Well, I guess I should do some work," I said, not because I really wanted to, but because I needed a reason to look away from her and think.

"Me, too," said Remy, and we swiveled around to face our respective computers. We hardly spoke for the rest of the shift, working hard or at least trying hard to seem like we were, but minutes after we'd said good-bye and she left, my phone lit up and I saw that she'd sent me a friend request on Facebook. For a moment I just stared at it, wondering what to do—wouldn't Keith see that we'd become friends? What would he think, and would he ask Remy about it? What if he *did* ask her about it, and she asked why he was asking, and then, hand forced, he explained it to her? He'd make it brief, dismissive, a wave of the hand. I felt sure of it.

But then, I thought, Keith hardly used Facebook in the first place. Even if he did somehow venture into Remy's activity and saw that she'd added me, I figured he was both bright enough to put together that she and I both worked at the library and simpleminded enough to assume that was all there was to it. And anyway, even if it came to that, maybe it wouldn't be so bad if he *did* have to explain how he knew me. I tapped "Accept" with my thumb, thinking *I would love to see him try.*

12

In theory, spring break began on Friday at 6:00 PM, the deadline by which professors were told their exams had to be completed and their grades turned in. In practice, it began in waves, the most blessed students finishing sometime Wednesday night, the same day midterms technically started. Some students (juniors and seniors, mostly) didn't have class on Fridays and were therefore shoo-ins for early escape. Others negotiated and asked to take their exams early; it was known to have happened, on more than one occasion, that an otherwise amorphous, ambivalent class organized in a sort of single-case union and petitioned a professor to move their test block up a day.

In theory, what kept me at school all week was my 5:00 PM Friday lit review deadline. In practice (because I could have turned it in earlier, if I'd wanted), what kept me at school was that I dragged my heels until the very end, since I had nowhere else to be. I was one of maybe three dozen or so students who would stay on campus over break. Most of them lived in foreign countries, and even among that group they were an anomaly; most of the international students had American friends whom they'd go home with rather than stay at school. My childhood home in Carbondale, a little over three hours south, was just far enough that I didn't want to ask my dad to come get me, and while I supposed I could have bought a bus ticket, I didn't even want to go home in the first place. My dad had picked me up for spring break freshman year and I'd spent the week lying on the floor of my childhood bedroom, staring at the magazine cutouts I'd taped to the ceiling and never took down if for no other reason than nobody had ever asked me to.

There was just no point to it; Tess, the only high school friend I still talked to (and that wasn't very often at all, anyway), had her spring break two weeks after mine. There was nothing else for me to do in Carbondale. So sophomore year, I'd decided I'd just spend my spring breaks at school and make a little extra money at the library, which stayed open year-round for researchers and grad students. Maybe I'd have gone home with Mel or Logan if they'd asked me to, but they hadn't—Mel's family went to Mexico every year, and Logan spent hers at her family's house south of Chicago playing RPGs with her sixteen-year-old brother and engaging in various sociopolitical debates with her parents. I imagined that if Logan had to host someone for a week, she'd kill them by the end of it.

On Thursday evening after their last test, the two of them left for Chicago together in Logan's car. I hugged them both before they left, and we all wished each other a good break. Whatever was still off between Mel and me was muted by Logan's presence and by the relief we all felt at being on the verge of vacation.

It was Friday at exactly six thirty when I felt a vibration beneath me, my phone having slipped under my side while I lay on the couch watching TV. I propped myself up on my elbow and pulled it out, unsurprised to see that the screen read "Dad."

"Hi, Dad," I said into the phone. Right away I heard rustling—when he called me he usually multitasked, working on one of the three crossword puzzles he completed daily.

"Hello, Harriet," he said. "All finished with exams?" He kept my academic calendar printed out and taped to the refrigerator, midterm and final deadlines circled in red pen.

"Yeah," I said. "Just turned in my last paper at five."

"Good," he said. "How do you think you did?"

"Um, fine," I said. Onscreen the perp was getting arrested, slammed facedown into the hood of a car. He was yelling, saying he had nothing to do with it, but it was obvious that he did. "I only had two exams, but I think I did all right."

"Good," he said. He cleared his throat, right into the phone, and I held the phone away from my face. "How're the girls?"

"They're good," I said. "They went home last night."

"Well," he said. "Just wanted to check in."

"Thanks," I said. "How're your other kids?" He taught anthropology at SIU, mostly to freshmen.

"Oh, you know," he said. "Just can't get enough of the Sumerians."

I laughed. "I'm not surprised," I said. We both paused, me watching the show, him scribbling a string of letters into their row.

"Do you have enough money?" he said, and I felt my jaw tighten, even though I knew he didn't mean to sound accusatory. At least not completely. When I was younger he'd encouraged me to go to SIU—because it was a good school, but also because I would've gotten reduced tuition. I'd wanted to go somewhere else, especially by the time I graduated. Not too far, but not Carbondale. I'd gotten a partial scholarship offer from Springfield, and a little money from life insurance, and in the end the cost worked out to be about the same, but my dad remained convinced I would have saved more if I'd stayed.

"Yes," I said, "I'm good."

"Good," he said. Then, "Well!" and I knew that was my cue, so I said thanks again for calling and that I hoped he'd have a good weekend. "Take care of yourself, Harriet," he said, and I told him that I would.

Before my shift the following Wednesday, the first sunny day of break, I took a walk around the empty campus. I walked figure-eights through the quad and around the loops of dorms and Greek housing, sometimes stopping to brush piles of wet leaves off the sidewalk back onto the grass with my sneaker. I walked for an hour and didn't see a single other human being, and imagined that I was the lone survivor of an apocalyptic event.

Once inside the library, I noticed how unusually clean and good it smelled—I looked around and saw that some of the windows were open, probably to air out the heavy-smelling sadness left behind by unshowered students suffering through midterms. I stood in the entryway and inhaled it and thought of how each spring my mom would run around our house throwing open all the windows the moment it seemed warm enough to her, and how I would close them an hour later, because it was too cold, too early.

I walked over to the circulation desk and saw the staff librarian, Deb, sitting in her office. She looked up at the sound of me sitting in my chair—the only sound amid complete silence. She stood up, walked over to her door, gave me a tight smile, and closed it.

I took my book out of my backpack, set it next to my computer, and opened up my email and Facebook accounts. There was nothing new in my inbox and very little on Facebook, apart from a few classmates who were already cross-posting vacation pictures from Instagram: pedicured feet on beaches and sunny cocktails and the pets people had left behind in their parents' homes. I closed out of the tab.

I'd only just plugged my earbuds into the monitor to watch a show when my eyes were drawn to the (1) that appeared next to the "Inbox" on my Dear Emma email tab. I was immediately excited, and a little nervous, because anyone who took a mid–spring break pause to write to their school's newspaper advice columnist had to be asking something good.

I clicked over to look at who that anyone was, and I saw that it was Remy.

For a second, I panicked. It felt like she could see me; if she'd written to me, and I looked at the message, surely she'd know that Emma was me. What if she already knew? Was that possible? She'd figured out Mel was dating someone before I did, and she didn't even know Mel. But no, she couldn't know. If she did, if she'd somehow learned that the column was mine, she'd have just told me. Right?

I scanned slowly over the subject line of the email.

Subject line: Problems With Boyzzzz.

It couldn't be about Keith. I mean, that was obviously the first thought, and the most logical, but it had to be wrong.

The preview line began: *Dear Emma, Soooo, I feel a little silly emailing this to you, because—*

OK, so maybe it was going to be about Keith, but it was going to be something annoying. A fake problem. Like, what to do if your hot new boyfriend loves you TOO much. Or like, what do you do if your boyfriend can't shut up about how beautiful you are? Maybe she was going to ask me if I thought it was possible to know you've found *the one* when you're twenty-two and it's only been about a month.

I rested my cursor over the email and pressed, holding it down as I took a deep breath. When my finger started to turn red and hurt a little, I let it go.

The email opened and I read:

Dear Emma,

Soooo, I feel a little silly emailing this to you, because so many of the questions you get are so interesting, and complicated, and mine is such a cliché that even I find it boring. Still, I've been obsessing about it, and I don't really know who else to talk to about it, so here I am with my boring cliché boy problem. I've been dating someone for just under a month. It's been really nice, and I've felt a strong connection/chemistry/whatever, and I think (or, thought) he feels (or, felt) the same way. In the very beginning we texted and talked constantly. After a couple weeks, it slowed down a little, but I told myself that was normal. But then it slowed a little more. And now it's been three days since I've heard anything from him (I was the one who started our most recent text conversation, and his last response was really brief), and I'm just wondering if this is another one of those things. Like, those kind of really intense three- or four-week things with a guy who is SUPER CRAZY about you until all of a sudden he's just gone. (Why do they do that? You don't have to answer that part.) I'm sick of these things. I don't have patience for them anymore. I've been through what feels like one million of them. So my question for you is: Should I, for once in my life, cut my losses now, to get to be the one who says "enough"?

Sincerely,
Sick of Scrubs

Reflexively I clicked the reply button, but I immediately closed out of it. I felt compelled to respond to her directly, which was probably just because I knew her. It was hard not to write something back right away, at least for a second, until I realized I had no idea what it was I even wanted to say. There was a burning little part of me that wanted to reply with a long string of capitalized, diabolical laughter. It was just so fucking rich.

I copied the text of Remy's email and pasted it into a new message from my personal account, typing Logan's and Mel's email addresses in the To: box. Then I deleted Mel's, hesitated, and put it back in. She was going to have to care about this, whether she had to fake it or not.

At the top of the message I added a short note: "YOU GUYS. OH MY GOD. What do I do? What do I write back? This is CRAZY, right? I mean, this is crazy. Help."

I stopped typing and rested my fingers on the keys. I added: "Miss you. Harriet."

Subject line: !!!!!!!!!!!!!!!!!!!!

I'd already sent the email off when it occurred to me that Mel, off in another country and never very attached to her phone anyway, wouldn't get the message until Sunday, when her family flew back. Thinking of my email, which contained the entire body of Remy's email, sitting openly and undealt with in Mel's inbox, made me wonder if I should have sent it at all. I'd never directly copy-pasted them a Dear Emma email before. I'd read them select excerpts a few times, while working on the column at home, and I'd definitely paraphrased plenty of letters to them. I'd always figured they'd get printed sooner or later anyway; all they were really getting was a preview. So why did this feel like crossing some imaginary line? Was I just worried Remy would somehow find out?

I checked my outbox, suddenly terrified I'd inadvertently added her name to the address field along with the others. But everything looked as it should; it had gone to Mel and to Logan and probably some database at Google, but not, from all available evidence, to Remy.

I did my best to distract myself. I turned on some music and told myself I wouldn't nudge Logan until at least three songs had gone by. I took out a notebook and tapped my pen against it, then doodled a series of loops and lines down the margins. I looked out over the desk for inspiration; there was nothing. Nobody had come in. I drew my computer, and then I set it on fire with cartoon flames. Stick figure me stood next to it, on my knees, wailing to the sky.

I put the pen down and looked at my email outbox. I had sent the message eight minutes earlier. Even I knew it would be crazy to expect Logan to respond in eight minutes.

I looked behind me, in search of the book cart, and found a single hardcover on its shelves. I'll put that away, I decided, and then, when I get back, if she still hasn't written back yet, I can text her.

Nine minutes later, I texted her. "Omg check your email please."

I stared at my phone screen, running my finger over it to keep it lit. Within half a minute, the little ellipses appeared to indicate that Logan was typing, and I was so relieved I half shouted "Thank god."

I watched, and waited. The ellipses disappeared. Had she started to write me and then thought better of it?

"What the fuck?" I said. But then it came back. A few seconds later, a text appeared.

"Hang on, looking."

This was infuriating to me. She could have easily opened and read the entire message in the amount of time it took her to send me that. But I texted back "OK," and waited.

"Oh, weird," came the next text.

Is that it? I thought. I started typing, but then a text popped up.

"Lol, I like how she just had to say 'by the way, I've had one million boyfriends.'"

"I know!" I wrote back, though really I'd hardly noticed that part.

"What are you gonna say," she wrote.

"I don't know!" I typed. "That's why I sent it to you."

"Well right," she wrote. "But you're the one who signed up for this."

"I know that, thanks," I typed. (The "thanks" was not sincere.) "It's just sort of a conflict of interest. Or, complicated, at least."

There was a long enough pause then that I set my phone down on the table. It was getting on my nerves, and I wanted it out of my hands.

When it buzzed I leaned over it and read: "Yeah. Well, I guess he has an MO."

I wrote: "Yeah, apparently. Ugh."

There was a lot more I wanted to say but it was too much for texting, so I figured that would be the end of it. But a few seconds later it buzzed again. "Just give it a few days," she wrote. "It's spring break."

I tried not to think about it. I went home, and I watched *Law & Order* and ate three-quarters of a frozen pizza, and I tried not to think about it, until it became so clear that I couldn't not think about it that I had to pause the episode and dedicate five minutes to thinking about it in peace. I finished a mystery novel, and added three more to my online shopping cart, and tried not to think about it. I started another one and set it in my lap two times per page, to think about it. I'd realize what I was doing, pick it back up, read slowly and determinedly for three or four paragraphs, and drop it again.

I was thrilled, or at least excited. I was happy-angry. This was what I'd been hoping for, even if I hadn't totally recognized it before now: their failure. I hadn't thought about how I wanted it to happen, though I now weighed the pros and cons of each possibility. If she dumped him, it was a sort of vicarious vengeance— if I never got the chance to break his heart, the next best thing might be witnessing another girl do it. But him getting dumped might also mean he'd still wanted her. If he dumped her, he was still the one in control—but at least I wouldn't feel like an anomaly. At least I'd know that it wasn't just me; two examples would be enough to argue that this was his thing. And maybe that was even better than revenge: to be on a team, with an enemy in common.

I opened up my email on my phone and typed a short response to Remy's email: "Hello there— Just wanted to let you know I'll be answering your question in the first column post-break." I paused. Most times I'd leave it at something like that, but here it felt strange not to say more. She didn't know I wasn't an impersonal soothsayer, but I did.

I typed: "Hang in there! xo, Emma," and pressed send.

*　　*　　*

Neither Logan nor Mel ever got anywhere any sooner than they needed to. Logan was more often the later of the two, so it was a surprise when she walked in the door first, and alone, on Sunday evening. I had woken up early and lounged around all morning, waiting for them on the couch so I could see the driveway from the windows, even though I knew they'd get back well after lunch, and always two or three hours later than they originally said.

As soon as I heard the side door open I was there, sliding into the kitchen on my socks.

"I thought you guys were going to leave at lunch!" I said.

"I was," she said, dropping her backpack and laundry bag on the floor. "And then I just...didn't."

She shrugged and put her hands on the place her hips would be, if she'd had any; she looked about the same as she had when she'd left, which made sense for the actual amount of time that had passed, but not for how long it seemed.

"Where's Mel?" I asked.

"I guess their flight back was delayed, so she wasn't quite ready when I wanted to leave. She took the bus."

"Did your mom give you any treats to bring back?"

Logan leaned over and unzipped her backpack, from which she produced a gallon-size Ziploc bag with an aluminum foil package inside it. "Chocolate chip cookies," she said. I took the bag and set it on the table, but we both knew what I was really waiting for. "And—" She leaned down and pulled out an enormous second plastic bag, filled with trail mix. I took it from her carefully, cradling it like a baby. It weighed as much as one. Logan's mom was famous, at least among the three of us, as a true innovator in the art of trail mix—though it probably wasn't even fair to call it that. She did not bother with nuts, or pieces of granola, or anything so basic as raisins and M&M's. There was no half-assed attempt at nutritional value; there were, instead, mini Oreos and chocolate-covered pretzels and Goldfish, sour strips and Licorice Nibs and sour balls, all among other types of candy and treats I had never even seen before. It seemed like it shouldn't taste good together but it did, so salty and so sugary that it hurt to eat.

When Mel got home half an hour later, she said, "Hey," dropped her bag by the door, and sat down next to Logan at the kitchen table, where we were still eating directly from the bag. She dug a hand in and brought it out full.

"How was Mexico?" I asked.

"The same," she said.

"How many boys did your sister make out with?" I asked.

"Two," she said. "Or—was it? No, yeah…I think two. One was really hot. Oh my god, he was so hot. I don't really remember the other one's face, but I think he was like. Kind of old."

"Wonderful," said Logan. She slid her hand down the table and cupped it around the small mountain of Oreos Mel was picking out of her pile. Logan herded them toward herself and stacked them into a small tower.

"How many guys did *you* make out with?" I asked. I was only teasing her, but I regretted it immediately. I brought Will into it, already, without even trying.

"Zero," said Mel.

"I was just kidding," I said.

"I know," she said. "I mean, I like, could have, but. Anyway, how was your guys' break?"

"Boring," said Logan.

"More boring than that," I said.

"My mom made me work on an MCAT prep book," Logan countered.

"On Tuesday morning I'd run out of so many ideas for things to do that I emptied my underwear drawer on my bed and folded all my underwear and unfolded and refolded all my socks," I said. "That drawer is pristine now. It looks like a department store."

"You win," said Mel. "Logan had Lucy and her mom's snacks." Lucy was Logan's family's Portuguese water dog.

"Thank you," I said.

"Fine," said Logan. Everyone took another handful.

"Did you get my email?" I asked Mel.

"Oh, yeah—I only just got it this morning, sorry," she said.

"No, it's OK," I said. "I figured."

"I was kind of surprised you sent the whole thing!" she said, and my heart sank. If Logan had any negative opinions as to the ethics of my email forwarding, she hadn't spoken them aloud. And because Logan didn't generally keep her negative opinions to herself, I'd assumed she didn't object. I'd stopped feeling guilty, forgetting I still didn't know what Mel would think.

"I know," I said, "I didn't really—it was like a reflex, I didn't think about it. You guys weren't here for me to indirectly outline it to you. But now I kind of feel bad."

"Oh, whatever," said Logan. "People who write in should know you're like, a person with friends. If it were really serious, they'd talk to a therapist."

"Yeah," I said, "I guess so." But I wasn't as placated by Logan's lack of judginess as I had been a few days earlier.

Mel shrugged. "Yeah, I mean, we're not going to tell anyone." She waved her hand, like *no big deal*, but I had the feeling she only did it to move us along, to prevent me from entering panic mode. "Did you already write the response?" she added.

"No," I sighed. "Logan told me to wait. Also I have no idea what to say anyway."

"But you're using it for this week?"

"That's the plan," I said. "I told her I would. I mean, like, Emma told her."

"I'm still not sure why she's so sure there's a problem," said Logan. "How long had it been since he texted? Three days?"

"Yeah."

"That's not *that* long," she said. "And it was spring break."

"Oh, true," said Mel. "What if he was just on vacation?"

"I feel like she must've known what his plans were and was accounting for that," I said. "Plus, I kind of *do* think three days is a long time."

"Yeah, true," said Mel. "If it were, like, two..."

"Even still!" I said. "Even still, that would be an annoying time to go without talking at all. You want the person you're hanging out with to want to talk to you." "Hanging out with" was easier for me to say than what I meant, which was "sleeping with."

"Well, sure," said Logan. "I mean, we already knew he was like this."

"I know," I said. "I just don't know how to tell her that."

"You'll figure it out."

"Maybe. I tried to write a few notes yesterday and literally wrote nothing."

"I think you're overthinking it," said Logan.

"I can't believe you'd accuse me of being capable of such a thing," I said.

"Maybe you have to pretend she's someone else," said Mel.

"Yeah," said Logan. "If she was just some random sad girl with some random asshole boyfriend, what would you tell her?"

But she isn't, I thought. *He's not.*
"Yeah, you're right," I said.

It was an hour later, after we'd eaten half the bag of trail mix and subsequently come to a mutual if reluctant agreement that we really shouldn't eat the entire thing in one sitting, and Logan had climbed onto the counter and "hidden" the rest on top of the cabinets as Mel and I watched, that I went into my bedroom to write the column.

I closed the door behind me and picked up my laptop with one hand, holding my stomach with the other. I propped up my pillows and slid into bed, shivering at the coolness of my sheets.

I opened a new document. At the top, I typed the date, and a line below that, I wrote, "Dear S. O. S."

Though I knew both parties, I decided it would be irresponsible not to check for any additional evidence, as I did for the rest of the advice-seekers. I pulled up Remy's Facebook page first, but found nothing new or relevant. So I went to Keith's: Since the last time I'd looked, two new items had appeared on his wall. One was an uncommented-upon link to a *New York Times* op-ed about gender inequality in filmmaking—*ugh,* I thought, *of course*—and the other was a picture he'd been tagged in. I clicked on it to get a better look, careful to avoid the like button, knowing full well that if I clicked on it by mistake, I would have to drop out of school immediately. The photo was old, it seemed, maybe by a year or two; it had been taken by a girl named Andrea Moore, evidently sometime over the summer. In it, Keith was holding an ice-cream sandwich, squinting and half smiling toward the lens. It looked like they'd been at a fair, and the photo was tagged to Milwaukee. I clicked on her name. Her profile was limited, but I could see she went to Michigan State. It was likely she was just a friend from high school, but I supposed it was possible she was an ex. It was somewhat odd for this girl to have uploaded and tagged him in this photo now. It violated the typical chronology of Facebook. It was just *there*—dropped, as far as anyone who didn't know this girl knew, at random, just four days ago. He looked so cute and so beamingly happy in it that you almost didn't have a choice but to be suspicious.

Four days ago—that was Wednesday. I wonder if Remy had seen it, if it had meant something to her. I checked the timestamp and compared it to her mail, but the photo was put up after she had written me. I couldn't decide whether, for Remy, that was better or worse.

I picked up my phone and checked both their Instagram accounts next; his had been updated a week ago, with a poorly filtered picture of a particularly sad-looking pile of melting snow. Hers, updated around the same time, possibly the same day, made me gasp: It was a picture she'd taken of them together, close together and close up, their eyes wide and peering over the edge of a table. It hurt to look at it. It felt personal, like they'd posed it and lit it and shot it in such a way to maximize my humiliation.

I tried to separate myself, to look at the picture as evidence. It was adorable, objectively, and anyone who saw it would think they looked like a couple who liked each other a lot. But you could never be sure. And if I once would have thought it impossible that two people could go from looking like they did in that photo to not speaking to each other in the span of a week, I didn't think so anymore. A week could be a really long time.

I dropped my phone next to me on my bed. I closed out of my Internet browser and stared at the nearly empty document in front of me. The clock in the corner of my screen read 10:22.

The column was due by midnight. I had never before missed my deadline, and the last thing I wanted to do was let Keith be indirectly responsible for the first time I did.

*   *   *

Dear S. O. S.,

There is no such thing as a boring question. Well—that's not quite true. I don't want to be too provocative, lest anyone set out to prove me wrong. Perhaps it is safer to say that cliché is unavoidable. If I had a dime for every time I've been sent some version of your letter, I'd probably have over three dollars. That little variations on the same dating crime are being perpetrated en masse is not your fault. That I could receive 30 or more letters from people (mostly girls, let's be honest) in different stages of this very situation is a crisis to be sure, but it's not one for which I plan to hold you responsible.

I get the sense that you consider your problem not only boring but also imaginary in some way, like you're making a big deal out of something that isn't. But your suspicion of yourself here isn't innate so much as it is a clever by-product of your boyfriend's behavior. He is (consciously or not) acting in a way meant to disarm you—to make you feel it is *you* who are needy, and bossy, and serious; that it is *you* who are dramatic should you wish to have this turn of events explained. But moving from frenzied romance and fanciful, long-term sentiment to chilly distance in the span of mere days is nuts. *That* is dramatic. But because all of this is happening over a relatively short span of time, he's able to convince himself that the entire thing must be unserious, and handled accordingly.

I am increasingly certain that young straight men view the approach of any relationship's one-month mark as a ticking time bomb. Why else would they act so crazy when they see it coming? What do they think is going to happen? (A Siamese twin-like fusing of your body to his? The implicit agreement to an unbreakable, eternal oath that states he may never realize his recently formed dream to one day backpack through Latin America, or buy a patch of farmland, or learn to build furniture, or become a firefighter or cross-country trucker? Honestly.) A friend of mine once told me a month is about how long it takes to begin seeing another person as another person instead of a character making a cameo appearance in your life. Maybe that's the problem—now you're real, and must be contended with.

So here you are, a few weeks in, facing this familiar quandary. You are on the cusp of knowing for sure, one way or the other. And that makes it somewhat difficult for me to answer this question, because what happened between the day you sent it and the day I write my response could, at least in theory, change your mind, and mine. Three days is a really long time to go without talking to someone you're dating, except for those specific cases when there's a really good (or at least sort of good) reason, and then it's not.

But the more time that passes and the more people I hear from, the less I believe in the probability of those exceptions. And that, more than anything else—more than the headache-inducing familiarity of the timeline you presented, more than the general hopelessness of boys aged 18–22(+?), more than my feeling that your having been through this "one million" times means that you're overdue for a break; though each of these things counts a little, too—is why I'm going to answer the way I'm going to answer.

Enough is enough, indeed. Once in a while things can get better after they get worse, but this early on, is it likely? If it did get better, would it be likely to stay that way for very long? There are wafflers who can waffle for just about forever. In my opinion, dear S. O. S., you're better off being resolute, and demanding resoluteness in return. You're better off looking for someone who is super super crazy about you in a way that sticks, who never leaves you counting days.

Most humbly yours,
Emma

13

By Wednesday the Remy problem had fallen to the back of my mind in favor of the unexpected intensity of my post-break workload; if I had been spoiled by the first half of the semester, my professors seemed intent on making up for it now. I had an essay-based Spanish Civ. exam in a week, the novel *Rebecca* to read by next Thursday, a poetry analysis due the Monday after that, and the first draft of the analysis portion of my writing seminar paper on the horizon. When I got to the library that afternoon, fifteen minutes before my shift—Professor Ferrer was in the midst of an "atrocious episode with pollen allergies" and had ended class early—I wasn't thinking about seeing Remy. Nia and Robert were still at the circulation desk, so I sat at a table nearby and wrote all my remaining deadlines into my planner in color code.

A few minutes later I noticed Nia stand up and start to pack up her things, so I hovered behind the desk until she walked out and then reclaimed my spot. When Robert left a few minutes after that, I was left with the circulation desk to myself. I settled in and looked up at the clock to see that it was 3:08, and Remy still hadn't shown up. It had hardly occurred to me to start wondering if she'd make it in when I noticed a little red notification appear on my Facebook page: Remy Roy had sent me an instant message.

"hey," she wrote. "sorry I'm not there."

"That's ok!" I typed. "Are you ok?" I felt panicky. What if she told me directly about her problems with Keith? What would I say if she did?

"yea just sick," she wrote. "i think i caught strep at home from my sister."

"Ohhh no, I'm sorry!" I typed. "Well, don't worry, there's like nobody here anyway."

"ha i figured."

The little window went still, each of us (I assumed) staring at it and waiting for the other to say something else. Even over the Internet the awkwardness was nearly unbearable. I started typing but then so did she, so I stopped.

"anyway just wanted to let you know," she wrote. And then: "did you have a good break?"

"Ummm it was OK," I wrote. "Haha. I was here the whole time, so it was…fine."

"you were??" she wrote.

"Yep."

"i'm always impressed by people who stay. it kind of seems like it would be fun. or relaxing, at least."

"It's a little fun," I wrote, feeling vaguely proud of something I hadn't previously considered an interesting choice. "It sort of feels dystopian. But also, boring."

"haha yeah," she wrote. "i guess it would get old by the end."

"I did a lot of weird, bad crafts," I typed.

"haha," she wrote. "well, i went back home to chicago and i was bored to death too, so maybe that's just the nature of spring break."

Bored to death or *heartbroken* to death? Now that it seemed almost certain she wasn't going to bring it up, I really wanted her to bring it up.

"Except for the kids who go to Mexico or Miami," I wrote.

"except for them. but I'm not a big beach party person anyway."

"Me neither," I wrote.

Another pause.

"Well, don't let me keep you, you should rest or something," I wrote. Then: "…Not that I'm your mom or doctor, sorry."

"haha no you're right," she said. "sometimes when i get sick i stay up even later than usual and think it's an excuse to eat macaroni and cheese 3 times a day and i just make it worse. so this is good."

"Well, in that case, boil some water and add lemon and honey," I typed. "Four glasses of cool water a day minimum. And definitely keep eating macaroni and cheese."

"yes ma'am. haha. thank you."

"No problem."

":) ok, see you sunday then! have a good rest of the weeeeeek," she wrote.

I'd have to wait two days until she read the column (if she read it on time—she had to read it on time, right?), and two more beyond that before there would be any chance of seeing her, and having her bring it up. I would have to bring it up, if she didn't.

"Thanks," I typed. "You too."

When I got home I found Logan and Mel making dinner in the kitchen.

"You're here!" I said.

"Yeah," said Logan. "We just probably failed an Orgo exam so we decided to come home and die rather than go to the library again."

"It was sooooooo bad," said Mel. "Like, so bad. And I knew

it would be! I swore I'd study over break! But did I?? No! I did not!"

"You were on the beach," I said. "Nobody can study on the beach."

"I could've stayed back in the hotel," said Mel. "Serves me right. Sitting in the sun! Basking, pretty much! What was I even thinking?"

"Maybe you did better than you think," I said.

"That only ever happens to her," said Mel, pointing a thumb in Logan's direction.

Logan shrugged. "I thought it was hard too," she said.

"Well," I said. "At least it's over."

"Until next week!!" said Mel. So many years of learned optimism (from her father, mostly) had taught her to smile even in circumstances like these, when it couldn't be clearer she was miserable; her mouth reached up and open so you could see all her very straight teeth, but the overall effect was more mania than mirth.

"Don't worry about that now," said Logan. "First we have to get through the weekend."

"What's this weekend?" I asked.

"Oh," said Mel. "We have that dance thing."

"Which?" I said. "Tri-Beta? That's this weekend?"

"Regretfully, yes," said Logan. Mel nodded.

"That's exciting," I said. "Or not," I added, both of them turning around to glare. "What are you guys going to wear?"

"Probably my dress," said Logan.

"Still just the one, huh?" I asked.

"Why would I need more than one?"

"Godddd, I forgot I have to go *shopping*," said Mel. She pressed her palms hard into her eyes and whimpered.

"Do you want me to come with?" I asked. If there was any tension between us still, it had to be set aside now, out of duty.

"Yeah," she sighed. "But I cannot spend more than fifty dollars."

"On a formal dress?" I asked. The annoying thing about this was that Mel had money. Her dad and his business partner co-owned a string of dental offices in the greater Chicagoland suburbs. The first time I'd seen her house, I'd gasped. She had a *canopy bed*, which was something I hadn't previously thought real people owned. Yet she existed in an alternate financial universe— one in which the tolerable price of goods and services was generally about one-third of what they actually cost. Her older sister might have spent money like a European duchess but Mel took after her mother, who grew up penny-pinching on a dairy farm.

"It's semiformal," she said. "That's totally reasonable."

I felt my lips retract into my face.

"*Fifty dollars?*" she asked.

"We'll do our best," I said. "It's on Saturday?"

"Yeah," she said.

"Are you bringing Will?" I asked.

"Yes," she said curtly. I could tell that was all I was allowed to ask right now.

"Oooooohhh," said Logan.

"Who are you bringing?" I asked her.

"Uh, no one," she said. "I do not want a repeat of the Theta incident."

The year before, in the fall, Logan had shocked us both by announcing she'd agreed to attend the Theta Xi winter formal with a freshman pledge named Connor. He was an engineering student in her calculus class. They'd hardly spoken, until he asked her. "I figured I might as well see what these things are like," she'd explained. So we helped her get ready and waited up for her to get back. Four hours later she walked into our dorm's living room and calmly told us that she'd had enough for one lifetime. We tried to get more information out of her, but as far as we could tell, her main objection was the way Connor followed her around all night, asking if she was having fun, and if he could get her another drink, or water, or anything.

"When do you want to go to the mall?" I asked Mel.

"Is Saturday morning crazy?"

"No," I said. "That'll be fine. Do you want to come?" I asked Logan, just as a formality. She'd worn the same short-sleeve red dress to every semiformal occasion that had arisen over the past two and a half years, and she looked so great every time that it seemed doubtful that anyone, if they noticed, would mind.

"Absolutely not," said Logan, "but you can take my car."

On Saturday morning I woke up early, well before the nine o'clock alarm I'd set the night before. I reached for my phone on my nightstand and scrolled through the alerts: a few Instagram likes, a few admin-type school emails, and a very dark Snapchat video of drunken dancing in the basement of what looked like the Phi Gamma house from this sophomore named Trisha. I had sat next to her two or three times in a creative writing class, which was apparently all it took to earn a spot on her Snapchat mailing list. "Wooooooo!" screamed Trisha, turning the camera around on her pink and shiny face. "[Unintelligible shrieking]!"

I got up from bed and went into the kitchen, making just a little more noise than I needed to in hopes I'd wake up Mel smoothly enough that she'd think she'd done it herself. I dropped a spoon into my bowl; I coughed; I let the cabinet doors fall shut against their frames. I sat down at the table to eat. I paused to listen but heard nothing. I looked at the clock: 8:52. I decided I would give her until 9:15.

When I was done eating, I decided 9:09 was closer to 9:15 than 9:00, and therefore close enough. After a few warning knocks I opened Mel's door to find her cocooned away in one of her contorted, uncomfortable-looking sleeping positions. Half her face was pressed flat into her paper-thin pillow, the comforter up around her head like a nun's habit so that only her mouth and right eye were visible. Her butt stuck up in the air, her right knee pulled up toward her elbow. She snored; not at this moment, but as a rule.

"Mellll," I sang. "Wake up! It's time to go shoppingggg."

"Unh," she said, and her head slipped backward into the duvet like a turtle.

"It's ten o'clock," I said, rounding up.

Beneath the puffy purple mounds I heard faint burbling.

"We should really go soon," I said. "It's not going to be easy to find a dress for eighty bucks that isn't trash."

"Fifty," said the bed.

"Well. We'll see what's even left by the time we get there."

I stepped closer, watching for signs of movement. After thirty seconds or so she seemed to sink deeper into the cocoon, perhaps believing that I'd left.

"Mel!" I said.

"FINE," she said, flipping the top half of her comforter over onto her legs. She picked up her phone from the wicker end table next to her bed. "It's nine thirteen," she said.

"I know," I said. "I thought you'd want to shower before we left."

Eyes still closed, she reached a hand into her hair and ran it through a few times.

"Yeah," she said. "You're right."

*   *   *

Nearly two hours later, we walked into the freezing fluorescence of Bergner's, the nicest of the shitty department stores in our shitty local mall. Scattered golden-yellow placards announced clearances of 30 to 50 percent—never more and never less. We were early enough that the only other people in the store were various combinations of moms, babies, and grandmothers. We walked in wary silence through Women's Contemporary and Women's Delicates, both of us trying to psych ourselves up for the strategic tug-of-war that was convincing Mel to spend money on clothing.

In one of the back corners of the store we found the small, squarish area devoted to formal dresses. Unhappily, we both noticed it was the one spot in the store without sale signs.

"OK," I said. "Most of these are going to be prom dresses."

"OK."

"Ninety-nine percent of prom dresses will not work for your dance. It's possible there might be a simple one somewhere in there. But I'm not confident."

"OK."

"Let's split up," I said. "To save time."

"OK," she sighed. She pulled her hair into a ponytail and immediately took it out.

For a while we patrolled our respective halves of the section, picking things off the racks and inspecting them more closely under the light. After I'd found two dresses I liked I looked over to check on Mel, who was standing very still facing a turquoise dress with a satin top and two feet of tulle layers that cascaded down from the waist.

"No," I said. She turned around to face me.

"It's sixty dollars."

"It's hideous," I said. She rolled her eyes.

"I give up!"

"Just do one last look-through," I said. "I'm almost done."

She sighed and turned back to the racks, dragging her hand along the fabrics as she passed them. I knew she probably wouldn't pick anything up. I knew that while she was trying on the dresses I picked out for her, I would go back over the ones she'd walked by and pick up a few more she'd passed over. I thought it was important that we both pretend she had some say.

I'd just added a short, charcoal-gray strapless dress to my pile when she reached the fitting rooms at the back, still empty-handed.

"Can I just take what you have?"

"Yes," I said. "I'll keep looking, but come out with each of them. Even if you think you hate it. Because you might be wrong." Mel was silent as she took the dresses off my arm and headed back into the fitting room.

While I waited for her to come back out, I picked up two more options: a red wrap dress that was borderline too casual but could be dressed up with shoes and jewelry; and a black-on-black brocade short-sleeve that was maybe too boxy, and also a little funereal, but it was only $75, and we didn't have much to work with.

When she came out a few moments later—in the royal-blue but unfortunately too-big A-line, which I'd predicted she'd try first as it was both her favorite color as well as the cheapest—I handed her the other dresses I'd found and sat down in one of the dingy velour chairs that were placed outside the waiting room for friends, family, and impassive boyfriends. Once, when Mel and I were in this same store, looking for swimsuits, a fitting room attendant had asked us if we wanted to share a fitting room.

It had always been my understanding that sharing rooms was against shopping mall law, if unevenly enforced—I'd worked in a Gap one summer in high school and we'd been told never to allow it. ("Even if it's two guys or two girls," the manager, Dawn, had said. "Anyone could be a couple planning to have sex these days.") The fact that someone in Bergner's had willingly offered it to us made it feel like a privilege, like she'd seen us walking in and right away known we deserved to stay together. I would have said OK, but Mel had replied, "No, separate's fine," and she was put in one little beige-carpeted room and me in another. But the nice thing about waiting was that it was a surprise each time she shuffled out through the curtains, and I liked the job of standing behind her at the mirror, pulling at hems and tucking pockets and holding hair back to see if having it up changed the way we felt about the outfit.

Mel worked her way through the pile, from the next-most cheap to cheapest after that. The funeral dress was too gloomy after all; the wrap dress was decent, but we agreed that it made her look a little lawyery, which was not a bad look, if not necessarily the one she wanted for tonight. She came out last in the gray silk strapless, which had been my favorite going in, and which cost $99. The look on her face when she walked out suggested that she knew it fit her perfectly, and she was not happy about it.

"That looks amazing on you and you know it," I said.

"I don't knowww," she said, though it was obvious she did. She stood up on the platform and turned side to side, hands clasped at the space just under her chest.

"You are the body type strapless dresses are made for," I said. Really it went beyond that—she was the body type *clothing* was made for. Five six, flat-chested, thin arms and legs, full hips and butt. She would look like this forever, I felt sure; her mom had the exact same body, and she was fifty-two.

"Is it too long?" she asked, facing the mirror straight on, lifting up on her toes and back down as if to mimic high-heeled shoes.

"You are making up problems."

"It's sooo expensive," she said, our eyes meeting in the mirror.

"It's a little expensive," I agreed, though inwardly I thought not really, not for her. "But you will be able to wear this like a hundred times. It's cheaper and smarter overall to buy fewer things that are versatile and good quality and cost a little more than a bunch of garbage you wear once and throw away." I gave a version of this spiel most times we went shopping. I tried not to call upon specific garbage she'd bought and thrown away unless I really had to.

"I knowwww," she said. "I just feel like I could practically make this myself."

"You definitely could not."

"Well, if I had a sewing machine."

"Still no."

She smiled at me in the mirror and then turned around.

"Do you really like it?" she asked.

"Yes," I said. "I love it, and I'm not just saying that because you have to get something today. I actually love it."

"It is really pretty," she said. She was softening. So far this had been the easiest it had ever been to convince her to buy something she needed and liked, and I wondered how much of it had to do with the fact that it was for a party she was going to with Will.

Like extravagantly bored royalty, we spent the entire day getting ready for the dance. I curled Mel's hair into waves while she braided Logan's hair into a tight crown, and when she and I were both done, I moved over to Logan, pulling out a selective few wisps to make her look more glamorous and less like Kirsten, the American Girl doll. They took turns going into the tub to shave their legs. I did their makeup while they sat on the couch in the living room watching a movie on TV, and when I was done we went into the kitchen to take preparatory shots of tequila. By then it was just after seven. The dance, which was being held at the golf club in town, started at eight.

"You guys look so good," I said.

"Thank you," said Logan.

"It's only thanks to you," said Mel, which was untrue, but nice.

"What do you think Will's gonna wear?" I asked. I'd never seen him out of basketball shorts and a T-shirt (in spring) or sweatpants and a hoodie (the rest of the year), and I could not imagine his wiry Gumby body in a suit. It could go either one direction or the other: would it make him look like a man, or a little boy?

"I dunno." Mel shrugged.

"I can see him wearing, like, a vest and bow tie," said Logan.

"Oh," I said. "Yeah. Yeah, me, too."

"Mm," said Mel. She didn't care much about the things boys wore—I think she actually liked Will's gym shorts, because they highlighted his butt—but this was a possibility she hadn't considered, and she didn't love it.

"Is Peter taking . . . what's that girl's name?"

"Nora," said Logan. "And no, thank god—did we not tell you about this??"

"No!" I said.

"She's bringing her ex-girlfriend who goes to ISU," said Mel. "Casey or something?"

"Yeah, Casey," said Logan. "She's super hot. Like, when they're side by side it's almost too much."

"Nora showed us pictures," Mel explained.

"Peter is going to light himself on fire," said Logan gleefully.

"Wow," I said. "Nora is so cool."

"I know," said Logan and Mel.

I wished then that I was going with them. But I was not, strictly speaking, a member of the biology honor society, and I knew that if I were to go, that fact would ruin it for me. In between moments of dancing and drinking and watching couples fight, they would talk about professors and medical schools. I knew this because I spent seventh grade feeling left out of the Bible study group that met for pizza parties every Wednesday night at Allison Burns's house, until one week I let her copy my civics worksheet and in return she invited me to Bible study. So I went, and I sat there for two hours with an empty juice box and two pizza crusts on a paper plate on the floor in front of me while people who weren't my friends talked about the Bible, and not at all to me. When my mom picked me up afterward I was confused and vaguely angry. How had those girls made that sound so exciting? It made no sense, and I'd told my mom as much.

"Are you interested in Christianity?" she'd asked.

"I don't know," I said. "No," I decided.

"Well," she said. "Then they're probably just not your crowd."

I hadn't replied, but I'd thought: *The whole point was that I wanted them to be.*

"Anyway, from everything you've told me, Allison Burns sounds like a brat," my mom had added.

I'd refused to agree, even though she was correct. Allison Burns was mean and didn't like me, just like everyone else I'd ever wanted to be friends with. Until I met Logan and Mel. My mom never met them; their timelines in my life didn't overlap. But from the beginning I was sure she would have loved them. I looked at them across the table from me, both antsy and hunched over and uncomfortable-looking in their dresses, and loved them so much I felt nauseous.

"You guys look so pretty," I said. "I know I already said that."

"I mean, I'm not going to put a limit on it," said Logan.

Mel looked over at the clock on the microwave, and I followed her gaze: It was 7:22. It would take them about fifteen minutes to walk over to the gym parking lot, where their shuttle was picking them up.

"We should probably head over soon," she said.

"Do you guys want another shot?" I asked. They both nodded and held up their glasses, which I filled up so full that a little bit of tequila spilled onto their hands. "Sorry!" I said. "I feel nervous and I'm not even going!"

"It's seriously not going to be that fun," said Mel. That she appeared to believe it only meant she was trying very hard not to hope for too much.

"I plan to have a great time," said Logan. "Which means I probably won't remember if I actually had fun or not."

"Well, text me," I said. "If you remember. If you get bored."

"I will," said Logan, standing up. Mel followed suit. They smoothed out their dresses, double-checking their bags for money, IDs, lip products, and phones.

"I feel like you guys are my husbands shipping off for the war or something," I said.

"Why husbands?" said Logan.

"You're right," I said. "Wives."

I hugged them, fixed a bobby pin in Logan's crown, and pushed them out the door. After it closed behind them I turned to face the empty kitchen, very quickly remembering I had nothing to do. And I was a little drunk.

"I guess I should read a book?" I asked the house. It had no opinion.

I decided that if I had another drink, I might come up with a good plan by the time I finished it. I took a beer from the refrigerator and uncapped it with Logan's refrigerator magnet bottle remover. I carried it to my desk, where I took a sip, said "Yuck," and then took another four. Logan kept telling me the taste would grow on me, but it had to be happening very slowly, because two years had gone by and I couldn't say I'd noticed any improvement at all.

14

It was the first image in my head when I woke up. An impersonal but undeniable memory, like a scene I'd watched in a movie about someone who looked an awful lot like me: me sliding into my room on my socks, half-drunk third beer in hand, picking up my laptop with the other and taking it into my bed. Logging onto Facebook. Typing in Keith's name. Seeing he'd written a new status earlier that afternoon.

And *liking it.*

I sprang up in my bed. A rush of air made cool contact with the back of my neck, which I realized was covered in sweat, at the same moment that my forehead pulsed in protest of the sudden movement. I kicked off my comforter, pulled off my T-shirt, and sat still for a moment in my sports bra and shorts. When my body had recalibrated, I gently leaned over to pick my phone up off the nightstand. It was only 7:14. I couldn't remember when exactly I fell asleep, but I saw that I had a new text from Logan, with a timestamp that read 2:12, so I knew it must have been before that. All her message said was "Lol."

Ominous. I would have to figure that out later.

I opened Facebook and went to Keith's page. Sure enough, there was a bright blue thumb under his status, which meant, against everything I knew to be right and true, that I had liked it. "Unlike," it offered, and I held my thumb over it for a second or two, but Facebook and I both knew it was far too late. Worse even than to have liked it and have him know would be to have liked it and, hours later, unliked it, and have him know. It was cruel, this false offering of a second chance. There was really no such thing.

I read the status for a second time, though I hardly remembered the first. It was a quote: "This deficiency in our ideas is not, indeed, perceived in common life, nor are we sensible, that in the most usual conjunctions of cause and effect we are as ignorant of the ultimate principle, which binds them together, as in the most unusual and extraordinary."

I read it three more times, quickly at first and then very slowly, mouthing each word as I went. I squinted at it, trying to remember what I thought when I saw it last night.

"What?" I whispered. *Why did I like this?*

I copied and pasted the sentence into Google, which informed me that it was by David Hume, from a book called *A Treatise of Human Nature*. I hadn't heard of it, much less read it, though it certainly fit the profile for something Keith would find quotable. Attempting to do so now, skimming through a few pages that were printed online, I couldn't imagine any reading material more torturous for someone in my condition. The run-on sentences (which were, as far as I could tell, about nothing) rolled over each other until I felt motion sick.

I closed my eyes and slid back down into bed, feeling chilled and clammy and horrible. When I opened them I looked one last time—I was one of *only two* people who'd liked it so far, I noted; just me and some idiot named "Grant"—and then carefully closed out of his page, afraid I'd somehow slip and click everything else there was to be clicked. I turned my phone off entirely, wiggled over to the edge of my bed, and slid it onto the floor underneath. I could only hope that when I woke back up, an hour or two from now, it would be gone.

"Ugggghhhhhhhhh," a voice moaned, dragging me out of an unintelligible hangover dream: the inside of my mouth and tongue coated in sand, me spitting over and over again but never able to get it all out.

I paused to listen, unsure whether the voice had been real.

There was a small scratching sound, which seemed to come from the bottom of my bedroom door. I looked over and saw a little shadow move just underneath it. Had the sun not been shining violently, unnecessarily brightly through my windows, were I not hungover, and had I not, hours earlier, committed a grievously mortifying social media error, I surely would have screamed. But all those things were true. If it was somehow a murderer outside my door, I wasn't sure I even cared.

"Harriettttt," the voice moaned. Logan.

"What," I croaked.

"Help."

"I can't get up."

"God!" she said, and then there was a smack against my door, like she'd used her last jolt of energy to fling her arm against it. "Ow," she said.

"Just come in."

She groaned, and a full minute of silence passed, each of us waiting for the other to cave. Then I heard fabric sliding over the floor, and my door swung open. Logan, her sweatshirt hood up, sat on the floor. Her makeup had migrated from above her eyes to below them. I raised a limp hand to wave hello. She closed her eyes and slid on her butt across the floor until she got to my bed, when she reached one arm up to me. I grabbed it and helped pull her up on the bed, like a mountaineer helping her partner up over a cliff. Finally she rolled onto my bed next to me, and we lay there facing each other, both in the fetal position.

"You smell like you ate a dead person," I said.

"Fuck you. You also smell terrible."

"I know."

"I want to die."

"Same."

"Wait—" she said, squinting at me through one open eye. "Why do YOU smell like booze? Just from two shots?"

"I drank three of your beers after you left," I said. "Sorry."

"That's OK," she said. Then: "The Coronas? Those were kind of old, I think."

"I honestly cannot ever tell either way."

"Well," she said. "That sounds fun."

"No," I said, grabbing her wrist. "Logan. I *liked* Keith's Facebook status."

She laughed, a single short "HA."

"That doesn't mean anything," she continued, lying.

"Yes, it does," I said. "It might be the worst thing I have ever done."

"What did it say?"

"Logan."

"What."

"It was a *David Hume quote.*"

"I don't know who that is."

"He's a philosopher. Was."

She laughed again. "Of course."

"I know. I read it again this morning and I don't even know

what it means. Like I 'get it,' on a basic English comprehension level. But also I literally don't think it means...anything."

"It probably doesn't," said Logan. "Just like 'I'm a man! I am uniquely able to notice that the world is not as it seems!'"

I laughed, feeling for one instant like it really wasn't a big deal.

"I just don't want him to think I want him to think about me," I said.

"What?"

"Ugh, nothing," I said. I was so thirsty.

"Harriet."

Logan took a deep breath and moved a sweatshirt-covered arm over her face.

"What! The dance? Tell me! Oh my god, did something happen?"

"Something terrible happened," she said. What I could see of her face was contorted in anguish.

I reached over and pulled her arm off. She looked at me, then quickly closed her eyes.

"I accidentally kissed Peter Dorffman," she wailed.

"With your own mouth??"

"Yes! Oh, *godddddd*." She rotated on her stomach, prostrating herself. She moaned unintelligibly into my pillow. Her hood slid partway off her head; pieces of hair stuck spikily out of the braided crown that Mel had so painstakingly created the night before, creating the effect of a lion's mane.

"But...how?" I asked. "Why?"

"I don't knowww," she said. "We were dancing near each other, I guess because we were like the only two people who didn't have dates? And then it just happened."

"What does that mean?" I asked. "People are always saying

stuff 'just happened' and I never know what that means. Someone
has to be doing something."

"I don't know," she said. "It just happened."

"Logan!"

"Like, one minute our faces were not touching, and then
they ... were."

"Oh," I said. "I get it now."

"Ugh," she groaned, burying her face again. "I just remembered that he licked my lips."

"What! No!"

She pulled her hands to the side of her face and whined for a
little bit.

"Someone else can't just lick your lips for you," I said.

"I know!" she said. "God, he's such a fucking twerp."

We looked at each other, both aware that neither of us had
heard, much less used, the word "twerp" in years or possibly ever,
surprised to find how effectively it summed everything up. Peter
was a twerp. Keith was a twerp too, I thought.

"The only relief in this," said Logan, "is that we were both
clearly just kissing out of boredom, or whatever."

"Are you sure about that?" I asked. Logan tended to ascribe
much more utilitarianism to other people's feelings and thought
processes than was actually there. Plus, Peter was a nerd—and
not like a hot one with interesting glasses—and Logan was a
pretty, cool girl who had kissed him.

Only one of us was surprised when he texted her ("good morning :)") an hour later.

I'd stayed in bed as long as I possibly could, getting up only
to make breakfast and then retreating back under the comforter
with it. There was no sign of Mel all morning. It didn't seem pos-

sible that she would stay at Will's this long, without any of her books and without a change of clothes. Logan and I figured that the likeliest possibility was that she'd come by early this morning while we were still asleep, changed, and left for the library. Around one thirty, we headed there, too. On the walk over, we discussed various options for handling what we'd already come to refer to as the Peter Problem.

"I'm just not gonna respond," said Logan.

"I think you should maybe respond once today," I said, "since you have to see him all the time, and you did just make out literally yesterday. But then after that, if he keeps texting you this week—"

"God! He's going to, isn't he. Jesus."

"Yes—and then you ignore him."

"Fuck! I'm such an idiot! What if he tells Nora?"

"I'm sure he won't," I said. I was not at all sure. "You just have to be very curt. Absolutely no emoticons—"

"Do you think I'm stupid??"

"—and no hahas or lols whatsoever," I said.

"I'm sure that won't be a problem."

By then we were inside the library's doors, and, with a dejected little wave, Logan headed upstairs to hide away at a third-floor desk. I looked over toward circulation; the 10–2 shift people were still sitting there, and Remy hadn't yet shown up. I was still ten minutes early, so I went downstairs to buy hangover salves (pretzels and a bottle of blue Gatorade) from the vending machines.

The basement was cool and dimly lit. It was also nearly empty—in most cases students found it too dark and depressing down there (though there were vague and unsubstantiated rumors of hidden make-out corners), but today I found the fallout shelter—like atmosphere soothing. I took my snacks and sat down on one of the dusky green couches in the rotunda, pulling my legs up under me. With the Gatorade I swallowed a pair of Advil from the travel-size pillbox I kept in my backpack. I went to pull out my phone but then remembered there was no reception. I looked around the room, and once I'd confirmed there was still nobody in the immediate vicinity, I arranged my backpack into a makeshift pillow and curled up into it. For a few minutes I lay there staring at the empty couch across from me, pretending my temporary inability to see the proof meant that last night hadn't ended the way it had. I'd finished that first beer, and then I'd gone to bed to read a book. I'd never liked Keith's Facebook status at all. Never even met him. Keith who?

My eyes opened at the same time a single jolt shook through my body. I looked straight ahead at the couch opposite mine, where an enormously muscular guy in sweats and a windbreaker sat chugging yellow Gatorade, his backpack still on. I watched him for a few seconds—was he going to finish it all in one go?—before realizing that I'd fallen asleep and was now probably late.

I shot up in my seat, drawing muscle guy's eyes in my direction. He stopped drinking and wiped his mouth with the sleeve of his jacket. He seemed surprised by my presence, which I found annoying given the fact that I'd been here longer. *I was here first,* I wanted to say. But instead I pulled out my phone: 2:13.

"Shit," I whispered. I didn't dare look up to see if muscle guy was still watching me. I pulled on my backpack and ran up the stairs two at a time. When I got to the top and walked around the corner, I saw Remy sitting there, hunched over her computer, and felt my head swim with anxiety. The last twenty-four hours had pushed the column to the back of my mind; now that I was here, seeing her for the first time in what felt like years but was really not even three weeks, I wasn't sure what exactly I hoped she'd say.

It wasn't until I'd pushed through the gate that Remy looked up from her notebook. We smiled at each other; hers looked somewhat strained. She was wearing a sweatshirt—an ordinary one, a pullover from our campus store—and she looked tired. Well, she'd been sick.

"I am so sorry," I said. "I got here early and went downstairs to buy Gatorade, because I'm hungover, and then I literally fell asleep on the couch downstairs, like a freshman."

Remy laughed. "It's OK!! You didn't miss anything."

"I woke up and there was some huge guy also drinking Gatorade on the couch across from me, and he was drinking the whole bottle at once, which I did not think was possible in real life. I think the sound of him gulping is what woke me up, that's how vigorous it was. But I like, jumped awake, and he didn't say sorry for waking me up. Which seems weird. Even though I am glad he did because I was late, obviously," I said, rambling and unpacking my bag in tandem.

"Hey, can I talk to you about something?" Remy said, swiveling in her chair to face me. I looked at her face, serious and anxious, and I felt my own drain of color.

"Sure," I said. I realized I was standing there still holding a textbook aloft over the desk, and I carefully set it down. I sat down in my chair, folding my hands in my lap like a TV therapist.

"I'm sorry," said Remy, self-conscious in a way she hadn't been seconds ago, pulling her expression into something less open. "I just completely cut you off."

"No!" I said. "I was done, and also I was talking about nothing. What is it?"

"OK," she said. "Sorry. With break and then being sick I haven't talked to hardly anyone in like two weeks and I think I've gone a little crazy, ha." Her voice sounded even throatier than normal, which I envied even though she just said she'd been sick.

"I bet," I said. "I felt that way over break and that was just one week."

"OK," she said. "Well. This might be weird, because we haven't known each other that long, but I don't really have a lot of close friends. Or like, any, really, anymore. And I think you're really nice and a good person to talk to." She blushed, and I felt like complete shit. I wasn't really nice. I'd just tricked her, some-how, into thinking I was.

"Thank you," I said.

"OK, so, anyway: I just broke up with my boyfriend," she said, smiling and throwing her hands in the air like it wasn't that big a deal at all, really, seriously.

"Oh!" I said, in my best and mildest feigned surprise. Don't look suspicious, I thought, though I wasn't sure exactly how to not. Great lengths of silent staring probably didn't help, I realized. "I'm sorry," I added, lamely. "That's . . . not fun."

"Thanks," she said. "I'm like, fine, it's just that it happened last night so it's all I can really think about right now." She looked at me in a way that made it clear she wanted to say more but was waiting to see what I said first. I thought I could feel Emma hovering there. Curiosity made me desperate to know whatever it was Remy might say about her, but some other un-named impulse made me want to hold my hand over her mouth so she couldn't. I'd imagined I'd have to slyly drag this confes-sion out of Remy, and now that she was offering it so willingly I wasn't sure I wanted to hear what she had to say.

"Of course," I said. "I'd be a wreck, too. Not that you seem like a wreck or anything—"

She smiled. "No," she said, "I mean, I kind of am."

"If you wanted to go home, I would understand. I could punch your timecard out," I said.

"That's so nice, thank you," she said. "But if I go home I'll just, like, pace around. At least being here is sort of a distraction." I felt as relieved at her staying as I had at the possibility of her leaving.

"Do you want me to pull the fire alarm?" I asked.

She laughed. "Maybe. Not yet. I'll let you know."

"OK," I said. "Well. You don't have to tell me anything you don't want, but if you want to tell me anything, you...can. I have very little interest in being productive today."

"Good," she said. "Me, too."

Her phone vibrated then, and she leaned over to look at it. Her expression upon seeing whatever she saw there was unreadable. She picked it up off the desk and dropped it on the pile made by her coat and book bag on the floor behind her chair.

"OK, so," she started. Involuntarily I took a deep breath, which I then tried to mask with a cough, which kind of made me choke. "Are you OK?"

"Yes," I wheezed. "Sorry. Talk."

"OK, so—you know *Dear Emma?*" she said.

I will die in this chair, I thought. I couldn't envision a future beyond this conversation, so it must've been true that there wasn't one. Not for me. Still, I arranged every bit of focus I had into seeming like an unconcerned, impartial, casual listener.

"Yes," I said. Keep it short. That was the way to go.

"So, this is kind of embarrassing," she said. "But I wrote to her about Keith—my boyfriend. Ex-boyfriend."

I nodded. *This is all new information to me!*

I should have let her keep going but I couldn't help myself. "I don't think that's embarrassing," I said. "I have plenty of friends who've written to her."

"Right," she said. "I know. I would never judge anyone else for writing to her. I don't know why I feel so lame about it. It's stupid. Anyway—"

"Yes, sorry, I cut you off. I'm doing it again right now!"

"It's OK!" She laughed. "So, anyway, I wrote to her basically being like, we've been dating a few weeks and he hasn't texted me in three days, should we break up?"

"Mmm."

"Because, like, that's a thing, right? The three- or four-week thing that starts dying the moment it begins?"

"I think so," I said. "I don't have a lot of personal experience, but...I think so."

"It is," she said. "I'm sure it is. It's happened to me like eight times. And the way it always starts—like, the way you know the end is coming—is they don't text you back for a few days. Sometimes they'll sputter on beyond that, but it's always really strained from that point on. Because they were trying to send you a message, by not sending you any actual messages, and now they're just waiting for you to get it and break up for them," she said.

"That's the most words I've ever heard you say in a row," I said.

She smiled. "I didn't sleep much last night, so I think I'm kind of hysterical."

"No," I said. "What you said made perfect sense."

She looked briefly disappointed, like she'd hoped that she really was just crazy.

"Well, anyway," she continued, "I wrote the letter over spring break, and she wrote back saying she'd answer my question, so I wanted to kind of stall until then. Even though I think I knew what she'd say."

"Sure," I said.

"But then break was over and Keith and I saw each other on . . . Tuesday, I think it was, and it was just weird. Like. I maybe was being weird, because I was just thinking about the letter the whole time. But he seemed weird too, and distant, and didn't say anything about not texting me. So I made up studying I had to do the next two nights and was like 'We'll hang out this weekend,' but on Friday I read her response and it just felt like, what's the point, you know? Did you read it?" she asked.

"Ummm, I think I skimmed part of it," I said.

"Well, basically she was like, 'It's not worth it. They're all the same.'"

It was unnerving, hearing my own letter summed up so tidily. Remy didn't seem unhappy with the advice; she was merely recounting it for my benefit, for context she didn't know I had. But surely there had been more to it than that.

"Hm," I said. "I mean, I don't doubt that."

"Me neither," she said. She slid her hands into the front pocket of her sweatshirt.

"So . . ." I started. "You broke up with him the next day?"

She nodded. "I went over to his house yesterday afternoon, after going back and forth for, like, literally twelve hours. And it just sucked. It sucked. I don't even really remember what either of us said."

She took her hands back out, folded them in her lap, then crossed them in front of her. I was afraid she wouldn't stop and I wouldn't know what to do. But she settled on a weird pose, one elbow on the back of the chair, her head in her hand, and the other draped across her torso, clasping the other arm. It couldn't have been comfortable. It looked like she was trying to be.

"Was he surprised?" I asked.

"Kind of?" she said. "He can get really quiet, and sometimes it's hard to tell why."

I had to stop the "Yeah, I know" from coming out of my mouth.

"Ah," I said. "That's ... annoying."

"It really is!"

"Do you—how do you feel about it now?"

"I can't tell," she said. "Right afterward, last night, I went home and felt sort of ... vindicated, or something. Because he didn't really fight me very hard on it. On breaking up. But then, this morning, I guess, that same thing just made me sad."

We sat there for a moment, each of us trying to decide whether there was anything else worth saying. Before I could make up my mind either way, she said, "Anyway, that's all," and shrugged. She looked like she was going to cry.

"I'm going to do something that might be weird, OK?" I said. "I'm going to come hug you."

She laughed in a way that suggested that was fine, so I slid off my chair and walked over to her. I bent over her awkwardly, and she reached her arms up into the spaces under my elbows. There was way too much space between us. But then again, we hadn't been friends for very long.

When I walked up our house's little driveway that evening, I felt like I'd been gone for three days. It was still light outside the way it hadn't been after 6:00 PM in months. It didn't feel possible that it was the same sunlight I'd woken up in.

I unlocked the side door, in a hurry to see who would be

home. Though I didn't want to be alone I tried to expect no one, but was relieved to see Mel at her desk with the bedroom door open as soon as I got inside. Her hair hung wet at her shoulders; it was the only time it was ever completely straight. She was wearing pajamas—her high school tennis team T-shirt and the now-ratty black Springfield sweatpants her parents had bought her on move-in day freshman year. A towel was folded over the back of her chair. I wondered if she'd only just gotten home, and if so, from where.

"Hey," she said, looking up only after I'd dropped my things on the kitchen table.

"Hi," I said. I walked into her room and sat on her bed, and she turned around to face me.

"How was work?"

"It was fine," I said. I felt that I should not go first. She could recount her night, and her morning, and *then* I would tell her about Keith, and Remy, and Keith and Remy. "How was the dance?"

"It was good!" she said. "Umm...I'm like, trying to remember any interesting parts...Oh!!! Well, you heard Logan made out with Peter Dorffman!" She smacked her hand onto the table gleefully, and I laughed.

"She told me," I said. "She was like, 'It's nothing, we both knew it was just the alcohol.' And then he texted her before noon."

"I know! She said you told her to text him back, and I was like, 'OK, I guess that makes sense,' but...mannnn, I do not think he is going to be easy to get rid of," she said.

"Really?" I asked. "Well. We'll just have to help her."

"YOU can help her," she said. "I have no idea how to deal with that kid."

"I mean, you could try," I said, feeling annoyed and not totally sure why. "You know him better than I do."

"OK, well, nothing else has happened yet," she said. "And Logan doesn't exactly have trouble telling people what she thinks. So there probably isn't any need to worry about it."

"I'm not worried about it, I was just trying to have a conversation about our friend," I said. "Who you brought up."

"I know," she said. "I just don't think it's our job to fix it for her."

"'Fix it for her'?" I said. "What is your deal all of a sudden? Like we haven't always constantly told each other what to do about everything?"

Mel was full of *shit*, I thought. Logan might have been blunt, but she had almost as much trouble getting rid of people she didn't like as anyone else did. And though she might not think she needed it anymore, now that she had an apparently perfectly figured out life, Mel had had plenty of crises of her own. And she had asked us to help her with them all.

"I just don't think everything needs, like, a strategy," she said.

I stared at her, trying to tell from the look on her face whether she understood how badly the thing she'd just said hurt me. Either she didn't, or, for the first time in her life, she'd learned how to keep the way she really felt off her face.

"OK," I said. "You're right! Why should we talk to each other about anything?" I stood up from her bed, knowing how childish I was being, but too stubborn to stop now that I'd started.

"Harriet—"

"I'm going to my room. I have a lot of work to do. Including writing my meddling column! So, I'll see you later," I said. I paused for less than half a second in her doorway, wanting her to stop me but determined not to let her. But all she said was "Fine."

I closed her door behind me, even though she'd had it open before. I wanted to be able to move around the kitchen without having to pretend she wasn't four feet away from me. I opened the cabinets and slammed them behind me, and I set a bowl hard on the table. I poured the milk as angrily as I possibly could, which made it come out too quickly, and some of it splashed onto the table. I said "Shit!" just loudly enough that Mel might've heard me through the door, assuming she hadn't already (angrily) put on headphones.

I carried the bowl into my room and set it down carefully. I sat down on the floor and started eating it, and then I pictured myself: dirty and hungover on the floor eating cereal, unceremoniously ghosted, having a simmering, weeks-long fight that I didn't quite understand with one of my best friends, one I'd thought was at least close to being resolved but clearly wasn't. And then I started to cry. And then the fact that I was crying into a bowl of Kix made me laugh a little. But then I thought of Mel, only maybe thirty feet away but so suddenly strange and unknowable, and I started crying again. I'd gone into her room to hear about her night and tell her about mine, and somehow I'd done neither.

*   *   *

Dear Emma,

I'm a theater major, and for the majority of the time I've been one, I have been thrilled about it. I am good at it. I get good roles. I get pretty good grades and my professors have nice things to say about my performances.

I think the main source of doubt for me is my family. I have three older siblings, all of whom work as or are studying to be doctors. This is something we joke about—they'll be rich and I'll be broke; they have to be straight-laced because I sucked up the whole family's creativity. None of that has ever bothered me much. But the last time I was home, it was implied by one of my brothers that there was another difference: they'll be helping people, and I will not.

I don't think it's true that art doesn't help people. I don't believe my classmates are selfish. But ever since that "joke" I've found myself setting myself apart—like it's not wrong for them to pursue this, but it is for me. This is going to sound narcissistic but I think part of that is for many of them, I can't see them doing anything else. I could have. I came in as a premed major and I was good at that, too. I could be learning how to save people's lives and I chose to stop. How do I stop feeling guilty about doing what I want to do? And, maybe harder, how do I know that I'm right about what it is I thought I wanted?

Sincerely,
Existential Black Sheep

Dear EBS,

There are probably three main ways to stop feeling guilty for something: first, to convince yourself that what you did was right and not wrong; second, to accept that what you did was a mistake, and making mistakes is part of the human experience, and all you can do from here on out is your best not to make them again; and third, to realize that the thing you're feeling guilty about doesn't really matter either way. So: You shouldn't feel guilty for wanting to study theater and not medicine because you tried both, and you liked one of them more. That means you're right. And you don't seem to think of your choice as a mistake, and neither do I, so this one doesn't apply. And finally: you shouldn't feel guilty for choosing theater over medicine because it doesn't really matter that much.

I hope that doesn't sound cruel. Bear with me.

What you do with your future does, of course, matter to you. And it matters, somewhat, to your family, as people who support you. But please don't allow yourself to indulge in any sort of self-pitying fantasy in which you're a would-be martyr who chose hedonism instead. You did well enough in your introductory coursework, but the truth is you might not have made it as a doctor. You might have failed the board exam— from what I understand, it's very difficult. You might not have gotten a job. Or you might have aced the program, gotten a job, and quit after a year because you couldn't take the suffering. You might have become a doctor and taken up community theater on the weekends, and found yourself loving that hobby so much you wished you'd taken it seriously sooner. You don't know.

Even if you did make it, who knows what kind of doctor you would've been? Not every doctor is literally saving people's lives. Don't trick yourself into believing that your siblings are capital-g Good because of their careers, and you aren't, or can't be. Your job is just one way to be good to other people. There are lots of others. One everyday one to start with, for you, is to think more highly of your classmates. What makes you think they couldn't be doing other things? Don't you conceive of them as "theater people" first and foremost because you know them in this confined context alone? Surely they think of you the same way. They don't know that you were once *almost* a doctor. That you feel the need to differentiate yourself from them as multitalented with a wide range of possible futures says something about you, not them.

I don't mean to be too hard on you. This is not an uncommon plight among arts and humanities students—and probably students and young people of all kinds, honestly. None of us is especially, uniquely uncertain. All of us have gone home to be asked "And what do you plan to do with that?" by other people, as if those people are now doing exactly what it is they thought they'd do at 19 or 20. As if they've lived out lives of perfect usefulness and unceasing integrity. Obviously, it's harder to hear it from three people at once—especially, I imagine, ones who share your genes. But you have to shut out what they said. Stop thinking of yourself as someone who deigned to study acting when you could have done more. Start thinking of yourself as someone who found something they wanted to do and chose to do it. It's just one choice out of many, neither all-important nor unimportant to the way the rest of your life will go.

You picked this path for a reason, and I think you know what it is. It's normal to start worrying about your future toward the end of college. It's going to keep happening to you. I couldn't stop you if I tried. But try not to worry too much about what's already behind you, particularly at the behest of other people. You have better things to do.

Most humbly yours,
Emma

15

Monday morning I woke up early, feeling calmer than my circumstances should have allowed. Everyone always said not to go to bed angry, but it seemed to me there was no better time to be full of rage than nighttime, swaddled in blankets, alone and glaring up at the ceiling. How much more harm could you do from there, reduced to the stature of a helpless, tired baby? It was hard, too, to keep it up over seven or eight hours of immobility. There had been times I went to bed angry and woke up still feeling it, but it was almost always lessened by then. Rain could make it worse, but it was raining out now, and even still I felt perfectly fine.

The reason I felt fine was that I was right about everything, and everyone else was an idiot who could go fuck themselves.

With my extra time, and the house to myself, I got ready slowly, deliberately. I would see Keith in class that afternoon, and he would see me. I had to look good, but casual. I had to look like an oxymoron: coincidentally perfect, thoughtlessly put together. I had to look like someone who'd known what I was doing when I clicked "like" so late on Saturday night but had already completely forgotten about it.

I decided that the outfit that said all this was black jeans and a striped T-shirt.

Despite my best efforts to arrive coolly on time, I got to class almost ten minutes early. I recognized the only two students who consistently got there before me, though I didn't know their names. In the front row sat a young-looking elfin girl, with very short strawberry-blond hair and thick, dark green glasses, who looked like someone who'd only recently recognized the potential of her face. Two rows back from her, slumped up against the right wall, was the guy who came to every class early in order to maximize the time he could spend sleeping through it.

I headed up the stairs toward the very back row, but three-quarters of the way there I changed my mind. The back row was for hiding. From it I could look straight ahead and see everyone else in the class, none of whom could see me. Someone who didn't care who saw her wouldn't always sit in the back. So I made myself stop three rows in front of the very back, and took the aisle seat there instead.

To prevent myself from staring at every person who walked through the door, I started writing unnecessary and nonbinding study plans in my planner. Monday night: *Read chapters 11–12 for Spanish Civil War. Tuesday: Read chapters 13–14 for Spanish Civil War. Wednesday: Day off from reading for Spanish Civil War, unless there is extra time and everything else for other classes is done.*

Two minutes before class started—the time I had intended to arrive—Keith walked in. I wasn't looking up at that moment; I identified him by the sound of his particular shuffling on the carpet through the door. He didn't pick up his feet all the way when he walked, and his shoelaces were never tight enough, so his shoes slipped around. I used to think it was cute, boyish. The last time we hung out we'd been walking from the library to the coffee shop for a study break, and I'd noticed how loose his shoes were and slowed down, falling behind him just a few steps. He was talking about something I couldn't remember now, probably because I was only half listening. With the tip of my boot I pressed down on the heel of his left shoe and laughed as he stepped right out of it. He'd laughed too, and fake-glared at me as he slid his foot back in. But he still didn't tie his shoes any tighter.

I watched him walk across the lecture room, past the first set of stairs and then up the next, right toward me, before he picked the aisle seat four rows ahead of mine. My staring was an accident at first, then intentional. If he noticed it, though, he didn't show it. He never looked over at me once. And as much as I knew I would have been embarrassed to be caught, I was furious when I wasn't. Why was it so easy for him to ignore me completely, even now? Liking a Facebook status was a dumb, drunken little gesture, but in doing so I had dared him to remember, to acknowledge that I existed. And now he wouldn't.

It was dumb to think I could cultivate an ice queen attitude with an outfit, I thought. A T-shirt and jeans, no less. I wasn't carefree, and I wasn't cold. I was fucking furious, and I was really, really hot. I felt my shirt cling to my underarms and I pulled it away from my body at the shoulder seams. I pulled my metal water bottle from my bag and surreptitiously held it against my cheek. I felt dizzy, and the thought of continuing like this for the next hour made me more panicky still. I looked up at the clock: It was 1:00, and Professor Ferrer hadn't come in yet. Now or never, I thought, and then I did something I'd never done in the entirety of my academic career: I threw my things back into my bag, stood up, and, without looking anywhere but straight ahead, I walked out.

I left the languages building on an adrenaline high. I hadn't run into Professor Ferrer, hadn't had to explain why I'd come to class only to leave it. It was early afternoon on a Monday and I was free. Gaining distance from something I hated. I sped toward the quad, which was empty: It was still too chilly for anyone to study outside, and still a few months yet before anyone could trick themselves into thinking they could get a tan. I was on autopilot toward home, but when I came up to the circle of stone memorial benches on the quad's center-west side, I stopped short. I didn't want to go home yet. I had too much energy. But Logan and Mel were in lab, and I didn't really want to see Mel anyway, and the campus was so small I didn't know where else to go. So I sat down on a bench for a while and imagined elaborate scenes in which Keith ran out after me and I listened stone-faced while he groveled at my feet, until the cold of the marble became too much for my butt to bear and I had to get up again.

I walked slowly in the direction of the coffee shop, more because it was straight ahead of me than anything else. I wanted to hang out with someone but wasn't sure I had options; it was Monday afternoon, and anyone I could think of who was even sort of my friend was either in class or, I feared, would find it strange to be asked to meet up with no notice. But then I remembered Remy saying something weeks ago about her weird class schedule and the permanent three-day weekends it gave her. I couldn't remember whether it was Friday or Monday she always had off, and I stopped still on the sidewalk and wondered whether I should message her to find out.

I opened Facebook on my phone and started to compose a new

message. Was this weird? Were we at the hanging-out-outside-of-work-study stage? I wanted to tell someone what I'd just done but if I told her I'd have to leave things out. Things like who, and why. *Whatever*, I thought, shrugging at no one. She was probably in class, or would say no anyway. It wouldn't hurt to just ask.

I typed: "Heyyyy Remy, this is maybe weird, but are you in class? I thought I remembered you saying something about having Mondays off, but I might be wrong. Anyway I just wondered if you were around and wanted to meet at the coffee shop to…get coffee. And hang out or something. I feel like I'm asking you out, haha. OK. I'll probably just be there for a few hours anyway so you can just stop by or something. If you want. OK byeee!"

I sent it before I could chicken out, then read it over and sighed. *I sound deranged*, I thought. Still, there was some comfort in knowing it was too late for me to pretend to be cooler.

When I got to the coffee shop, I found it empty save for a couple studying together on the couches by the window. The boy sat facing forward with his legs on the floor, and the girl sat on the other end, facing him, her feet resting on his lap. He was holding a textbook up in front of him like a novel, obviously straining to make this arrangement work. She was leaning against the back of the couch, head in folded arm, an actual novel in the other hand. When I walked past them I looked over, and they looked back at me in a way that made me feel as if I had wandered into their private living room.

I bought a hot chocolate and pulled my phone out of my coat pocket. I saw that Remy had responded to my message: "ha. hi! yes, i'm out of class today! i was just in the art building avoiding work so this is perfect. be there in 10."

I sat down at a table toward the back windows and took off my coat and bag. A few copies of last week's paper were strewn messily over the top, and I leaned forward to arrange them into a neat pile. I pulled the top copy toward me and was midway through reading point/counterpoint op-eds about getting gender-neutral bathrooms on campus when I noticed Remy coming down the stairs. I set down the paper and waved.

"Hey," she said, breezing past the couch couple and snaking through the tables toward mine. "I've had two coffees already today but I think I'm going to get another one." She laughed and flung her bag over the chair next to mine. I watched her approach the counter and, glancing behind her, noticed that the guy behind it was doing the same thing. He smiled, and she asked for something I couldn't hear, paying for the drink with a crumpled bill and change she fished out of her back pocket.

"OK, hi," she said, walking back over. She sat down and blew into the cup, still holding the lid in her hand. Black coffee.

"Hi," I said. "I'm so glad you were around!"

"Me, too!" she said. "I was just sitting in paint lab trying not to fall asleep. The piece isn't even due for like two weeks."

"I normally have class now but I walked out before it started!" I said immediately, even though I'd decided beforehand to not tell her that specific thing. "I don't know why," I lied. "But I didn't want to be there and I didn't want to go home either for some reason."

"Probably spring fever."

"Yeah," I said. "Like real spring, not spring break."

"Exactly."

We paused to take sips of our drinks, both of us realizing that we'd met up to sit down together for an indefinite amount of time, and now we were going to have to talk our way through it.

"I walked out of a class once," said Remy. "But it was like, halfway into it. It was a tiny studio class, so my teacher saw me bolt for the door and was like, 'Everything OK?' But I don't think I even responded. I left all my paint supplies there."

"What happened?"

"A guy from class collected them for me."

"No, I mean, what was wrong?" I said.

"Ohhh, ha," she said. "I was just having a panic attack."

"Oh," I said. "What exactly does that...involve?"

"I just get really light-headed and dizzy out of nowhere, even though I'm sitting. And my hands get clammy, and my heart races," said Remy. "But they're also different for different people," she added, and I knew then that she knew I was wondering if this was more or less what had just happened to me.

"I was just really hot all of a sudden," I said. "And I felt like I needed to be somewhere else, as quickly as possible."

She nodded. "I used to get them a lot, and my therapist always told me I needed to wait it out. So I try. But sometimes it happens at parties and I just go home without telling anyone."

In my head I saw that picture of her, standing over the beer pong table, smiling with her mouth closed.

"It felt kind of exhilarating to just leave," I said.

"Leaving is always good," she said. "But then I always feel bad later. I get home, and I'm like, 'OK, now what?'"

"Yeah," I said, and she watched me take another drink from my now-lukewarm cocoa. "God, I hope I didn't lose participation points," I said, and she laughed. I thought, *I hope Keith spent all of class wondering why I left.* "Anyway, how are you doing?"

"Oh," she said. "I'm...OK. I don't know if you can tell from the three coffees and the gigantic circles under my eyes, but I haven't been sleeping all that well."

"I don't think you look tired," I said. "I mean, I think your eyes look normal and good."

She smiled; it looked difficult. "Thanks."

"Because of—because of your breakup, you mean?" I couldn't bring myself to say his name out loud to her.

"Yeah, I guess," she said. "I mean, definitely. I don't want that to be the reason, but obviously it is."

"Have you talked to him any more?"

"Sort of," she said. "I still had a couple of his sweatshirts in my room so I texted him to ask if I could return them. But he just told me to leave them in a bag on his porch."

"Jeez. I'm sorry."

"It's OK," she said. "It's done. Now I just have to kind of . . . suffer through it."

"Unfortunately, I think that is true," I said. "And it's only been a couple of days. It's going to take a little while before you feel good about it."

"Yeah," she said. "I just wish he would've at least let me give him his stuff back in person."

"Maybe it's better not to see him," I said. I wasn't sure why she was dwelling on this point, or what reason she could have for still wanting to talk to him. If it were me, I would have wanted to leave the clothes in a neutral territory, like maybe the center of the track at the gym. I would have sprinted there and dropped it off and sprinted away, like I was leaving a briefcase full of ransom cash. I would have hoped never to see him again. I *had* hoped never to see him again. And she'd been the one to break up with him. Hadn't she already said everything there was to say? Part of me thought: *she should feel lucky she got to talk to him about it at all.*

"Yeah, well," she said. "He made it clear I won't be."

"I'm sorry," I said, feeling horrible. "I'm not—that wasn't very sympathetic of me. I can't say what I'd do in your situation. I've never had to break up with anyone before."

"Really?" she said.

"Nope," I said. "It is my impression that to break up with someone would require me to date them first."

She laughed. "I mean, I have imaginary breakups all the time. On the El especially. I always see a hot guy get on, and everything's going great, and all of a sudden he's pulling, like, *On the Road* out of his bag, and bam, we're divorced." I laughed. She took another long drink. "I'm glad you messaged me," she added. "I actually wasn't sure if you liked me."

I felt like I had just reached out and slapped her across the face—shocked, mortified, forced to recognize myself as someone who was capable of bad things. It had never occurred to me that she could tell I'd hated her; I'd assumed she didn't notice, wasn't capable of noticing, didn't care enough. I pictured the whiteboard on the back of my closet door: Reasons Remy Is The Worst. I realized I'd never erased it, and I felt a brief and ridiculous panic that if I looked her too long in the eyes, she'd be able to see it.

"Of course I do!" I said. "I'm just. Awkward, sometimes. Like now, for example." Right after this I'd go home and erase the list on my whiteboard, I thought. Nobody would ever have to know. Except for me. And Logan and Mel, who'd huddled around my closet door with me, agreeing that if we knew one thing for sure it was that it was all true.

"Well, me, too." She laughed.

"If you want to hang out again at all, outside the library, or just like, talk to me. About...the breakup, but also whatever else, you can always message me. Or, wait—actually, what's your number? I feel like we're at the texting stage. And I really have been wanting to use Facebook less," I said, leaning over slowly to pick up my phone from my bag. I slid it over to

Remy and she filled in her number, then texted me so I had hers. "Hi it's Remy."

"Cool," she said. "I might just sulk all week—"

"Oh, that's okay too, of course—"

"—no, but, thank you," she said, and smiled.

"Sure," I said. "Well, I'll see you at the library, anyway."

"Yes," she said. "Um. Maybe not Wednesday? Just because I have this paper due Thursday that I was supposed to start last weekend, but...that didn't happen, ha."

"Oh," I said. I was a little surprised, and kind of impressed, by her willingness to miss shifts, and to tell me to my face that she was planning to do so. "Yeah, of course. Sunday, then."

"Sunday," she said. "I have no excuse not to be there."

I thought about telling her about Mel. I had thought about it when I sent her the message asking to meet up. But that fight suddenly felt too particular and personal—too dependent on knowing more about me—to tell Remy. She wouldn't understand why it was so mean of Mel to, basically, tell me to butt out of other people's lives. That I couldn't explain it to her bothered me, but I ignored it. Instead I asked her if she'd heard that Nia and Robert (of Wednesday-shift-before-ours fame) were hooking up. There had been speculation that they were doing it in the library break room, which I didn't think was possible because of the windows, and Remy agreed.

The days between Monday and Friday felt not like three separate entities but one long cycle, between waking up and going to sleep and waking up again. I spent nearly every free hour I had in a cubby on the second floor of the library, because I didn't want to see Mel, but I did want her to notice how long she'd gone without seeing me. After getting coffee with Remy, I'd gone home, waiting for Logan and Mel to get there so we could eat pizza together. But Logan had texted me to tell me their lab was running long, and they were going to just get food at the sandwich shop instead, and I thought, *Fine. I will be home even less.*

Two downsides to my hideout plan quickly revealed themselves: first, that I didn't have enough to do to keep me busy in the library for approximately six to nine hours a day. On Tuesday I finished all my work for the week, and a little of the next week's work, too. On Wednesday I looked up every student I could remember graduating high school with on Facebook, drew a sketch of the sophomores sitting at the long table that sat between rows SA and SR of the World History racks, spent my shift mostly staring, and tried to teach myself French from a textbook I checked out in a late-night delirium. "La nourriture est empoisonnée," I repeated, whispering. The food is poisoned.

On Thursday morning, when I was walking to class, Logan emailed me. "I just realized I haven't seen you in . . . days?" it said. "Please confirm that you are still alive. Also, PD is still texting me. Help." Vindicated—at least by her—I read the email over three times.

"I'm alive," I wrote back. "I just have kind of a crazy week, so I've been studying a lot. [Well, sort of.] What is he saying?"

When I checked my phone after class, she'd written back "Literally nothing."

I started a sentence four or five different ways before erasing each one. In the end I just sent back a frowny face.

By the time I got to the library on Friday afternoon, I felt like I was in a trance. My arms and legs tingled, my ears buzzed, and I felt like I hadn't blinked in over a year, though, technically speaking, I probably had. I imagined two little creatures standing in the cave-like recesses behind each eyeball, pushing them forward with their tiny hands. I hadn't been sleeping very well; I woke up in the middle of each night and lay awake thinking, OK, if I'm still awake in half an hour, I'll get up and make use of this wasted time. I will read a book, or at least watch TV. Then half an hour would pass and I would think, OK, if I'm still awake half an hour from now, then I'll get up. I'd go through four or five rounds, becoming increasingly certain that I'd never, ever fall asleep again, until I did.

Outside it was beautiful. I didn't notice until I was standing at the top of the steps in front of the library. I got to the top, realized I was squinting, and turned around to face the sun straight on. For a moment we glared at each other until my eyes started to water, and I looked down the brick path, which, on the other side of the arts building, opened up onto the quad. There were buds on the trees that lined the sidewalk that I could have sworn weren't there a day earlier. *Good*, I thought—nobody will be inside on an afternoon like this one, and I will be left alone.

I pushed open the doors and then the gate and enjoyed about ten seconds of having the circulation desk to myself before David rushed in behind me, rustling. He made so much goddamn noise when he walked—his too-big black windbreaker coat and too-big jeans and too-big tennis shoes, all that extra material flopping around and rubbing against itself.

I turned to face my computer and the room beyond it, which was empty. I had hoped for this without thinking about the fact that with nobody here to watch, I'd have even less to do with myself. Three open hours stretched out in front of me and I realized just how tired I really was. Ridiculously, I wondered what Emma would tell me to do—"Get over yourself," most likely. Take a nap and get over yourself.

I missed my friends, even though, for all I knew, they could be here, in the same building, right now, somewhere upstairs. Much to my alarm, I felt my eyes start to well up. David was the least likely person I knew to notice if I started to cry, but to make absolutely sure that he didn't, I quickly slid off my chair, grabbed my wallet, and walked toward the stairs. When I got to the basement, I looked all around me and, finding it empty as far as I could see, walked to the vending machines. I pressed my forehead against the cool glass. I took a few deep breaths. And then I bought a Diet Coke and a bag of M&M's.

Halfway up the steps I was reenergized by anger. At Keith, at Mel, at Logan for not knowing to be mad at Mel, even though she probably wouldn't have been anyway. At Remy, for feeling sad about Keith instead of hating him. I kicked the gate open with my shoe, looking behind me to see if David noticed. (He hadn't.) I sank into my chair and opened my email accounts. I had a new Emma email. I read it with my mouth agape, and I realized I knew what I was going to do for the rest of my shift.

*　　*　　*

Dear Emma,

I have a problem perhaps as old as man himself: I have feelings for two different women, and somehow I must choose. It isn't so simple as one good girl and one bad. (Alas, they are each both.) Rather, one is one of my oldest friends—I'll call her Éponine—and one is new to my life—I'll call her Cosette.

Éponine and I went to high school together, and though we always had a flirtatious relationship, we were always dating other people. A few weeks ago, she and her boyfriend broke up. We got drunk at a party and nature took its course: We made out, and talked about our feelings for each other. Since then we've been together a few times, and it has been, in a word, transcendent. She is thoughtful, clever, and adorably stubborn.

But then there is Cosette, who I met in Survey of College Mathematics. After being paired together for a project, we, more left-brained creatures than right, discovered and bonded over our shared disinterest in the rigidity of equations. We have spent several delightful afternoons in the coffee shop—the last of which found us expressing our unexpected sadness that the project was almost over. We haven't kissed, but the way she looked at me at the end of that meeting made it clear that we both wanted to. She is quiet, free-spirited, and, I suspect, a little dark.

I can tell you have an appreciation for classical romance, and hope you will therefore both enjoy my letter and help me find a way forward. I don't want to hurt either of these two amazing women.

Yours,
Marius in Ambiguity

Dear MIA,

Oh, spare me. If I didn't think it was important to answer male students' and female students' questions in equal or near-equal ratios, and if I had any other question from any other male student this week, I would have printed out your email just to set it on fire. I mean it. Why would you assume I'd enjoy this? Because you can name characters from a book you were assigned to read in Honors English in high school? Please. I wish with all my heart that some freshman boy would have emailed me to ask which pair of shoes go with the new sweater his mom got him for his birthday so that I could have devoted 600–750 words to answering that instead.

Alas, here we are.

Here's what I would like for you to do: Finish your project with "Cosette." Don't be rude, but don't go out of your way to be your undoubtedly twisted idea of "nice," either. Just get it done, and smile or nod at her when you see her in class, but unless she asks you to talk, don't sit there ruminating on whatever you think might be going on between you and then bring it up to her out of nowhere. Under no circumstances are you to let yourself get all whipped into a frenzy of imagined romantic distress wherein you feel you must dramatically confront her about this alleged way she looked at you. She looked at you because you're her project partner and sometimes you have to look at your project partner to get a project done. Stop thinking of her as a wood nymph who flitted into your life just to make it sparkle. Get a grip.

Your problem (one of your problems) is that you find your own interest in Cosette (and all the other Cosettes you'll meet after this one) fascinating. I promise you it is not. I think you believe yourself to be too layered a man for someone who likes you as simply and openly as Éponine, for God knows what reason, seems to like you. (Although, let's neither of us assume her to be your equal in starry-eyed lunacy: Have you considered the possibility that she's not so much desperately in love with you as she is content to hook up a few more times here and there? Have you considered the fact that chronology and circumstance make you a likely candidate for her rebound? She and her boyfriend broke up a few weeks ago, for God's sake.)

You need to disabuse yourself immediately of the notion that your predicament is interesting. That is a fantasy, and it's clouding your vision. Either you like Éponine enough to keep seeing her, or you don't. Either option is permissible, and believe you me, I'd sooner see you decide you didn't, and have an honest conversation with her about it, than have you wriggle pathetically for weeks and months on end. Stay in the water or get out and stay out, but don't grant yourself so much tortured complexity that you make her suffer through your indecisive pity party. You may not have any technical exclusivity obligations to her right now, but you're coming up to that line real quick. This is someone who, for whatever else she might or might not be to you, has been your friend for years. You owe her more than the basic minimum of common decency.

Please don't misinterpret my response as me picking Éponine over Cosette on your behalf—I can't do that for you. (In truth, who I really want you to pick is neither. No one. Find a nuclear fallout shelter and stay there.) You are not a helpless infant. Stop acting like one.

Also, *Les Misérables* is a terrible literary analogy for this situation. Congratulations on your self-regard being so abundant that you can readily consider yourself analogous to a revolutionary hero admired by two little beggar girls, one of whom is a near-silent doll and another who literally dies for you.

Most humbly yours,
Emma

Email FROM: <Alexia E. Collins>
Email TO: <Dear Emma>
Re: Column!
   H—Lol. Everything OK????
   — A

Email FROM: <Dear Emma>
Email TO: <Alexia E. Collins>
Re: re: Column!

Yep! Great!

Harriet

Email FROM: <Alexia E. Collins>
Email TO: <Dear Emma>
Re: re: re: Column!

Just want to make sure, NO pressure, but are you sure you don't want to give this another read-through before I pass it on to copy? It's tooootally up to you, of COURSE, but…if you do want another pass, I just need it by Monday morning. But it's your call, obviously!!

— A

Email FROM: <Dear Emma>
Email TO: <Alexia E. Collins>
Re: re: re: re: Column!

Nope, I'm all set. Thanks!

Harriet

Email FROM: <Alexia E. Collins>
Email TO: <Dear Emma>
Re: re: re: re: re: Column!

OK!!!! Awesome. Good thing we don't allow comments, right? Lol.

16

At the end of my shift, I texted Logan to see where she was. "3rd floor," read her reply. "Wanna go home?"

I paused, weighing the pros and cons of texting her back to ask if Mel was with her. Pro: I would find out if Mel was with her. (Con: If she was, would I just leave? Walk home a block ahead of them?) Con: Logan would almost certainly take that question to mean I was mad at Mel. (Pro: Maybe Logan would take my side.) I decided it would be cowardly and overly dramatic to ask—it took so little time to walk home, and anyway Logan would be there as a buffer—so I texted back "YES, I'll come get you."

I nearly jogged the whole way up, until I got close enough to her study spot to get nervous, and then I stopped. I rounded the corner on tiptoe like someone expecting land mines, but it was for nothing: Though her table was covered in enough books and candy wrappers and scattered papers for a study group of four, Logan was alone. My whole body unclenched. Her back was to me, and when I walked up behind her I cupped the back of her neck.

"AGH," she yelped, and I laughed.

"Sorry! You knew I was coming!"

"I didn't know you'd sneak up! Only predators approach from the rear."

"Well, or, people who are coming from the stairs behind you."

"Still. You could've announced yourself." She stood up and started gathering her things, sweeping her long arm across the table like a snowplow, the books falling into her huge messenger bag at all angles.

"Where's Mel?"

"She left maybe an hour ago to take a nap. I think she wasn't feeling well."

I allowed myself a brief moment to imagine this meant not that she was sick but that she was having as hard a time as I was. Harder, even.

"Oh, that's too bad," I said. "She must be really sick to let herself miss these valuable study hours."

"She'll be fine. I think she just needed sleep."

"Me, too," I said. "I feel a little crazy."

"You look a little crazy."

"Do I?" I realized I couldn't remember the last time I'd looked in a mirror.

"Yeah," said Logan. "But I haven't seen you in a few days. Maybe you've always looked like this, and I just forgot."

Logan and I were halfway through dinner when Mel barged out of her room. Logan stopped halfway into a sentence at the sight of her—ponytail shifted forward so that it seemed to emerge directly from the left side of her head, sweatshirt tucked into her leggings, one sock on and the other, gone missing. All of that gathered, I looked back at my plate.

"Hi," she croaked.

"Good morning, sunshine," said Logan. "How'd you sleep?"

"Ugh," she said. "I don't even know." She moved to sit at the table with us and then seemed to think better of it. "Actually—"

"...Yes?" said Logan.

"I should probably shower first. Sorry. I'm thinking out loud."

"That's OK," said Logan. "I agree you should shower."

Mel retreated into her room to grab her bathrobe and towel. Neither she nor I said a word as she came back out and walked directly behind me to the bathroom.

As soon as she pulled the door closed behind her and turned on the shower, Logan reached across the table and poked me on the wrist.

"What's going on?" she whispered.

"Nothing. It's dumb," I whispered back. Chances were Mel couldn't have heard us at anything less than shouting volume, but she was so close it was hard not to worry.

"Is it nothing or is it dumb?"

"Dumb."

"I'll decide for myself," she said, and raised her eyebrows in waiting.

"She didn't tell you about it already?"

"I literally have no idea what it is, so."

"OK, but, this is like the cop rule. If I ask you if you're a cop, you have to tell me if you are. I mean, if she already talked to you about this, you have to tell me."

"I'm not a cop," said Logan, "but just so you know, that rule isn't real."

"Well, OK," I said. I paused to scoot my chair in closer until the edge of the table dug into my stomach. "Basically, we had a fight about you and Peter."

"Ew, what? Nobody should care enough about Peter to fight about him. Including his parents."

"Well, it was sort of more about giving you advice about him."

"Like how?"

"Like, I just casually said something to her about us needing to strategize—or, I don't know, I can't remember what exactly I said. I just know her response was 'Not everything needs a strategy,' like I was overinvolving myself just by suggesting we help you get rid of Peter. So I got pissed."

"That's dumb," she said. "I *will* take your help getting rid of Peter. I will take any help I can get."

"That's what I thought!" I hissed. I paused to listen. The water was still running. "But she made it seem like, I don't know. Like I was trying to say you couldn't possibly know what to do so I had to fix it for you."

"OK, well, a), I *don't* know what to do. I barely ever respond, and if I do it's a single word, and somehow he keeps thinking that means he should say more. I am worried he thinks I'm being mysterious and flirty when really, I find him repulsive. And b), I don't know why she'd care if you want to help me. It's not like she thinks I should be asking her instead. She knows she sucks at texting," she said.

"I don't think that's why it bothered her," I said. "I think it's because she and Will are just SO in love now that somehow, in a matter of frickin' weeks, she no longer relates to anyone having boy problems."

Logan laughed. "Well," she said. "Good for her, then, I guess."

"NOT good for her! Doesn't it bother you if she thinks your problem is stupid?"

"My problem IS stupid," she said, shrugging.

"I don't think it is," I said.

"Well, either way," she said, "I'm sure you guys will make up soon."

"She thinks my column is pointless and meddlesome," I said, in a rush, exaggerating and knowing it, unwilling to let her perpetual chill smooth over this topic. I wanted something to faze her.

"She said that?"

"Well, no. But—"

"Harriet. There is no way she thinks that."

"She does," I said. "It was strongly implied."

"Harriet, Mel has read your column every week for the entire time you've written it. She would never read the paper for any other reason." She looked at me, waiting for me to acknowledge what she'd said. But I didn't say anything. I knew that should count for more than I let it. I knew that. "You're being too sensitive. OK?"

We heard the shower turn off and the curtain slide open across the metal rod. I turned back to look, or to pretend to look, but I felt Logan still looking at me, waiting.

"OK," I said finally, but I didn't mean it.

Mel came out of the bathroom in her bathrobe, her hair tied up in a towel, and walked silently into her room. Once her door was closed I got up, washed my plate, and took two cookies from the package on top of our refrigerator. I was halfway to my room when I stopped and turned back, deciding it was only fair—given my emotional state—that I got one more. I sped to my room and ate them like a squirrel, nibbling all around their edges to make them last as long as possible. I changed into sweatpants and a tank top and climbed into bed intending to read. It was seven thirty-five. Some time later—I guessed about two hours—when Logan knocked on my door to tell me she and Mel were going to Mavericks, and did I want to come with, I said no, I'd already fallen asleep once, but have fun. After I heard them leave I lay awake for what felt like a year.

The weird, angry, improbably loud bird that lived in the rafters of my spiderweb-strewn palace morphed slowly as I woke, sounding more and more like a buzz until it became clear that it was my phone. I reached over and fumbled around my phone's edges in the dark until I managed to stop the sound. I left it sitting there while I blinked my eyes open and peered into the total darkness around me. What time was it, two? Three? If I saw Logan's name on that screen, I'd be pissed. I turned over onto my stomach and slid over to the edge of the bed, grumbling to myself in anticipation.

When I picked up my phone, I made myself read the screenful of information there from top to bottom: Time—just 10:43. Then, a series of texts from: DEAD TO YOU. Four of them. DEAD TO YOU, DEAD TO YOU, DEAD TO YOU, DEAD TO YOU. I stared at it for a moment, horrified. And then I laughed. It was sort of funny, seeing them all lined up like that. He always texted like that, line by line, creating as much suspense as possible.

Then shock hit me and I woke up more completely: It was Keith. Keith was texting me. I'd changed his name in my phone after he stopped texting me, when I wasn't yet ready to delete him entirely but hoped I could at least dissuade myself from ever texting him. It had worked, I guess, until now.

Though I could see previews of the messages on my screen, I unlocked it, not wanting to give myself even a few seconds in which I might wonder what the rest said and come up with something better than what was really there. The messages came in quick succession:

10:40: Hey

(Ugh.)

10:40: It's Keith

(Duh.)

10:41: You up/around?

(Rude, to assume I might be asleep before eleven on a Friday night.)

10:42: Can you meet me for a drink? I'm at Butler's…

(WHAT?)

As I read over the series once more, the little typing ellipses popped up and I gasped. I dropped the phone on the nightstand. I pressed a finger to its screen to keep it lit, and watched as the bubble flickered, went away, came back, went away.

10:45: Sorry. I know this is random…

I held my finger there, watching to see if the bubble came back and trying to decide as quickly as possible what to do. I was in pajamas, in bed. Going to meet him would violate several of my protocols, not the least of which was that I didn't leave the house after I'd gotten into my pajamas, no matter the time. And what if there were other people I knew there? (What if Mel and Logan had migrated from Mavericks?) What if there were people Remy knew? (What if Remy herself was there, and this was some kind of terrible prank?) Furthermore, if I responded now and said I'd meet him, it would be a concession that I hadn't been doing anything better.

Then, also, there was the fact that he was a fucking shit-for-brains idiot whom I hated.

On the other hand: What could he possibly want to meet me for, now? I knew, on some abstract level, that texting one's exes was a thing people did late at night when they were drunk, sometimes months and months after the fact, but it wasn't all that late, and it didn't seem like enough time had gone by for him to find me interesting again. I supposed he could have been drunk—he hid it well, never once made a typo—but even if that was true, there would have to be some other reason. Did he want to apologize? And: Was the "Sorry." perfunctory or multipurpose?? When I looked at it a certain way, the period at the end seemed curt, insincere, borderline cruel; a way to let me know that was all the apology I was going to get. But maybe it was just a way to end a sentence.

Did he miss me? Maybe it was just how I'd pictured it happening, early on, when he started dating Remy, and all it had taken was another girl (the wrong girl) to realize I was the right one the whole time. Maybe he'd been hoping and planning to break up with her for me, and then she'd done it for him. I felt a little flutter rise up in my chest, against all my better instincts.

Three full minutes passed and the bubble never came back. That was going to be it: his entire olive branch. More of a twig, really.

I typed out "Hey" and pressed send before I had a chance to erase it. Oh god, I thought. Now I had to answer, one way or the other.

"Sorry, but I was sleeping–" I typed out, then backspaced it entirely. Don't say sorry.

"I don't think–"

"What do you–"

"Why–"

Then I stopped. Why was I rushing? Let him watch that bubble disappear. I waited for another thirty seconds or so. He probably wasn't even looking at his phone. He probably put it right back into his pocket, unconcerned as to when or even if I would respond. For that reason alone, I shouldn't go. But I was wide awake now, sitting upright in my bed. If I didn't go, I would maybe never stop wondering what he would have said. I jumped out of bed to get dressed, first trying on a sweater he'd told me he loved—that he'd stuck his hands up inside because the inside was fleecey and soft—and then decided that was too obvious, and too nice, and put on a shirt instead, buttoned all the way up to the neck as if to say *Stay out*. I pulled my hair up into a ponytail as I walked to the kitchen, removing the tequila bottle from the freezer to take a quick half shot. And then another.

When I'd closed and locked the side door behind me, I wrote back. "Yeah, I'll meet you there in a bit." Period.

On the walk there I practiced a few options for what I might say depending on what he might say. I checked my phone—it was close to 11:00 PM.

If he tried to hug me, I would keep one arm firmly attached to my side. If he tried to kiss me on the cheek, I would run right out of there. But he probably wouldn't try to kiss me on the cheek.

If he told me he wanted me back, I would ask him why. I would need to hear a good, convincing argument before I even considered considering it. He couldn't just say it and expect me to fall into line.

If he just wanted to say he was sorry for how he treated me— I imagined him saying "I'm so sorry, I never meant to hurt you, I fucked up"—I would listen quietly and answer in a way that demonstrated both gracious forgiveness and a small but unalleviated woundedness, so he'd always have to live with knowing how he hurt me but wouldn't get to feel justified in feeling bitter about it. I wasn't sure yet exactly how I'd accomplish this, but I hoped that by selecting the desired message now, it would be more likely to come to me when I wanted it to.

My feet reached the curb and I looked up to see Butler's across

the street. I stood there for a minute, gathering as much information about its interior as I could before I went in. The crowd
looked just slightly smaller than average. A tower of coats had
overtaken a corner table by the window, blocking my view of the
booths that ran along the left side of the bar behind it. I didn't
see Mel or Logan, or Keith for that matter, but it was possible
that all of them were inside. I took out my phone, checking to see
if Logan had somehow texted me a location update (she hadn't)
and considering texting her to ask (I didn't). I clasped it in my
left hand and, with my right, reached up to feel the pulse in my
neck; 13 beats in 10 seconds = 78. I was almost disappointed it
wasn't higher.

I stepped into the street without thinking, pushed forward by
a deep impatience with myself. And then I was walking across it,
and up to the door, and pulling it open, and there was no other
choice but to keep moving ahead.

Butler's liked an early-aughts soundtrack, and as I stood in
the entryway to pull off my coat I identified the frantic, high-
pitched strings of "Toxic." *Jesus*, I thought, rubbing at my
temples and trying to survey the room without anyone seeing
me do so. No Mel, no Logan. No Keith, until there was—on
my tiptoes I could see him sitting at a high-top table just past
the dartboard, his back to the door. I nearly genuflected, grateful that I wouldn't have to cross the bar with him able to watch
me the whole time.

I pushed through the crowd between us as if politely hacking
my way into rain forest with a machete. "Excuse me," I said, to
no one in particular. "Excuse meeee, ahh. Excuse me. Thanks. Excuse me."

And then I was standing two feet behind him. I had the
strange urge to reach out and pull on a piece of his hair. Instead

I steeled myself, wiped under my eyes for errant mascara, and stepped forward until I felt him look up.

"Hi," he said.

"Hey," I said.

"Sit down," he said, gesturing at the chair across from him, which I was in the act of pulling out from the table.

"Really?" I asked, contorting my face into an exaggerated expression of profound gratitude. "This one? Are you *sure*?"

He half nodded, made a sound halfway between a chuckle and clearing his throat. I sat down, feeling both annoyed at him—for not giving what I thought was a pretty gracious joke, all things considered, a better reception—and unwillingly softened by his apparent nervousness. I'd been afraid I'd come in here and just start crying, or throwing things, or both. I'd expected to come here and hate seeing the front of his head as much as I'd hated seeing the back of it every Monday and Wednesday for weeks. But I watched him fidget, looking down and scratching at the back of his neck and taking a sip of beer, and I felt calmer than he looked.

"Are you—do you want a drink?" he said finally.

"Yeah—is there a server back here tonight, or do I have to go up?" I asked.

"There is, I got mine from—" He craned around, looking. "Yeah, she's over there, but I think she'll be back around soon."

"OK, then I'll wait."

"You sure?" he asked. I could tell that he would have been happy for me to get up again, to delay whatever conversation we were going to have for another five minutes.

"Yes," I said. "I'm sure."

"Great," he said. He took another drink of his beer and rubbed at his face, drawing attention to the fact that it was covered in a few-days'-old beard. I averted my eyes.

"What did you want to see me for?" I said, more to the table than to him. When I looked up he was looking back, peering up at me from his hunched-over position, still holding on to his own head for support.

"I don't know," he said, swiveling around to look at the dartboard and behind him, apparently in search of the server. "I just—"

"Can you stop?" I asked. "Just sit still for a second."

He turned back around, slowly.

"Sorry," I said. "I'm just. Wondering why I'm here."

"It's OK." He laughed a little, but it soon turned into more of a groan. "Aghgh, this is— um, I don't really— I don't think I have a good, specific reason for you," he said.

"OK..." *Don't finish the thought for him*, I thought to myself. I wouldn't humiliate myself by guessing his motive only to have him insist that wasn't it.

"I was just... here, and I felt bad, and I wanted to talk to you," he said, shrugging.

"Felt bad?"

"Yeah," he said. "For, I don't know. You know."

"I really don't," I said. "I really don't know." My face was hot; I was angry again. I thought, *Where is my drink?* I could've thrown my drink, if I had it. I could have gripped it, anyway, and thought about it.

"Where is she?" he said again, craning. "This is, like..."

"Keith," I said.

"Sorry," he said. "I'm bad at this."

"What, talking?" My voice got a little louder, there, but the bar was so noisy anyway that nobody noticed but Keith, who just looked at me.

"Yeah," he said. He looked down, shifted up in his seat, took another drink. *He needs a straitjacket*, I thought. I should have agreed to come here only under the condition that he wore a straitjacket.

"Hellooooo," croaked the server, who was pretty and raspy-voiced, wearing an apron that stopped just short of her nipples over a deep V-neck T-shirt that stopped just above them. "Sorry about the wait—can I get you a drink?"

"Um, yeahhh," I said, but I couldn't think of anything. Lighter fluid? Could I order a container of lighter fluid and some matches?

"Tequila?" Keith asked me, cocking an eyebrow and half grinning. How dare he.

"No, uh—an old-fashioned, please." I had never ordered that before in my life. Did that make sense? I vaguely remembered standing near someone tall and cool-looking at a bar once and hearing her tell the bartender "old-fashioned" with an even, authoritative tone. No "please." That's right: It was Logan. I looked nervously at the server. She nodded and walked away, which seemed like a good sign.

"Fancy," said Keith.

"Mm," I said. Seconds later I felt my mouth staying like that, pulled into a tight, straight line with my lips inverted into my face, and I tried to rearrange it into anything that might not seem so sexless—biting the lower, resting them slightly open. What would it look like, to be unattainably hot and bored by all this? *Gone*, I decided. Somewhere else.

But I was already here. So I waited.

"I just—" he started. "I—"

The server came by, slid my drink onto the table in front of me, took the $10 bill I handed her, telling her to keep it. I took a sip and thought, nice, she brought me lighter fluid after all.

If I made a face Keith let it go, which frankly was the least he could do.

"Go on," I said.

"I—when we were, whatever, hanging out or whatever, I met this other girl and I didn't know what or how to tell you," he said, all in one breath. I waited a moment, in case there was more.

"Any words," I said. "Like, any words would have been good."

"I know," he said. "I just—I know."

I watched his face, wondering if he'd put it together that I knew "this other girl," if it had come up between them. But no, I thought, no way. I was an unnecessary disclosure. And if he hadn't figured it out already, I wouldn't be the one to tell him that Remy and I had met. That we were kind of friends. I didn't want to risk the possibility that him knowing that might make him feel less guilty.

I took another sip of my horrible-tasting drink, and he took another sip of his. We set down our glasses at the exact same moment, which I found inexplicably embarrassing.

"Anyway, she broke up with me," he said.

And that's when I knew: that if I stayed here for a while, especially if I had another drink and he had one too, he would kiss me. Maybe he would even walk me home, or ask me to walk with him to his—that I wasn't sure about. But he would kiss me. If I encouraged him, if I put myself in front of his sad face at the end of the night and I waited, he'd do it.

I felt more depressed than vindicated. By how easy it'd be. And not because I was the one he was actually sad about, but because he wanted a placeholder and I could fill that role.

"Is that it?" I asked.

"What do you mean?"

He knew what I meant. He was just surprised. So was I. I felt like I was in shock. Absurdly, I pictured the server coming back over, wrapping me in a silver space blanket. I started again.

"Have you said everything you have to say to me?"

He ran his hand through his hair, shook his head a little.

"I guess," he said finally. A beat. "Sorry."

"OK," I said. I stood up from my chair, bumping the table a little as I did. I dropped my purse strap over my shoulder. "Then bye."

And then I walked off. I couldn't tell if he said anything back; I hadn't wanted to hear it if he did. I got to the door before I remembered my coat and walked back over to the mountain in the corner, the top of it caving in and downward as I rooted into its middle to pull mine out. A few slid to the floor and I bent over to pick them up and threw them back on top again, once again grateful Keith's back was to me. I knew he wouldn't have turned around to watch me go.

Once I had my coat, I bolted out the door. I jogged all eight blocks home with it flopping around in my hand. I kept thinking I should just put it on, but I didn't want to stop.

17

I woke up the next morning to the sound of laughter in the kitchen. I lay there motionless for a minute or two, trying to make out what was so funny, but their voices were muffled—halfheartedly trying not to wake me up, I figured. I reached for my phone in mock apathy, pretending (for whom?) that I didn't care if I'd gotten any follow-up text messages from anyone in particular later in the night after I'd fallen asleep.

It was 10:32 AM, and no, I did not have any messages. I was mostly relieved (it wasn't like I didn't have enough to think about) but a little disappointed, too. He could have said sorry one more time, or five. He couldn't even manage to exceed the below-zero expectations I'd come to assign him since he stopped acknowledging my existence.

I slid out of bed and stuck my phone in the waistband of my pants. I pulled my hair up into a ponytail as I walked out into the kitchen. Logan was leaning against the counter, wearing workout clothes and tennis shoes. Mel was sitting at the table with a bowl of cereal, still wearing her glasses and her bathrobe.

"Good morning!" said Logan. Mel smiled, sort of.

"Hey," I said. "Did you work out already?"

"No, I was about to go for a run."

"OK, well, it's going to have to wait a minute," I said. I took out my phone and slid it slowly onto the table, like a crime scene photograph. Logan and Mel looked at it, and then at each other, and then at me.

"Last night, between the hours of ten forty and ten forty-five—"

"So, minutes—"

"Between ten forty and ten forty-five, this phone received no fewer than five text messages from one Keith Rapp," I said.

"Whaaaat?" said Mel.

"You want us to read?" asked Logan. I nodded and she picked up my phone, the two of them scooting closer and reading through them together. "Why so many ellipses?" she said.

"I know," I said. "I don't think he knows what they're for."

"Did you go?" asked Mel, though it seemed like she already knew. I nodded and her mouth dropped open into a perfect O.

"I thought about not going, but I just...I don't know. I was too curious to know what he was going to say, I guess, because I had no idea. And I THOUGHT, incorrectly, that even if it was stupid, it would be better than not knowing," I said. *And I thought he might want me back*, I thought, but that I could not say to them now.

"So what happened?" asked Mel.

"I got there around eleven and sat down, and he just said... nothing."

"What do you mean?"

"Like...I'm trying to think about it now, and I don't remember a single full sentence he said. He can't have said more than two," I said. "He just kept looking for the server, acting all worried I didn't have a drink yet."

"Did he pay for it?" asked Logan.

"My drink?" I hadn't even thought of that. "No, I did."

"Did he even offer??" she asked.

"No! Is that weird?"

"That is fucked up," said Logan, shaking her head.

"What, why? She can pay for herself," said Mel.

"No," said Logan. "Any guy who's going to drag a girl out of bed so he can make half-assed amends for his own sake owes her eight dollars for a drink."

"I don't know," said Mel, "I think it's more independent—"

"Fuck independent," said Logan. "This is about fair."

"OK, whatever," said Mel, waving her hand. "You have to remember *something* he said."

"Basically, 'I met another girl and I didn't know how to tell you.'"

"Right," said Logan. "Cool story."

"And later he was like, 'But then she broke up with me, so...'" Remembering that part made me furious now. I should have been madder at the time.

"He DID NOT," said Logan.

"Whaaaaaaat," said Mel.

"And I kind of think...I don't know," I said, hesitant to say the next part but knowing I couldn't not, "I think if I'd stayed there longer, something could have happened," I said.

"Oh, I'm *sure*," said Logan. "Definitely. That's just, like, Newton's law of universal gravitation. He's a guy, and you were right in front of him. At night."

"Totally. That's where I thought this story was going, actually," said Mel. "Just because, why else would he want to apologize when it's kind of late on a Friday night?"

"*Bats*," said Logan.

"You were so right," I said.

"So what did you say?"

"I said, 'Is that it?' And he was like, 'I guess, sorry.' So I said, 'OK, then, bye,' and I walked out," I said.

"Whoa," said Mel.

"You just like walked off?" asked Logan.

"Yeah."

"Wow," said Logan. "That's, like, an alpha bitch move."

"Really?" I asked. I'd thought I'd just wanted to get out of there as quickly as possible.

"Oh, definitely," said Mel. "It's like, 'You wasted enough of my time already, asshole! I'm out! Boom!'" She raised both hands into the air, mimicked pulling the triggers of two guns. "Pchew, pchew, pchew, pchew."

"Am I shooting the ceiling?" I said.

"Yeah," she said. "Very cool."

"I'm just amazed you didn't cry," said Logan.

"Well, *thank you*, I didn't," I said. "I just ran."

"Speaking of," Logan said, pushing her chair back to stand up. "I've gotta go do this now or it's not going to happen."

"OK, fiiiiiine."

"See you guys later," she said, taking a drink out of her giant jug of water. When she opened the door and slid out, the air that rushed in behind her was warm. Somehow, it had gotten to be almost May.

"I guess I'm going to take a shower…" said Mel. At the sound of her voice I jumped in my seat. "Did I just scare you?" she asked, laughing.

"Apparently," I said. Somehow I'd been surprised to find her still there, across from me, the two of us alone together in a room.

"Hey," she said. "I'm sorry about the other week."

I felt this stream of pressure drain out of me, like a valve I didn't know I had opened up, like my muscles and my skeleton finally fit properly inside my body.

"It's OK," I said, because it was. Mel's apology, unlike Keith's, did not require specificity for me to know that she meant it. "I'm sorry, too."

"You don't need to apologize," she said. "I was being a bitch. All you did was suggest helping Logan in response to me bringing up the fact that Logan probably needed our help. Which makes sense."

"I know, I don't mean that. That fight was a hundred percent your fault," I said. We both paused, grinned. "I mean from before."

"Oh," she said, nodding. Then: "I still don't actually know what you mean."

"I'm sorry for making you feel like you couldn't tell me about Will, and also for making you tell me anyway," I said.

"You didn't," she said, but she looked relieved, too. "Or if you did make me feel that way, I made me feel that way, too. I don't know why I haven't really wanted to talk about it."

"You don't need a reason. I mean, I want you to feel like you can, and historically we have always told each other pretty much everything, so I think it's just been kind of surprising? And a little hard, just because you're my best friend and I feel like there's this whole part of your life I don't know anything about now," I said.

"I know."

"But I don't want you to be telling me anything out of obligation."

"I wouldn't," she said. "I never feel like telling you things is an obligation, I swear."

"OK," I said. I swallowed a few times, quickly, trying to keep every last bit of moisture I had far away from my face.

"I think…" she said. She shifted in her seat, took a strand of hair between her fingers, and twirled it. Fifteen or twenty seconds passed.

"Mel."

"Sorry, I think…I don't know. I just think that I haven't really had anything to complain about yet. With Will, I mean. So I just haven't brought it up," she said. She looked embarrassed, and I felt awful.

"Do you feel like we don't want to talk about boy stuff if it's going well?"

"Kind of?" she said. "I mean, even I don't! It's not as much fun! Like, what, 'Today I had a nice afternoon studying the French past perfect with Will, and then we went to his house and ordered pizza'? Kill me!"

I laughed.

"I don't know," she said. "This is the first time in a long time that anything like this has seemed like it might really happen, or something—"

"Which is why you should be able to talk about it, if you want!"

"I know. And I guess I used to assume I'd want to, or that it would just be, like, new and different kinds of things to worry about and talk to you guys about. And I'm almost disappointed, because I think I was kind of looking forward to that part of it," she said.

We sat there a moment not saying anything. I couldn't even picture myself there, feeling the way she did. She seemed so much older than me, and so calm. And she didn't need my help. For her to tell me even a part of her wished she did was the nicest thing she could have said.

"But it's good, right?" I asked. "It's good if he doesn't make you confused or sad."

"Yeah," she said, letting herself smile only just a little. "It's good."

"Will you tell me a nice thing about him?" I asked.

"Will?"

"No, your dad."

"Haha, well, I don't know. OK, sure, ummmm…" She thought. "Uhhhhhhh. This is weirdly hard? Please don't ever tell him I said that."

"I promise."

"Oh, I know, OK, one thing is that he waits for me in line at the cafeteria. Whenever we get breakfast. I get very overwhelmed by the number of options, and he always gets the same thing. But instead of just getting it and going to sit down, he walks around with me while I go back and forth between all the lines trying to decide what I want," she said. "And, um." She paused, evidently trying to decide whether to tell me whatever thing she'd just thought of in addition. "This might be TMI…"

"No," I said. "No such thing."

"He's really good at taking my pants off," she said, grinning.

"How much can there be to master?" I said, though I then remembered that I had taken off my own pants for Scott Dunleavy, who had seemed afraid to touch them.

"He just makes it seem like it's something he's been wanting to do for years," she said. "And it's been like that every time."

"That is really nice," I said. "Both of those things."

"Yeah."

"I am happy for you, Mel."

She smiled. "I know." Too embarrassed to allow both of us to feel pleased with her for too long, she took her hand from her hair and rested it on her table, using the nail of her thumb to pick at the corner where the white finish had started to chip off.

Mel got in the shower and I went to my room and closed the door behind me. I sat on the farthest corner of my bed with my back pressed up against the wall and my knees pulled into my chest—the position I assumed whenever I had to think about something I didn't really want to think about. I listened to the water running through the bathroom door, Mel's humming just barely audible over it. Later she was meeting Will in the dugout to get a sandwich and study.

I replayed the conversation with Keith in my head from start to finish, and then did it again, and again. I was looking for deeper meanings in what he said—had it meant something that he'd suggested I get tequila, or was he just trying to lessen the tension? It had felt like he was trying to remind me that he knew me.

When he told me Remy had broken up with him, what did he want me to feel then? Pity? Like we could relate—she had left him, so he could understand how I'd felt? He had to, whether he knew it or not, he had to have wanted me to feel a little hope right then. For me to have thought, oh, you're single again? I can't believe my luck. I should have said something. I should have said, "I don't give a fuck," or "Do you want me to feel sorry for you?" or "What's her email, I'd love to congratulate her." But then, if I'd been much meaner, or a little more dramatic, he would've just gone home feeling relieved he'd stopped talking to me when he did. I would have given him all the permission he needed to feel a little less sorry for himself. She was *crazy*, he'd tell his friends, and they'd believe him, even though it was him who was the crazy one.

Better to just not respond, to ignore him and then leave and then keep ignoring him for the rest of my life.

I leaned forward across my bed, picked up my phone from my nightstand, and erased Keith from my contacts—*dead* to me, I meant it this time. I opened my texts and swiped Keith away there, too. I crossed the room for my laptop and brought it back to my bed, opened Facebook, unfriended him. Deleted Gchat archives and emails. A minute or two and every last trace was gone. I looked around my room, hoping to see some printed-out picture of us I could rip up, even though I knew no such pictures existed. I thought of the little library slip I'd taken from him; it had fallen out of my bag weeks ago now. It wasn't as satisfying, just clicking all these dumb links. I tore a sheet of paper from a notebook and drew a gravestone poking up out of some grass. "RIP Keith," I wrote. "Everyone agrees he sucked." I taped it to the wall above my desk.

The water in the shower turned off, the curtain slid open. I tried to remember when it was that I last showered. Yesterday? No, Thursday. Morning.

I thought of Remy. I was going to have to sit next to her for four hours the next day. I clicked back over to Facebook and went to her page. There was nothing different or new; she hadn't changed her profile picture for a "fresh start," or posted a seemingly vague but actually pointed status, or otherwise marked herself as over it in any way. Which made me wonder if she wasn't. I checked—she and Keith were still friends. I felt vaguely betrayed by this, as if she was supposed to be on my side, to be as mad at him as I was, both on her own behalf and, less sensibly, on mine. But I supposed I'd stayed fake-friends with him for weeks. I'd been furious and hurt and still preoccupied, keeping the line open not just to be able to look over his life in the only way I still could but also as a little window, just in case. If she was doing the same thing, I guessed it wasn't fair to blame her for being no better than me.

"I'm going!" Mel yelled, her voice slightly muffled from somewhere on the other side of my bedroom door.

"See you later!" I yelled. The kitchen door slammed shut.

I checked the time and figured I could fit in a shower before Logan got home from her run. I closed my laptop and got my towel from the hook on the inside of my closet door. (When was the last time I had washed my towel?) The bathroom was still steamy from Mel, several strands of her hair stuck to the tiled wall of the shower, where she placed them to avoid clogging the drain, always with every intention to clean them up. I wiped them up with a tissue, turned on the water, and put my face directly under the faucet. I stood there for a long time, replaying the night prior over and over again, increasing the drama each time, so that by the time I heard Logan open the door I'd started picturing me taking his drink and spitting into it, me driving away from the table on a motorcycle, me holding him off the edge of a roof while he begged me to save him and me whispering *No*.

18

Around nine that evening, someone knocked on my door.
"Come in," I said. I was lying in bed with my laptop sitting on my belly, watching a documentary about historical plagues on Netflix. My voice, unused for hours, came out in a croak.

Logan opened the door and came in, Mel behind her.

"Hi," said Logan. "We're going out."

"Are you asking me or telling me?" I said.

"Telling."

"We haven't gone out all of us together in like, seventeen years," said Mel.

"Whose fault is that??" I said, looking at Mel, but everyone, including me, knew the truest answer was: mine.

"Come on," said Logan. "Pretty soon it'll be finals. We all need this. You, obviously. Mel has a 'boyfriend' now, so we know *she's* been quietly suffering." Around the word "boyfriend" Logan made air quotes, and Mel rolled her eyes. "Me, I haven't had any beer yet today. That's good enough. We're going."

"Which bar?" I said. I sat up to get out of bed but wouldn't until she told me. Mavericks was too risky. And I would never go to Butler's again for as long as I lived. Or at least until next year, when Keith would be gone.

"We were kind of thinking Acadia," said Mel, grinning.

"*Acadia?*"

They both nodded. Acadia was new, put in place of a used bookstore that had closed the summer before. It was a freshman bar—the twenty-three-year-old bouncers "checked" IDs but did not really look at them. They played loud, European house music that nobody had ever heard before. When you walked by it on the way to the real bars on the main stretch, you could feel the place pulsing. It was nightmarish. But it was also safe. There was simply no way we would see anyone else we knew.

"OK," I said. "I'm in."

An hour later we were outside, having scrambled into our most passably clubby outfits and taken two shots of tequila each standing over the kitchen sink. Logan had let me put a stripe of metallic teal eyeliner over each of her lids and tease her hair into a high ponytail. Mel was wearing a sequined tank top I hadn't seen on her since the first week of college. I had worn my lone pair of four-inch heels I'd ordered for $19 online once when I was drunk. From the way we kept picking at our outfits, it was clear that each of us felt like we were in costume, but I thought Logan and Mel looked like naturals and could only hope anyone who saw me would therefore think the same.

We walked alongside the bar's wholly unnecessary velvet rope and handed our IDs over to the bouncer, who was tall and pimply and visibly relieved to let in a group of legitimately legal customers. We pushed through the double doors and surveyed the half-empty room.

"They need to make better use of their space," said Logan.

Acadia still felt like a venue better suited to daytime, reading, and sobriety. They had piled it in with black pleather booths and black lights and vaguely industrial metal light fixtures, but all of it felt fake. But that was probably because we had extra context. The current freshmen, and all the ones who came after them, would think of Acadia as having always been there.

We ordered a round of shots plus a pitcher of beer at the bar and walked to a corner booth in the back, where the music was marginally less cacophonous and we could look out on the burgeoning dance floor and judge people.

"Where is everyone? When we were freshmen we were always at the bars by ten," said Mel. She picked up her shot glass and Logan and I watched her press its rim to her mouth, tilt her head back, and proceed to swish the tequila around a few times like mouthwash before swallowing it.

"Whyyyy do you do that?" I said. I'd watched her take shots this way for more than two years, and it never got any less horrifying.

"It doesn't have to be like this," said Logan. "Just swallow it."

"You don't have to taste it."

"I know," she said. "My mouth just does it."

Logan took her shot and bit into the lime, easy and quick. I held mine with two fingers, eyeing it warily. I needed a minute.

"Do you guys think I should talk to Remy?"

"Why?" said Logan.

"Like, tell her what happened with Keith?" said Mel.

"Well, that, but more so the...Emma thing," I said. I hesitated, still not able (or maybe not willing) to articulate what exactly felt wrong about it. I only knew that the feeling something was wrong was growing, pressing at the inside of my chest whenever I thought about it.

"Oh," said Logan. "I don't know, it's sort of pointless by now, isn't it? They broke up. It's done."

"I guess," I said. "I just feel like she and I are kind of friends now, and if she found out I'm Emma, I think she would think it was weird I never said anything."

"How would she find out?" said Logan. "*We* aren't going to tell her."

"To the grave!" said Mel. She mimicked locking her mouth with a key.

"And anyway, he's a piece of shit, and you were doing your job," said Logan. "Good riddance."

"Yeah," said Mel. "It was probably only a matter of time. And like, yes, maaaaybe they could have worked it out and been happy together for a while."

Logan and I both looked at her, waiting.

"...But??" I asked.

"That was it I think," said Mel.

"So, just, yes, you agree they should have broken up, but also maybe they shouldn't have?" I asked.

"I don't know," she said. "You know better than I do."

"You guys always say that but, I'm just some person," I said. "It's not like I've experienced exactly the same things most people ask me about. I barely even know what I'm basing my answers on. Like, sometimes, I find myself writing these opinions and I don't even know where they come from."

"Yeah, but, you're still an authority," said Mel. "You have a column."

"But is that it?" I said. "Is that the only reason people let me give them advice is because of the column?"

"I mean, yes, that is why people ask you for advice..." said Logan. "Because you have an advice column..."

"You know what I mean!" I said. "Is there anything about me—just me—that makes me qualified to tell people what to do?"

"I don't think anyone is really qualified to tell people what to do," said Logan.

"You're going to be a doctor!"

"Yeah, but, that won't mean anyone has to listen to me," she said. "Just because you answer a letter and tell someone what to do one way or another doesn't mean they do it."

I stared at her for a second, then looked down and realized I was still holding on to my shot. I took it and put the lime wedge in my mouth and chewed on it, squinting through the sourness. Had I been thinking of my advice as verdicts? Off and on I'd wondered what became of the problems people wrote to me with, but it was more in a "what were the consequences of doing exactly as I said?" kind of way. All this time people might have been ignoring me left and right. Willy-nilly. I couldn't believe it.

"I don't know, I think probably a lot of them do follow it," said Mel. Somehow she was already three-quarters of the way into a beer, so I poured myself a cup.

"THANK you," I said.

"I'm just saying, if, for example, Remy read your letter, and she did break up with Keith afterward, that doesn't mean there was a causal relationship between those two events," said Logan. "She wrote to you when she'd already started thinking about it. You didn't plant that thought in her head."

"Yeah," I said. "I guess."

"People write to you because something is wrong," said Logan. "Nobody's going to write to you to be, like, 'Hey, just wanted to let you know everything with me is pretty good.'"

"Sometimes I wish they would," I said.

"Your advice was sound," she said. She could tell I was not at all mollified. "That is the reason people trust you. Your advice is clear and sound."

"Yeah," said Mel. "If I were the one giving advice, I would never actually give anyone advice at all."

"You'd be like, 'Hmm, I see your point.' That's the whole letter," I said.

"'On the one hand, yes, but on the other hand, no.'"

We laughed, drank our beer, looked over again at the rest of the bar. A little crowd of girls in seasonally preemptive strapless tops and dresses bobbed at the center of the dance floor, all of them pretending not to be on surveillance duty. A group of freshmen frat pledges pushed through the door, and I watched as one of the girls grabbed another's arm, alerting her. It was clear the girl who was grabbed knew immediately what the touch meant; she glanced over at the pack of boys, now migrating in toward the bar in a wide berth around the dance floor, all of them oblivious, or pretending to be.

"Um, speaking of crises," said Mel, and I snapped out of it, turning back around to face her. She glanced at us nervously, me then Logan, then glued her eyes back on her plastic cup, grinning sheepishly.

"Uh-oh," said Logan.

"What is it?" I said.

"Something . . . weird happened, with Will," she said.

"Oh god," said Logan. "I'm afraid."

"Just tell us!" I said.

She pressed her fingertips into her forehead, covering her eyes, and started to laugh.

"Oh my god, Mel," I said. "Just say it, we're dying."

"Not me," said Logan. "I can already tell I do not want to know."

Mel took a deep breath and dropped her hands back to the table. "OK," she said. "Well. As you may have noticed, I slept over at his place last night. It just makes sense, on Thursdays, because he's so much closer to the science building anyway, so I can just kind of roll out of there at seven fifty-three and make it to class on time."

"Sure," said Logan.

"So, anyway, we were um, hooking up, um, in his bed—"

"In his bed? You don't say."

"I'm painting you a picture. You're going to need it."

"Go on," I said. "Ignore her."

"So we're hooking up, in his bed. He's on top of me. At this point both our shirts are off and he's just wearing boxers."

"Is he *so* skinny?" said Logan. "I feel like, without clothes on, he'd just disappear."

"So everything is going pretty normally," continued Mel. "Pretty basic, um, making-out–type activities. Uhhh. I mean, good, but. Anyway, so I'm lying there like, 'OK, hot, good, normal,' but then he stops kissing me and sort of starts to like . . . crawl upward?"

"What?" we said.

"Like, he's on his elbows, and he sort of crawls. What I thought of was those army guys, you know, in an obstacle course? Like that. Just, a little bit. Toward the headboard."

"I mean, how far was there to go?"

"Not very!" said Mel. "I was like, maybe six inches away from the top of the bed."

I looked over at Logan, who now looked like a horror film audience member, her shoulders raised to her ears, watching Mel through the gaps between her fingers. "OK," I said. "And what are you doing at this point?"

"I have no idea," she said, eyes widened. "I just kind of let my hands trail down his sides as he slid upward, like, looming over me." She held her hands in the air and looked up, and I thought that if anyone looked over they might have thought she was praising the Lord. "And that," Mel went on, "is when I realized"—Logan pressed her fingers together, whimpering a little—"that his crotch is moving toward my face, and his body is not as completely inside his boxers as I had previously believed."

"No," I said.

"Yes," she said.

"No," said Logan, shaking her head back and forth. "Nope."

"So he was trying to, like..." I said, but I didn't really know how to finish the question.

"Yep," said Mel.

"From above you."

"Apparently."

"And Jacob never did anything like...that?" I asked.

"No!!" she said. "I could barely get Jacob to *move*." She paused, shaking her head. "Poor guy." We all took drinks, Logan and I exchanging a look and smiling into our cups. Even three years later, Mel felt compelled to take pity on Jacob any time he was mentioned. But then, if anyone could get away with believing the high school boyfriend she dumped years earlier would carry on pining after her indefinitely, it was Mel. He probably would.

"So what did you do?" I said.

"I mean, I tried, sort of," she said. "For like, ten seconds." Logan shuddered. "And then I think he realized that it was not really going to happen in any, um . . . successful way. Also, I think his arms got tired. He was practically hanging off the head-board."

"That makes no sense," I said. "Where did he even get this idea? Are aerial blow jobs a thing now?"

"I don't know!" she said. "I really hope not, because I just don't think I can do it from that angle. It's too alarming."

"I am not sure there are any *good* angles," said Logan, and Mel and I both agreed that was probably true.

Before long we'd finished our first pitcher of beer and gotten a second. When we got home almost two hours later, we were drunk and starving. We ordered pizza from the worst pizza place in Springfield, which, as the only one in town that stayed open until 3:00 AM, was also the most popular. While we waited for it to come we gathered in Mel's bedroom to make her reenact for us what Logan had nicknamed "The Enterprise," as in the spaceship, gliding silently overhead. But seeing it live only made it more confusing, and Mel's various attempts to clarify made all three of us laugh so hard and for so long that we forgot we'd ordered pizza altogether, and its arrival was a wonderful surprise.

I spent the better part of Sunday morning making a slow loop between my bedroom, the bathroom, and the kitchen, my body curled over like I was the Hunchback of Notre Dame. Logan's and Mel's doors stayed closed for hours after I woke up. They were able to hibernate in their hangovers, lying there knocked out and motionless until the point at which their bodies knew they'd gotten as much sleep as they possibly could, and the next necessary stage was food. As far as I could tell, neither of them had ever had to pee.

But they were out by noon, so we made toast and eggs and ate it with juice in our living room, in our pajamas, watching *Law & Order*. It was an episode I felt positive we'd all seen, probably even together, probably even on this couch, but nobody raised any objections. Nobody said anything at all, too hungover to speak unless we had to. But the companionable suffering was pleasant in a way, and when it got to be almost time to go to the library I was jealous of them for getting to wallow in self-pity, drinking small sips of water and whining and eating crackers all afternoon. I thought about calling in sick, but I knew this was my best chance to talk to Remy. I put off getting up until I was border-line running late and then I wrenched myself off the couch, took two more Advil, and got dressed.

"Will you guys be here when I get back?" I said, and they nodded in a way that suggested that yes, literally, they would be right here.

Remy was already at the desk when I got there, and looked up right when I walked in the door, like it had gotten to the point where she was starting to wonder if I'd show up. She smiled, and I made a face like *Yikes, I'm a mess, I'm sorry.*

"I was getting worried!" she said when I pushed through the gate. I dropped my bag, shook off my coat, and collapsed dramatically onto the floor, which made her laugh.

"Oh nooo," she said. "That bad?"

"I'm a ghost."

"Are you going to be OK?"

"Well, when I fell down here it was a joke," I said, dragging myself over to lean against the book return shelf under the desk. "But, now that I'm on the floor, I don't actually know if I can get back up."

"I don't think you have to," she said, looking out at the rest of the room. "There's like nobody here."

"Great, then I will take my time."

I closed my eyes and rubbed at them, sighing. I was buying myself time while I tried to figure out what to say to her.

"This is awful," I said.

"What did you do last night?"

I laughed. "I went to Acadia."

"Acadia?"

I looked up at her. Her face really did have a way of making what I now knew to be generic surprise look like disgust—it was her mouth, I thought, the corners curving downward.

"Yes," I said. "Don't ask me why."

"I've never actually been inside," she said. "The outside frightens me."

"Me, too," I said. "There's no real reason for you to go. It's exactly what you'd expect from looking in the windows."

"I really liked the bookstore that was there before," she said. "I always sold books there when I was feeling broke. I mean, I think the most I ever got was like seven dollars, but having it there felt sort of like a nice safety net."

"Yeah," I said. "I liked it, too. I got really into *Sweet Valley High* freshman year because I found a bunch of old copies there. The order was all over the place, so I think I ended up skipping from number three to six, but to be honest I don't think it really mattered, plot-wise."

"I still haven't read those," she said. "My sister's nine years older and she loved them, so when I was younger I wanted to do the exact opposite of whatever she'd done."

"That is my general understanding of what it's like having a sister."

"Pretty much." She laughed.

"You should read them, though," I said. "I think I still have the first three. I'll bring them for you."

"Oh, that's so nice! I will read them this summer when I am destitute."

"Oh yeah!" I kept forgetting she was going to be gone in less than a month. "Er—like, 'oh yeah,' you're graduating, not 'oh yeah' like yes, that does accurately describe your future."

"Well, we'll see!" she said, fake-cheerily, the way you'd say the same thing to your aunt at Thanksgiving, when you wanted her to stop asking what was going to happen to you because you didn't know what was going to happen to you, either.

"When I graduate I'll probably just slowly transform into Deb," I said, nodding at her closed door. "I'll just never leave. You'll come back for your twenty-fifth-year reunion and stop by the library and I'll be shushing kids in the history stacks. Wearing glasses on a chain."

"Does she have those?" Remy laughed.

"I don't actually know," I said. "It seems like she should."

"It does."

The thinly carpeted floor started to hurt my butt and I realized it was probably weird that I was still sitting on the floor. I stood up too fast, sending my head swimming.

"Are you OK?"

"Ugh. Yes," I said. "But I'm never drinking again."

"Um, I was gonna go downstairs and get a snack from the vending machines. Do you want anything? . . . Gatorade?"

I could have cried.

"Oh, that would be great," I said. "Thank you. Gatorade and . . . Cheez-Its, I think. I think I have a couple ones—" I reached for my key chain, but stopped, remembering I'd used the last of my cash last night. I'd told the bartender I thought $2 was fair for five extra lime wedges to go with the tequila shots we bought after our second pitcher of beer. I'd set the money down on the bar and scooped the pieces of lime out of their plastic compartment but I couldn't remember now if he'd even responded.

"It's OK," she said, getting up from her chair. "I got you."

"Thank you," I said. She shrugged.

Her departure only reminded me of the conversation I needed to have when she returned, and I started to feel nervous all over again. I took off my sweatshirt and touched the damp patches of T-shirt under my arms. I took my hair out of its ponytail and remade it, likely more crazily than I had before. I pulled a leg up onto my chair and hugged my knee, thinking over what Logan and Mel had said last night. They were ambivalent as to what (if anything) I owed Remy. They did not think I had made Remy break up with Keith, and they were probably right. But I couldn't decide if that was good enough.

I had thought it wouldn't matter that much that I knew her, and knew him, because I was sure I'd see her after they broke up and she'd be relieved. Sad at first, maybe, but then, soon after, certain she'd done the right thing. But, so far, she didn't seem all that relieved. All this time I'd thought I was helping people decide to do the right thing. Or to at least act in that direction. But what if I was wrong about what the right thing was?

When I looked up and saw her walking back toward the desk, carrying the snacks she'd bought for me, with her own money, like some kind of saint I could no longer force myself to resent, I whispered "Shit." Because I knew that no matter what my friends had thought I needed to do, I wanted to say something to her about Keith. Or, I didn't want to. But I would.

"Thank youuuuu," I said when she set my Gatorade and

Cheez-Its on the desk. She'd gotten me blue Gatorade, and I wondered if she remembered me drinking it in front of her a few weeks before or if she'd just made a lucky guess. I was too embarrassed to ask her and risk imparting a utilitarian snack decision with sentimental meaning. I wondered if I was maybe getting my period.

"No problem," she said. "I got Coke and Skittles, because I'm eight."

We opened our drinks and snacks and chewed for a minute or two. I was hoping that the bright blue liquid and the bright orange food would work like a potion on me, and not only lift my headache but also tell me exactly what to say to her. And they did help a little, but not that much. *Just start talking*, I thought. That's what I always told people who wrote to me feeling afraid of some discussion they needed to have with someone. *It only gets worse the longer you go without starting to talk.*

"Um," I said. "I— agh." My mouth was dry immediately. I took another sip while Remy watched me. It was already so horrible and I had not even said a recognizable word yet.

"I have something kind of awkward I have to tell you."

She laughed, kind of. "OK. Shoot."

"You know that letter you wrote to *Dear Emma*?"

"Yes..."

"I mean, obviously you know your own letter, ha. I just mean. Um. OK, well, this is a secret, but—"

"It's you?" she said. Her expression was unreadable.

"I— how did you know that?"

"I didn't," she said. "I was guessing."

"Oh," I said. "Well, you're correct." Perhaps she would fill in the rest out on her own, I thought, if I just sat here waiting.

"So..." she said. *Dammit.*

"So, I knew about you and Keith before you told me about it in person, which is weird, and I'm sorry that that's ... weird," I said.

"Oh, right," she said. "Huh. OK. Well, I mean, it's her—your job to be anonymous, so ... I guess, that makes sense to me. Gosh, I never thought about the fact that she—you would get letters from people you know. I don't know how you don't tell everyone all the time!" She wasn't bothered, not really. Just a little surprised. The trouble was that I hadn't said any of the hard stuff yet.

"Well, my two best friends know it's me," I said. "But actually it doesn't happen too often that I know the person very well. You're kind of the first where it seemed ... like I should tell you."

"I feel so special."

"Don't," I said, before I could stop it. "I mean, it's just, there is a little bit more to it that I should explain."

She waited.

"I also know Keith, kind of," I said.

"Oh," she said. "That I did know."

What? What???

"What?" I said.

"When I added you on Facebook, I saw him in our mutual friends," she said, like it was nothing, like it was the most obvious thing in the world. That I had somehow overlooked. I had worried about Keith noticing, but somehow I hadn't really thought to wonder if she would.

"Oh," I said. "Yeah."

"Do you guys have a class together?" she asked casually. Fake-casually.

"Yeah," I said. "Spanish Civil War."

"Oh right," she said. "He loves that class."

"Yeah, it's all right," I said.

I could end it right here, I thought. I could say, "Anyway, just wanted to let you know," and then change the subject back to hangovers, or to finals. I could say I thought it would help me feel better to move around a little, and I could get up to go return some books.

"So you knew it was him, then? When I wrote in?"

"Yeah," I said. "I mean, I was pretty sure. I had seen you guys on St. Patrick's and I kind of put two and two together."

"Oh, funny," she said.

"Um, but, the other thing, is that. We—he and I—I mean, not like, 'we,' that is literally too strong a term to even use, but, he and I sort of...hung out. Not for very long. A couple weeks, maybe. Before he started dating you. Before I knew you," I said, all in one breath. The terror I felt for what she might say was overwhelmed by a relief so strong it felt like a fever finally breaking. I said it, out loud.

"Oh!" she said. "Really?"

"Yeah," I said. "I mean, sort of. Definitely not to the extent you guys are—or, were, I guess. We weren't, like, quote-unquote official. It was nothing." Well, not nothing to me, I thought. Nothing to everyone else. "We didn't sleep together," I added, embarrassingly, preemptively, because I didn't want her to ask me if we had, didn't want to have to say "No."

"You don't have to— "

"I know," I said. "Or, I don't know, I sort of feel like I do, actually. I feel like I'm telling you this way too late, so now it just seems dumb and weird for me to bring it up, like I want credit for something that doesn't matter. But that's not why I'm telling you," I said.

"OK," she said, then waited.

"So, when you wrote to me, and it was about him, there was probably—definitely—a conflict of interest. And maybe I should have told you then who I was, or maybe I just shouldn't have answered your question," I said, pausing, I guess, to let her object. She didn't. "But I guess I just thought it was my job to answer it as best I could," I continued. "And I wanted to write back to you. I felt like I knew how you felt."

She paused again to think and I bit my lip to keep myself from filling the silence myself. "So . . ." she started, "when you told me you agreed we should break up, was it because of what I wrote in my letter? Or was it also because of whatever happened with you guys?"

"I guess it was probably both," I said. "At the time I just thought I was being practical. Or, that's what I told myself. Because I get letters about guys acting shitty all the time. Just, all the time. And then sometimes I get letters *from* guys who want me to tell them that it's OK they're acting shitty. It just never stops. And it used to be kind of funny—or not *funny*, but good material, because that was the kind of letter I liked writing. Like 'Dump that loser!' But they just kept coming in, and they all kind of blend together. Everyone's always like 'Should I try texting him again, or wait and see if he texts me? How long?' They're always written like it's just a matter of this one small thing, like it's just a matter of logistics. But I feel like now I can tell. I can tell that they can tell it's the end, and this letter is sort of this last-ditch CPR that probably won't do anything, but they feel like they have to try. And I'm not blaming anyone for that, because that's what I wanted, too. I wanted to come up with the perfect text, and the perfect time to send it, and to know what the exact right move was to keep him from just . . . *ignoring* me."

She'd been staring at me intently but on this she looked down at her hands, clasped together in her lap. She seemed embarrassed—for me or with me, I couldn't tell.

"I'm sorry," I said. "That was a major tangent."

"Did he?" she said.

"Ignore me?"

"Yeah."

"I mean," I said. "Yeah. At the end, yeah."

"That's rude," she said slowly. "He's not—he's kind of shockingly bad at communication, sometimes."

I wasn't sure how much I was allowed to agree with this, so I just nodded.

"Anyway," I said, "that doesn't matter now. I'm not trying to make excuses for myself. Or I guess maybe I am, I don't know. I'm just trying to explain what made me write you back, and do it the way I did. I thought what happened to me was happening to you."

"Well, that's not exactly unreasonable, given what you knew and what I told you."

"But I was *relieved*," I said. "In a grim way, maybe, but I felt relieved. Or vindicated, almost. Because if he did the same thing to you, the way he treated me didn't have to be about me anymore. And I guess that means I'd been hoping he would hurt you, too."

I stopped, waiting for her to yell or roll her eyes or laugh or get up and hit me. But she just stared, and waited.

"I hated you," I said. "Before I even met you, and then for a little while after, too. When I found out he was dating you—when I saw you guys out at the bar. I hated you. And I was mean." I pictured the whiteboard list and swallowed hard.

She looked down at her lap. "I'm not sure what to say," she said. And then: "Thank you for being honest." I thought about sitting across from Keith just like this—how he didn't have any

of these proper little graces ready to go, hadn't had practice saying *thank you* and *I'm sorry and I understand where you're coming from*,
regardless of whether he really meant it or not.

"You're being a lot calmer about this than I expected," I said.

"Well, how long have you been imagining this conversation?"
she said, sharp.

"Not very long," I said, looking at my own legs and hands.
"But too long, I know. I should have . . . it shouldn't have taken
me this long to tell you. You should be mad at me."

"I mean, it's not like I haven't been there," she said, sighing,
like she couldn't help but be understanding, and that was exhausting to her. "I've hated plenty of my exes' new girlfriends. A
lot."

"Yeah, but you're my friend," I said. "I think. Or I hope so, anyway. Not that it's, like, okay to hate people you don't know, but
maybe it's more natural? I don't know. Maybe it's less. It's easier,
anyway. Because I couldn't even conceive of you as someone I'd
like, or who'd like me. Or know that we would know each other
in this context outside our connection to this person who hurt me.
I thought you had a terrible personality but I made it up, because
I was jealous of you. And that is mortifying to me," I said.

"I *knew* you didn't like me," she said, and she smiled with her
mouth closed tight. By now I knew that kind didn't count.

"I'm so sorry," I said, my jaw starting to shake. I wanted to
say more but I was afraid that if I did I would start to cry, and I
didn't want to put her in the position of feeling like she had to
comfort me just because I was upset and near her.

"I just wish you would have said something sooner," she said.

"I should have. I'm sorry," I said, and I meant it, but I also
wondered if it would have made a difference. Was the timing
really offensive, or was it that it had happened at all? I thought

about Mel not telling me about Will. Probably I would have been upset whenever she told me, I thought. Maybe less, if it had been right away, but it would have stung a little no matter what, and not for any good reason except that something between us had shifted.

"Do you still like him?" she said.

I thought about it for a second.

"No, I don't," I said. I was surprised by how sure I felt. "I'm just angry."

"OK," she said.

"Not that I have any right to be asking you this now, but just because, I don't know if this is the reason you don't want to say much about it, but—do you?"

"I guess so, yeah," she said. "I don't want to, but."

I nodded, my stomach sinking a little.

"We actually had a talk yesterday," she said. "In the spirit of full disclosure."

"Oh," I said. I hoped she'd tell me everything but I also hoped that a hurricane would blow through the library at the same time so I couldn't hear it.

"Not that that means anything definite. I don't know." She was flustered, clicking rapidly at something on her computer screen.

"Are you...I don't know. I'm embarrassed asking this, but, are you mad?"

She looked over at me, appraising me, as if trying to decide the answer to that herself.

"No," she said, finally. "Not mad."

"But not thrilled," I said.

"Yeah," she said, sounding at least a little mad. "That seems right."

"OK," I said.

She stood up suddenly, turned off her computer screen. "I'm going to go return books for a while, I think," she said. "Sorry."

"Don't apologize—"

"I just mean, I know I'm acting weird and not saying much. I just want—I'm just going to do some reshelving for a little bit." She walked over to the cart, which was only about a quarter full. "Can you—" she said, pointing at the shelf under our desk. I opened it, pulled out the four hardcovers at the bottom. I held them out to her, and she took them without meeting my eyes. It felt weird to turn away from her with her standing so close, so I watched her put the books down on the shelf, then quickly organize them by call number, then push the cart toward the gate, stopping to grab her phone and put it in the back pocket of her jeans. On the other side of the gate, she paused and turned back to look at me.

"I'll be back in a little bit," she said.

I nodded. "OK."

But it wasn't a little bit, it was three hours. Six PM came, and then 6:03, and 6:08, and she still hadn't come back to the desk. Her backpack and coat were where she left them; she'd have to come back for them at some point. Unless she'd scaled the building or disabled the alarm on a fire door, I could be sure she was still there, because I sat next to the main exit. But she knew I'd be done half an hour before her, and if she hadn't come back by the end of my shift I figured I shouldn't wait around until the end of hers. I put my things away slowly, shut down my computer, and walked out, looking over my shoulder just in case.

19

A week and a half before the seniors graduated I sat on my bed with my laptop on my legs, trying to will myself to finish my last paper. We had until the following Monday at five to turn it in, so I knew I wouldn't work on it in earnest until Sunday morning, but I thought it was important to make a show of thinking about it now. It was so close to done; all I needed to do was bring it all together into something like a conclusion. I kept typing and deleting the beginnings of sentences like "As examined earlier," and "Having considered," and "In conclusion."

On the other side of my closed door, Logan and Mel were studying at the kitchen table. When I stopped typing I could hear them testing each other, Mel frenziedly explaining each term she was given as if she were being timed, and then Logan, calmly adding the one or two pieces of information Mel left out. Even they had worn themselves out of the ability to carry their bodies to the library, or the science building, or anywhere not within ten feet. Their last final (biochemistry, if I remembered correctly) was the next morning at eight. Under my bed was a secret box of blueberry pancake mix I'd bought at the Hy-Vee after dinner. I'd washed their dishes and mine and then not-very-coyly told them I was "going for a walk," but I hadn't especially needed a cover; they'd hardly looked up from their flashcards.

I'd walked the five blocks there and stood mesmerized for twenty minutes in the baked goods aisle, staring at the cookies and brownies and cakes and cups of frosting. I forgot about baking for most of the year, but every time finals came around I went crazy for it. I added six boxes of mix to my basket—key lime bars, peanut butter cookies, tiramisu, cake, chocolate chip scones, and pancakes—and then put them back one by one until the pancakes were all that was left. I thought I'd make them while Mel and Logan took their last test. I could set the table with the place mats from Mel's mom (from a garage sale), and maybe sneak a few peonies from one of the bushes alongside the house next door. The senior boys who lived there never did anything with them, and they'd started to droop.

The day before, I'd had my Spanish Civil War exam, my last one. I thought I'd done just OK on the short answers, better on the essay. In the hall afterward I'd run into this girl Anna who'd finished just moments before me and was filling up her water bottle at the fountain. We'd worked on an in-class assignment once, earlier in the semester.

"That was roughhhh," she said, and I made a face and said "I knowww."

"I really bullshitted that essay," she said.

"Oh, meeeee, too," I said.

"I think I made up a word. Is 'convergently' a word?"

"I think so? I don't know. I'm not sure at this point in the year."

She shrugged and I bent over to tie my shoe, which did need to be tied but was more an excuse to let her go ahead without me so I could walk through campus alone. I meant what I said to Anna. I'd always thought of myself as someone who was good at bullshitting an essay. But I wasn't sure why. I wondered if it was possible that I was actually just good at writing them. I still wasn't exactly sure what the difference was.

I'd walked from the language building to the library and found David sitting in Remy's spot at the circulation desk. After standing in front of him for nearly a minute, waiting for him to take his headphones off, I asked him what he was doing there, and he said Remy had enlisted him as a sub over email the night before. When I asked him if he knew why, he looked at me like he'd never seen anyone dumber and said, "It's finals week and she's a senior." Both facts I already knew and understood, but still I was surprised not to see her. I hadn't heard anything from her since Sunday, and it was now Thursday night. Around Tuesday I'd started wondering if I should text her or email her to apologize again and see how her finals were going, but Logan and Mel had told me to give it time. "The ball's in her court," Logan had said, using my least favorite phrase in the entire English language.

From the kitchen, I heard the microwave door open and close, the beeps of numbers being pressed, and, several seconds later, popcorn popping. I slid my laptop off my lap and walked out to the kitchen.

"Hi," I said. "How's it going?"

"Did you come out here because you heard popcorn?" said Logan.

"Yes."

"I don't know a *single thing*," said Mel. She was frizzy-haired and wild-eyed, holding her knees up to her chest, her sweatshirt sleeves pulled far past her hands. "I'm serious! It's like I've never seen this fucking book in my entire life!" She picked up the textbook in one hand and struggled to wave it around.

"You've known plenty of things," said Logan. "Somebody's overtired," she said to me, whispering on one side of the hand she held up to her mouth.

"I'm not tired, I'm an idiot."

"You're not an idiot," I said. "Everyone panics about everything late at night."

"That's true," said Logan. "It's because we're afraid the sun won't come up again and we'll just die."

"I just need more time," said Mel. "If just this one time, a day could be, like, fifty-six hours long, I would be fine."

"You're going to be fine anyway," I said. "You're almost done."

Mel moaned, pulling her hood up over her head and yanking on the drawstrings until all that was visible of her face was her nose and mouth. Logan took the bag of popcorn out of the microwave, opened it, and held it open in front of Mel's face until she came back out.

I ripped three sheets off the paper towel roll we kept on the counter and put them down like table settings. Logan poured a little pile of popcorn on each and for a couple minutes we ate it in silence. Mel worrying about her test. Me worrying about Remy. Logan, not worrying at all. Logan, thinking about . . . I had no idea. Maybe just the popcorn.

"Should I make another one?" she said, eyeing all our empty towels. Mel and I nodded and she got up.

"I'm sad," I said.

"About Remy?" said Mel. "I'm sure it's going to be fine."

"Not that," I said, though it was a little that. "Just, the year ending. This semester wasn't even very good and I still don't want it to be over."

"Aren't you excited Keith will be gone, though?" said Logan.

"Yes. Aren't you excited Peter will be gone?"

"*Ecstatic*," she said. "Although he hasn't texted me in a little over a week, I realized!"

"Was the last one the one where he asked you to be treasurer?" I asked.

Logan nodded. They'd held elections already—Mel was the new recruitment officer, which she'd be great at. Logan had declined to run for anything, though about half the group had nominated her for president. She'd told them she was morally opposed to holding political office. (Privately, I thought she had a lot of opinions about how the various offices were run for someone who didn't believe in holding them herself.) They were still without a treasurer, which was what led Peter to beg—not that he could've cared much, because he was graduating, but more likely because it had been a good enough excuse to text her again. She'd ignored him. "We'll just get some loser freshman to do it," she'd told me.

"Never again," she said. After a moment she rapped her knuckles on the cabinet behind her to prevent a jinx.

"Well, *I'm* excited for summer," said Mel, pushing her paper towel toward Logan for her seconds. She was going to spend it working as an assistant at one of her dad's dental offices, making appointments and helping with cleanings. I wondered how often she'd hang out with Will, whose family was from a suburb just fifteen minutes away from hers. I'd asked her recently if they were official yet, but she'd only smiled and shrugged it off, saying she was sure they'd see each other "a couple times" over the summer.

"But I'm going to miss our little house," she added.

"I'm just so happy we get to live here another year," I said. I was staying in the house over the summer too, working full-time at the library. It paid me $5 more per hour than any job

I'd have found at home would, and anyway, my dad was leaving in June to teach a seven-week study abroad program in Turkey. I would not be alone: Mel's parents were covering her rent for the summer, but Logan was subletting her room to her cousin Marie, who went to ISU and would be working as an intern at the capitol for—Logan had warned me gravely—a Republican. Most of me dreaded living with someone who wasn't Logan or Mel, but I supposed (or hoped) it would be at least slightly better than having the house to myself for three months.

"I'll miss it, too," said Logan. "But next year, for real, we should actually have parties." We'd said this the spring before we moved in, too, when we signed our leases, and then again in August when we moved in. We'd gotten there all at once— I'd gotten a ride with Mel's family—and we walked around our empty new house picking out our bedrooms and feeling so adult, even as their parents stood just outside in the driveway, taking the furniture they were loaning us out of their cars.

"Definitely," said Mel, and I nodded, but I didn't care if nobody else ever came in this house next year except the three of us.

Back in my room, I thought about the letter I'd been drafting in my head. It would be my last of the year—the Friday before graduation was the last paper we ran. The concept of campus news ceased to exist every year in mid-May, not to be revived until the first week of September. The last paper of the year was therefore treated as a sort of send-off; a quarter of its potential readership would never read it nor think of it ever again.

I pulled my laptop back onto my legs and looked at the empty document in front of me, the empty email drafted to Alexia. It was 12:23 AM now. A new day, technically. Five, not four, days since I'd talked to Remy. I opened an Internet window and found myself on her Facebook page before I registered the thought to go there—R-E-M- and it filled right in. At the very top of her wall was a YouTube link, a music video by some band I'd never heard of called Paces, the thumbnail frozen on some jagged neon-striped light pattern. She'd posted it an hour ago. Sometime between then and now, I saw, Keith had liked it.

At first I gasped, looking up and down the page around the post as if more information would reveal itself through the manic speed of my scrolling. And then I stopped, looked at the little list of likers again, reading Keith's name among them. And then I laugh-yelled. "HA! HAHAHAHAHA." I laughed and laughed until I was blinking through tears, until I heard a knock on my bedroom door—the one attached to the bathroom, the one ad-dressed only in cases of possible emergency.

"Harriet?" came Mel's voice from the other side.

"Yeah," I said, "come in!"

She opened the door and came in, Logan behind her in the doorway.

"Are you OK?"

"Yeah," I said, wiping at my eyes.

"It sounded like you were screaming."

"No, just...laughing," I said. "Sorry."

"At what?" said Logan.

"Nothing, really," I said, closing my laptop. "I think I'm delirious."

"Well, join the party," said Mel. "I just made a sandwich of a piece of ham between two Cool Ranch Doritos."

"Gross."

"It was pretty good actually."

"I think I should just go to bed," I said. I could write my email and my letter in the morning. It would almost certainly come out saner if I did.

Mel sighed. "I hope to do that too, someday."

*   *   *

Email FROM: <Dear Emma>
Email TO: <Alexia E. Collins>
Subject: last column!!

Hi Alexia!

My column for next week is attached! Let me know if you have any questions or anything.

Also: I think this is going to be my last letter. For good, I mean. I have had so much fun writing it, and I'm so grateful to you for giving me the opportunity to anonymously boss around our peers for two years. It's been great, but I think I've reached the point where, if I were to continue writing it, it would get worse. Or repetitive, or something. And I want to leave it on a high note, both personally and for the sake of the paper. I hope that makes sense to you. I mean, I know you won't actually be here next year, so maybe you're like "ok, whatever!" but I haven't been "introduced" to the new editor yet so I thought I'd let you know now, and then maybe you can just let him know. Maybe he'll want to find a replacement. Although honestly, I kind of hope not, because I'll feel compelled to hate whoever it was, and then I'd just feel mad every week that I let someone else take over. Ha-ha, as you can see, this has been a really easy, emotionless decision for me. It's totally fine!!!!!!!!

Anyway, I hope you understand and aren't too disappointed. And thanks again. And I hope you like this last one.

— H

Email FROM: <Alexia E. Collins>
Email TO: <Dear Emma>
Re: last column!!

HARRIET!

This is terrible news. Of COURSE I care even though I'm graduating, are you kidding? I'm like you: I'll probably enlist one of my AGD underlings to mail me hard copies of the paper at j-school so I can scrutinize Mike's page design, lol. The paper just won't be the same without me.

Anyway, I hear what you're saying about feeling burnt out, but don't you think three months of summer vacation will help? Three whole months without writing it! That's 12 columns!! OK, you get what I'm saying.

As far as repetition goes...I mean, there are probably only so many problems a student here is realistically going to have/ write to you about, but that's not your fault!!

Seriously—any way I can talk you out of this?

Alexia

Email FROM: <Dear Emma>
Email TO: <Alexia E. Collins>
Re: re: last column!!

Ahhhhh, thank you, but I don't think so. I can't promise I won't have second thoughts after summer break, but...I don't think so. But thank you.

Email FROM: <Alexia E. Collins>
Email TO: <Dear Emma>
Re: re: re: last column!!

I'm not giving up yet.

But, keeping that in mind—there is no way in hell we'd run

the column without you writing it. That happens over my dead body. I'll tell Mike that myself. I'll issue an outgoing executive editor's order. That's not a real thing, but he's afraid of me.

Email FROM: <Dear Emma>
Email TO: <Alexia E. Collins>
Re: re: re: re: last column!!
  Haha. Thank you, Alexia, so much. I'm really going to miss you!!

Email FROM: <Alexia E. Collins>
Email TO: <Dear Emma>
Re: re: re: re: re: last column!!
  And I'll let you know if I have any questions or cuts! I'm planning to read everything for the issue tomorrow. First I have to finish my Earth Science final, which is a fucking PowerPoint, to be presented to nobody, which I got a one-day extension on by telling my professor that my grandfather died. Which he DID, but 12 years ago. I've killed him off like four extra times, lol.

Email FROM: <Alexia E. Collins>
Email TO: <Dear Emma>
Re: re: re: re: re: last column!!
  I'll miss you too.

*　　*　　*

Dear Everyone,

Instead of responding to a student question this week, I wanted to write a letter to all of you. To be honest, I haven't gotten any emails in the last few days, anyway—it seems every one of us has the same most urgent problem, and that is getting through finals. Everything else will have to wait.

To the seniors who are graduating this weekend, I want to say good-bye and good luck. And to everyone else, I want to say the same. We may not be going anywhere just yet, but this is the last you'll be hearing from me. This version of me, anyway. This will be the last Dear Emma column I write. It's been a very fun and illuminating two years, but it's time for me to leave Emma behind.

There are several reasons for this, none of them especially dramatic. There has been no crisis or grand-scale change of heart. I'm just afraid of becoming repetitive and boring. I'm afraid if I keep it up, advice-giving will become an obligation I resent.

I'm also quitting now because it has recently come to my attention that I have basically no idea what I'm talking about. This is a huge surprise to me. When I pitched the idea for this column to my editor, I was certain I had some special psychic insight into the minds and hearts of my peers. I spent my whole life before college quietly watching people. Probably because I had so little to say myself, I became a lot of people's confidante. That this wasn't the same thing as having friends only occurred to me after I made some real ones here. In my many years of observing and listening, I learned just about everything there was to know about any permutation of human-to-human interpersonal conflict you could think up—except what it was like to be part of them myself.

I've written *Dear Emma* for two years, amounting to 52 questions. On 52 occasions I gave you the best advice I could think to give you. 52 times I sent my answers to my editor, read them over again on Fridays, and wondered if I might hear any more from you. Maybe you'd tell me you followed my advice, and your talk/breakup/date/fight/registration went so much better than you ever could have dreamed, and thus today began the rest of your life. Or maybe, though it seemed less likely, you'd tell me I'd gotten it all terribly wrong. But neither of those things ever happened. I never heard back at all.

That this is the nature of semi-professional advice-giving is perhaps not so surprising as I often found it. After all, you don't know who I am. If I were your friend, you'd ask me follow-up questions. If I were your friend, and you didn't like what I had to tell you, you'd try to convince me your situation is different. If you were my friend, I would try to believe you. But I'm a stranger with a word limit. So my answers were also pretty cut-and-dried, likely more than they would have been if our relationship were different. And I think I kind of forgot that wasn't really the end of whatever it was you'd written to me about. For me it was, but not for you. And that's part of the problem with this whole setup, because giving the first response to the first question about something is super, super easy. He's not texting you back? He's not interested. Your friend is bothering you in some way? Well, go talk to her already. Someone you're dating cheated on you, or made you feel badly about yourself, or is boring you to death? Probably you should just break up with them. Today, if possible. It's not like any of this is bad advice, necessarily—in fact, I still think it's all generally good. Before writing this I looked back over every answer I wrote, and I stand by every one. It's just that I've finally realized that it often only gets more complicated after I sign off.

People do things that don't make sense all the time. Sometimes you don't ever get a real explanation. For all the rules and guidelines and flags, for all the generally good principles we can try to use to guide our decisions, and by which we can tell each other what to do, there is still a portion of human behavior that will remain incomprehensible and surprising. What a relief.

Still, I will miss it. And I hope more than anything that I was useful to you in some way. Of course I'd prefer if you agreed with me completely, but if not, I hope you disagreed so fervently you set out to prove me wrong. Earlier this spring I was proven wrong about someone—someone great, whom I wasted time disliking, for reasons I never would have tolerated from any of you—and while I can't say I cared for that feeling, I'm sure it would be good for me to experience it again. A few times, anyway.

Thank you for reading, and thank you especially for writing to me. I've learned so many things from so many of you, and hope I will remember them in my own, real life, off the page.

May your advice-givers be thoughtful and generous with their time, observant and wise, funny, and just a little mean when you really need it—

Slightly more humbly yours,
Emma

20

The day after the seniors graduated Logan and Mel left for home, piling into the car with their summer clothes half packed (by me) and half thrown in (by them) over the top of their suitcases in the backseat, promising to try to text me and email me sometimes on weekdays, too, from their respective clinic jobs. But even if they didn't, I knew it was because they'd never be the type of people to whom it would occur to just start up an email or text conversation for no real reason, and that was OK, or at least more OK with me than it used to be.

I hunched over the passenger-side window while they idled in the driveway and when I said, "OK, see you in three months," Mel said, "Oh, shit!" For a second I thought she was surprised to hear the length of time we'd go without seeing each other spoken out loud and I felt touched, but she leaned forward, digging around in the backpack at her feet. She produced a white envelope, my name written on the front in handwriting that wasn't hers.

"It's from my mom," she said, shrugging and smiling.

"Aw," I said, turning it over and then back, pretending to reread my name and really take it in. I wanted to buy even just two or three seconds of time before I opened it, worried that as soon as I saw whatever was inside—and it could have been anything, anything from someone else's mother—I would collapse right there on the gravel. But then Logan said "Just open it!" so I did.

Inside were two tickets, a pink Post-it attached to the front. In bright purple ink, in straight up-and-down handwriting so perfectly aligned it was like she'd used a ruler, the note read: "Please come visit and relieve Melania from having to spend all her free time with her parents and brothers and sister. I'll have the guest room all ready for you and Logan. Bring a swimsuit. :) Mrs. Alves." The tickets were for the bus, one to Chicago and one back, for the weekend of the Fourth of July.

I didn't fall but I did cry, and Logan turned off the car and they both got out again, and we went through the same good-bye routine we'd choreographed twenty minutes earlier, hugging each other individually and then together, and then once more individually.

"OK," said Logan, addressing the airspace over my head. "Get your shit together." But her grip around my back didn't get any looser, and may in fact have gotten tighter.

A week later, Marie arrived. I was sitting on the couch in front of two screens: the TV, playing *Law & Order*, and my laptop, playing an instructional YouTube video on how to bind off knitting. A few days earlier I had decided I wanted something new to keep my hands busy at the library. After work I'd walked downtown to a yarn store called Cast Away, bought three skeins of bright blue yarn, and had since then made most of one very bad, baby-sized scarf. For whom, I had no idea.

I heard two knocks on the side door and jumped, having forgotten I was expecting her. I paused the video and got up to open it. Even knowing the details I'd been given, I was surprised by the person I saw through the windowpanes, surprised that some-one like this could be related in any way to Logan: She was a tiny and blown-out brunette, wearing a white sundress and a thin strand of pearls around her neck. Over her arm was one of those quilted, floral tote bags that were somehow both girlish and geri-atric. She smiled at me with her mouth closed, and I opened the door.

"Hey," I said. "I'm Harriet."

"Marie," she said, extending her hand and giving me, I sup-posed not unsurprisingly, a very senatorial handshake.

"Well, welcome," I said. "I'll show you your room."

"Actually, would you mind grabbing my other bag first?" said Marie. "It's in the backseat."

"Oh," I said. I looked pointedly at the relatively small tote in her hand and then at the wide-open kitchen table, a surface upon which another person might place one bag in order to retrieve another that belonged to her. But Marie didn't move, so I added, "Um, sure."

"Thank you *soooo* much," she said, holding the door open for me.

I walked down the steps and into the driveway, opening the back door of her BMW to find a suitcase the size of a small planet wedged into the backseat. *Why do I have to do this?* I wondered. Was it because I was marginally taller than her, and therefore pre-sumed to be stronger? How had she gotten it into her car in the first place? Had she strained her wrist in the process of loading it in, and was too proud to tell me? Or was she just spoiled, the type of girl who didn't carry her own things and still called her father "Daddy"?

I tried yanking the suitcase out by its handle but it did not budge. I leaned my body in over it and tried sliding it back toward me, and it didn't move then, either. I walked around to the other back door, now facing the house, and saw that Marie was watching me. When she saw me look up, she waved. I opened the door and leaned into the backseat so she wouldn't see me ask myself if she was fucking kidding me.

I poked and tugged at the bag until it came loose from the grip of the backseat's leather, eventually lying flat on my stomach to push it across the seat until the suitcase slid out the other door and onto the driveway below.

"Yay!" said Marie from the doorway. She walked down the steps, bent over, and lifted the bag upright by its handle. She then wheeled it toward the house, pausing at the stairs. "Could you just—"

"Sure thing!!" I said, lifting the bottom of the suitcase as she hoisted it the last bit up into the house. "Your room is the one right off the kitchen." She looked at me and I pointed but stayed on the stoop outside, needing a moment to catch my breath and be a little bit farther away from Marie.

"Awesome," she said. I watched her disappear from the doorway and, moments later, heard a little "It's so *tiny*."

I pressed my hands over my face to keep from screaming. I reached for my back pocket, wanting to send Logan a text message asking her to confirm that this person was definitely the person who would be staying here, with me, for three months. But my phone wasn't there, and I realized I'd left it on the coffee table by my laptop. Knowing I could not stay outside forever (and especially not without my phone), I grabbed the handle of the door, took a deep breath, and went inside.

I walked over to the doorway of Logan's room and saw that Marie was neatly folding a stack of cardigan sweaters and camisoles into the drawer Logan had left empty for her. When she noticed I was there she looked up and said, "It'll be tight, but I think I can make it work."

"Well," I said, after a few moments, "if you need more space, we can probably put some of Logan's stuff in Mel's room."

"Oh, really?" she said. "I might take you up on that. I brought a *lot* of stuff."

"Yeah," I said. "It's no problem." It wasn't, really. Everything would be where it belonged soon enough.

I turned to walk back to the living room, anxious to resume my scarf and my show. But then I made myself turn back.

"Hey," I said, and Marie, now placing precisely ironed and folded slacks onto hangers, looked up again. "Would you want to get dinner later? When you're all unpacked?"

"Oooh, sure!" she said. She grabbed her purse off Logan's bed and removed a day planner, opening it to a page she'd marked with a tiny purple plastic tab. "I looked up like *all* the restaurants in town and made a list of the ones I want to try." She smiled and held the planner out for me to look at. The list was numbered, and went up to seventeen.

"You pick," I said.

"Are you sure?" she asked. "You don't want to look?"

"Yeah," I said. "It's your first day."

"OK," she said. "Then you can pick next time."

"Deal," I said, and she grinned, and bent over to resume working on the massive suitcase sitting open on the floor.

I returned to the living room and sat down on the couch, reaching forward to touch the home button on my phone. When the screen lit up, I saw that I had a new email. And when I opened my inbox, I saw that it was from Remy.

I closed my eyes and then blinked rapidly for a few seconds, vaguely worried that I'd invented it, like a mirage. But when I stopped, it was still there, the only unread message I had standing out in bold.

I held my thumb down on the message for a few moments, took a deep breath, and then let it go. And then the email was sitting there, open on my screen, and it was too late to decide to read it later (not that I'd ever really considered waiting, there was no reason to, but sometimes it was nice to pretend I was capable of such breeziness, of not swallowing whole each new piece of information that became available to me the moment it became available), so I read:

Well hello there. I've wanted to email you for a little bit now, but it's taken me this long for two reasons: 1) moving back home (however temporarily—please, God that I don't believe in, please, please let it be very temporarily) has been A CHALLENGE, to say the least, and all I did the first week was try to find reasons to leave my parents' house, which mostly turned into going to the strip mall all day, like three days in a row, which is a super cool thing for a newly graduated unemployed person to do with her free time. At Target, I bought lip gloss and candy. At Barnes & Noble, I bought a planner (for when I have a job and therefore "plans"). At Michael's, I bought an arrangement of fake flowers. (???)

2) I was thinking about your last Emma letter. I had thought of texting you or something before that, too, but as soon as I saw it, I was glad I'd waited.

(Does this make me the first person to write back? That part really surprised me. But then, I guess I hadn't written back at the time, either. For me, at least, it felt needy. You answered my question—if I wrote back AGAIN, then maybe you'd feel like you'd have to write back to me, again, personally, and that wasn't your job. Or something.)

Thank you for saying I'm great. (I'm assuming that was directed at least partly at me…? Ha, what if you wrote back like "uhhhhh, no, not you." I don't think I'm wrong, but if I am, maybe just let me have this one.) I think I more or less said this that day in the library, but just for emphasis: I am not (and was never) mad that you'd advised me to break up with Keith. Based on the information I gave you (and what I myself thought at the time), you were right. Or at least, not wrong. I wasn't even really mad that you said you used to hate me. I would have hated me, too. There is probably some perfectly Zen balance wherein we both accept and legitimize our own feelings but also make sure we're not jealous or projecting or bitter or desperate or participating in our own brand of fucked-up Hunger Games in which every woman is essentially just one more woman in the way of your boyfriend/ survival, but oh my god is all of it exhausting sometimes. Sometimes I think it just has to be OK to dislike someone until you don't.

All I was ever really mad about was the idea of there being some like…"secret wall" between us. If that makes any sense? Just, the idea that you had this extra context, but I didn't know you had it. Which made me feel like I'd been unknowingly exposed. Like the time I walked two blocks from my house toward school with my skirt tucked into the back of my tights. (Like the TWO times this happened, actually! Ha.)

I also wanted to say a couple more things. One is—(ahhhhh, this is the hard part for me, and the part that makes me see why you didn't tell me sooner, and maybe you'll be like "why so far into the email???" and I will have no answer): I got back together with Keith. We're both still living at our parents' houses, and they're almost an hour apart, and he's going to grad school in Michigan, so who knows what will happen anyway, but I thought I should let you know. If you want, this can be the very last thing either of us says about him ever again. I hope this doesn't sound weird, or like I want to keep anything from you, but I think you and I can have a friendship that doesn't have anything to do with him.

Another thing is: Even if I didn't stick to the advice you gave me, or even the advice I gave myself for that matter, there was a part of your response that stuck with me, and that was when you told me it wasn't dramatic to want an explanation for something that bothered me. I have spent way too much of my life trying not to be "dramatic." I feel like your letter let me give myself permission to leave that behind. I think that for most people who wrote in, regardless of whether or not they agreed with the larger point of your response, there will be that one thing they'll remember.

In my mind, as I've been writing this email, I've been picturing you reading it while sitting in the library at the same spot you always do, one leg up on the chair and the other hanging down. I hope you aren't too bored. Like I said, I'm unemployed, sooo…if you ARE too bored, and ever want to email me…it's pretty much guaranteed I'll be at or very near my computer.

OK, I guess that's it for now.

Your pal,

Remy

I'd skimmed the body of it right down to the end, searching for anything shocking or upsetting, trying to prepare myself for what it would feel like to read it by, essentially, reading it. When I was done, I scrolled up to read it again.

It was only then that I saw the very first line of the email, which, in my eagerness to get to the end, to find out everything it was going to say, I'd missed.

It began: "Dear Harriet."

ACKNOWLEDGMENTS

Many thanks to my always encouraging and very patient agent, Allison Hunter, and the rest of the team at the Stuart Krichevsky Literary Agency. Thank you to my editor, Emily Griffin, for giving me the kind of extremely specific feedback that I love, as well as the rest of the amazing team at Grand Central Publishing. Thanks, too, to Sara Weiss, whom I cannot help but trust implicitly.

Thank you to Jane Austen, for the inspiration.

Thanks to all the young women (and not-quite-as-young women) who read *Never Have I Ever,* and an extra thanks to the ones who wrote to me about it. Your messages alone made it worthwhile.

I want to thank the cool people I work with at BuzzFeed, for being so supportive of my books, and of me in general.

I also want to thank my friends, especially: Chiara Atik, who makes me want to write more and better, and who knows what to tell me so I do; Arianna Rebolini, for talking to me all day every day, and usually across three or four forms of communication; Silvia Killingsworth, for getting it; Rachel Sanders, for being a paragon of fearsomeness; and Colleen McShane, the best storyteller I know, and the worst texter. Thank you always, for everything, to Rylee Main. And special thanks to Regan Smith—for her friendship, her book-length emails, and for being a really good example of how to be.

Thank you to my mom and dad, who taught me how to be a good friend, and to my brothers, Joe and Dan, for being mine.

A CONVERSATION WITH THE AUTHOR

1. **What gave you the idea for *DEAR EMMA*? Are there any elements that are based on your own story?**

In part, it's inspired by *Emma* by Jane Austen, which I've been obsessed with since I first read it years ago. I love all her books, but *Emma* is endlessly captivating to me. The book as a whole, but also Emma the character. She's such a brat! I love her, but she's a brat. She's just beautiful and charming and mean and smart and she doesn't have to lift a finger for the whole town to fall in love with her. She is the type of girl I envy. So when I read *Emma*, or watch one of the many movie versions, I empathize more with Harriet Smith, who's the inspiration for my own Harriet. Like, what a terrible turn of events *Emma* is for her. One crush after another, all of them encouraged by her best friend, all falling for that same best friend instead of her. How does she not hold that against Emma? I think she would, really, if the book were more about her than it were Emma. That dynamic is super interesting to me, and something I think most women have experienced in their friendships with other women. I definitely have.

2. **Why did you choose to write about people in college, and how did the campus setting affect your plotting?**

I think of college (or at least, my time in college) as an extremely romantic time. Everyone is so young and so hot (way more than anyone realizes at the time, I think), and you're somehow both constantly stressed out and constantly bored. And, in smallish schools at least, everyone knows what's going on with everyone else. It's its own weird little ecosystem. And so everything is just running at this very high frequency, high tension. Timelines are very compressed—just like in the book, two weeks is a really long time. I'd solidified new best friendships in that amount of time. I remember friends having entire relationships in that time, easy. It's like one four-year soap opera. But I also think that so much of what we did in college was to hang out in the library, talking and eating junk food, sometimes hungover, and that obviously shows up in the book.

3. Are you someone from whom friends seek advice? Have you ever gotten in trouble giving advice?

I think I am! I hope so, it seems that way. I really like giving advice, though I think I used to like it even more. I wouldn't say I've gotten into trouble with it—at least not so directly as maybe Harriet does—but I have definitely, over the years, come to question the way I give it, and perhaps become more hesitant to leap to severe conclusions. I think I was a real hardliner when I was younger. I am probably still a hardliner, but I am trying to embrace gray areas. It's tough. I think one of the most interesting things I've witnessed as I come to be friends with people for three, five, ten years, is the way you mold your advice-giving styles to each other. And you start to be able to tell what the other person is hoping you'll say, and, sometimes conversely, you start to know what the most effective way to break it to someone gently is. It's so complicated! Clearly I am still fascinated by this topic.

4. **Keith is such a real-seeming character—we've all known someone like him. Did you struggle more with showing his good side or his not-so-good one?**

I guess I think it was harder to show his good side, in a way, because we mostly see him through the rearview mirror as someone who has hurt Harriet, and who behaved immaturely. As outsiders we're able to look at the way he treated her and probably pretty easily say he's an asshole—which, make no mistake, I definitely think he's an asshole—but I wanted to make it plausible that he could be both an asshole and also someone that Harriet liked, and someone she was right to believe liked her back. And I think that goes back to the advice thing—it's easy to be the friend who's like, "He sucks so much, what's wrong with you?" but unfortunately, people who suck often have a few really compelling traits, too.

5. ***DEAR EMMA* is your first novel, though you've also written a memoir (*NEVER HAVE I EVER*). How was the process of writing fiction different for you?**

I loved it so much. I think that getting started with this one was much harder, because I had to really invent and then nail down the plot and outline every major event and character pretty specifically up front, whereas with *Never Have I Ever* I knew the plot, because it was just my life. It took a while to get all the details ironed out; I think I agonized over it for at least a month. I did a lot of hand-wringing and angrily squinting at Word documents. But then it came to me, finally, and once I started, I found it surprisingly easy (most of the time) to get immersed in the world. I always thought it was a lie when writers talked about "getting to know" their characters as they write them, but it turns out that is real.

6. What should we expect next from you? Are you more interested in fiction or nonfiction right now?

I am more interested in fiction right now. I still take inspiration from my real life, my friendships and interests and things I think about, but after writing something as personal as my memoir, I have really enjoyed having the freedom to make things up. I'll always be interested in writing things that are honest and real and personal to me, but at the moment I feel I'm actually better able to do that through fiction.

QUESTIONS FOR
FURTHER DISCUSSION

1. Harriet often struggles with what she believes she *should* do (her internal Emma voice) and what she *wants* to do. Do you ever struggle with your own internal "Emma"? How do you resolve such struggles?

2. Harriet believes social media can be representative of how we want to be seen by the world at large. Do you agree? What do you think your social media says about you? What do you think it says when someone doesn't use social media at all?

3. When Mel doesn't tell Harriet about her new relationship with Will to spare Harriet's feelings, Harriet is both hurt and angry. How would you feel if you were Harriet? Is it ever okay to withhold the truth or lie to a friend, even to protect them?

4. Harriet sees Keith at bars or in class, but she never approaches him, afraid that she'll look "crazy." Do you think she did the right thing or should she have confronted him? What would you have done if you were in her shoes?

5. "Emma" tells a freshman thinking of transferring that good friendships take time and patience, and she gives a list of what she looks for in a friendship. Think about your closest friends. What drew you together? Was it an instant bond or did it grow over time?

6. Mel accuses Harriet of "strategizing" too much in relationships. Do you agree or disagree? How much do you "strategize" about relationships, both romantic and otherwise?

7. Harriet gives Remy advice as Emma, even though she's not sure if she's being objective enough. Would you have answered Remy's letter? What advice would you give her, if you were Harriet?

8. Remy was graduating, and it was possible she and Harriet would never see each other again. Was Harriet being a responsible friend by telling Remy the truth or should she have kept it to herself? What would you have done?

9. Before they become friends, Harriet worries a bit that she dislikes Remy for the wrong reasons. Later, Remy tells Harriet it should sometimes be OK to dislike someone until you don't. Do you think that's true? What are "good" reasons to dislike someone?

10. In the end, Remy and Keith are back together. Do you think that relationship will last? What about the friendship between Remy and Harriet?

11. Harriet and Remy are able to become friends despite having dated the same guy—have you ever made friends with an ex's girlfriend, past or present? How does it differ from other friendships, if at all?